# THE LINE, THE BITCH AND THE WARDROBE

ROBERT COMMON

Troubador Publishing Ltd
Unit E2 Airfield Business Park,
Harrison Road, Market Harborough,
Leicestershire. LE16 7UL
Tel: 0116 2792299
Email: books@troubador.co.uk
Web: www.troubador.co.uk


ISBN 978 1805143 079


British Library Cataloguing in Publication Data.
A catalogue record for this book is available from the British Library.

Printed and bound in Great Britain by 4edge Limited
Typeset in 11pt Minion Pro by Troubador Publishing Ltd, Leicester, UK

*"If you think that I am only this body,*
*then you have not truly seen me."*
– Thich Nhat Hanh

# ONE

# A HOSPITAL IN NAME ONLY

A life-altering event doesn't happen all at once. It usually begins as small moments of alarm that add up to some massive outcome, and you don't have the capacity to see the whole thing for what it is until sometime later, or maybe you never will. At first, everything is loud and up close, with people, images, and sounds blurring together. There can be an incredible amount of dreadful waiting, like waiting for your friend and colleague's parents to find out about her death and come claim her body. That's what Milo was doing in this remote referral hospital in Cambodia. Waiting seemed so regimented, especially when everything had exploded into chaos.

At the moment, Milo wasn't checking the time with impatience or contemplating the larger meaning of what had transpired. Where any sense of consideration should be was a dull hole. He must have nodded off. But that wasn't quite right either. In that surreal space right before waking, all he was aware of was a pervasive blackness and a ringing in his ears that covered the chaos surrounding him. As he tried to wrestle himself back to consciousness, his body struggled against a wave of pain. His breathing felt laboured as he tried to make sense of what was going on. Breathing out through his mouth, the metallic taste of chaos was heavy on his tongue. His throbbing head was beating in time to the off-kilter fan above him. With what little awareness he had, he tried to press his hand to his forehead to ease the pressure. He couldn't move.

Was it sleep paralysis or some weird nightmare where he'd traded places with his friends, the ones that didn't make it, like Maly? Remembering his small but powerful co-worker was like a jolt of adrenaline to his system. Her delicate body lifeless on a bed like this one while Milo had been working to keep her covered and out of the way.

Hadn't he just been fine, though, at least physically? Mentally scanning his body in panic, his confusion mounted. The stiff, still silence pressed through the darkness.

If he could only open his eyes to see or his mouth to speak. With effort, one eye let through a slit of light, the other still black. What he saw confused him. Actually, it was what he didn't see. Where was everyone? The bare fluorescent bulb flickered its last glimmer of light. The shutter-stop effect put extra strain on his one good eye.

Where was Gia? He knew he had been searching for her. They must have been sitting together on the bus. No, that didn't fit what happened, either. He tried to find thought through the searing pain. Something wasn't right, and it wasn't only that he hadn't yet seen a nurse or doctor; medical professionals were sparse in many far-flung places around the world.

The last thing he remembered was the aftermath of the accident. The survivors were brought to this rural hospital in Kep, a coastal town, hours from Phnom Penh, down the end of the road in Cambodia. It was a hospital in name only. The sparse staff had limited supplies and was overwhelmed trying to handle being inundated with trauma of this magnitude. Shrouding the devastation, there was a sense of order. Gathering critical information was made more challenging because of the language barrier.

Milo had been in reaction mode, trying to assess who among the badly injured most desperately needed medical attention. He was doing his best to stabilise his colleagues. These people he worked side-by-side with helping families and children now needed help of their own, and Milo was desperate to do whatever he could. They'd already lost Maly. And Heng, an incredibly kind and patient child protection worker, had been blood-soaked, barely recognisable, and struggling to breathe.

Milo had felt a distinct sense of urgency as lives were on the line. Yet, he was able to find equilibrium amidst the horror with an ability to see everything at once. While assessing the situation, he was able to take in how many people were in dire need of help, notice the dynamics of the hospital staff, and be aware of the people and families who were there seeking other, more mundane medical procedures. The look in the eyes of the people who had survived the accident was sheer panic but also with a glimmer of relief that someone was taking control of the situation.

There is a strange calmness when you are a trained medic in the midst of a chaotic traumatic event, especially when it is intensely personal. Helping strangers, Milo could remain clinical and follow procedure. With friends and loved ones in the fray, an isolated part of his brain screamed with grief, overcome with emotion that remained locked away while trying to mitigate disaster. His ability to compartmentalise, separate himself from the trauma and do what was required of him came from a dark place, but it also came in handy.

There was a blank space from then to now. He was alone, and the silence emphasised the absence of the others. How many of them had been on the bus together? He couldn't remember. A big chunk of his memory was missing, along with a portion of his face if how profusely he was bleeding told him anything. The bus accident had been fatal, but who was hurt and how many were missing? It was all a blur. They couldn't all have gone on to the Royal Phnom Penh Hospital and left him there. The muggy air and the heat of the day pressing through the open windows of the hospital weighed him down.

"Why can't I move my arms?" It took a second for him to realise he'd said that out loud. Then, sucking moisture into his parched mouth, he tried yelling, "Hello."

His surroundings were still blurry, his body radiating pain as he looked around the room. His skin was sticky, yet he didn't remember getting wet. The more awareness he gained, the more unpleasant things got. The fan spinning above his head made him nauseous. He squeezed his eyes shut to block out the sound, sensing more clearly one eye caked shut and broken in some way he was only beginning to fathom through the wrongness of how it felt. Taking a long, low breath, he tried calling out again and managed a quiet croak. Inside, he was fighting to come to the surface as he pushed the air out of his mouth, in through his nose, trying to find rhythm.

As his eyes rested against the strain of the light, he tried to figure out what happened to him. It seemed like moments ago, the night had been thick around him, and he was surrounded by carnage, begging for help because his two hands were insufficient. Medical supplies of any sort would have helped, but all Milo would have given anything for at that moment was transportation; to get people medical attention before they bled out on a metal bed. Doctors had been working on one of his child protection workers who had half his head cut open to relieve pressure from a brain bleed. Meanwhile, he had been doing his best to triage the rest of his friends and staff members, moving back and forth between them. At the time, he had been uninjured.

It was supposed to have been an agency workshop, a morale booster to encourage the team. Instead, he had been working alongside Rith, his program manager, to determine who needed urgent attention first. Taking over patient management and, at times, pushing doctors out of their way, they had held back the blood, assessed internal injuries, and rushed to get seven of their colleagues to the Royal Phnom Penh Hospital if they had any hope of saving them.

They had worked side by side just as they had in the

office at World Children's Services and in the field so many times. With lives on the line, it was always high stakes, only now it was their team whose lives were hanging in the balance.

He remembered how his husband, Ra, and close friends in Cambodia had come to meet him amid the chaos but sat out of the way of the injured, helpless to do anything other than be there for support. There was only one so-called ambulance, which was really a small van with a light on the roof. At that point, it didn't matter. They had to make do with anything they could get to take people to the Royal Phnom Penh Hospital, nearly four hours away but much more equipped to handle this level of trauma.

The medical staff on hand were limited in the help they had been able to provide, not only by a language barrier but also lack of access to life-saving supplies. Milo had taken it upon himself to object rather firmly because no one at the Kep hospital had allowed them to move the injured a few hours northeast to Phnom Penh, the capital of Cambodia. The doctor on duty slowed progress because he had so focused on preventing them from taking people out of the hospital, regardless of their medical needs.

Milo didn't remember what he had said to get the doctor to back off, but it wasn't polite. He had known that some people didn't have long left. They had internal injuries, and there was no surgical theatre, no anaesthesia or sterile equipment. While he had gotten used to taking charge, compartmentalising the chaos and handling whatever happened, this was much more immediate, up close, and so personal.

That's where he last remembered being; surrounded by the sound of people crying out in pain; friends, co-workers, people he had lived and worked alongside. When did he lie down in this empty room, like a meat slab on a table? Was his head bleeding earlier, and he had simply ignored it? And now it was daytime. It made sense while making no sense. He had been moving, helping, and supporting. He had held Maly in his arms only moments ago. The feeling of urgency to respond returned. Even as half his world was black, he pushed himself to focus.

He nudged at the corner the haze to try to remember the bus accident, where it happened, and what had happened. He remembered the hospital he was in now but couldn't fathom how calm it seemed. Now, from what he could hear, the hospital's silence was only rarely interrupted by infrequent footsteps in the hall that seemed to speed up when he tried to call for help.

Feeling dizzy, he closed his eye under the rising tension. Blackness overtook him for hours he was unaware of. He was waiting for Gia now in another place and time, on a bench by the sea. Here in-between reality, he could smell the salt waves licking the shore. They were talking about hair, of all things. He mentioned that the only time he missed his long locks was feeling the ocean breeze flow through them. It made him feel connected, like each strand was a nerve ending communicating with the wind and the waves. She scrunched up her nose and leaned into his shoulder as, laughing, she told him she was the opposite. She couldn't stand the fluttering feeling of hair in her eyes.

When they met, he had liked Gia right away, but he was like that with most people. It was a way of giving people the benefit of the doubt with an initial friendly acceptance. Letting them into his inner circle was a more selective process, and it was rare for him to establish such a close connection with a colleague. Most people didn't last long working in child and family care, so he was used to being polite and friendly in a professional setting with a high turnover rate. But Gia had been different.

If he was going to spend his life with any woman, it would have been with someone like her. He would have first noticed her radiant smile if he'd been paying attention the day they met. Instead, he had been scowling into the meeting agenda, wondering why the people who had no idea what they were doing were making the decisions. More specifically, he wondered why it surprised him since it was nothing new.

When she said something witty, deftly pointing out how the deficit of services would only be made worse by the proposed program, Milo let out a snicker because he had been thinking the same thing. They had become fast friends after that, and he was so thankful for an intensely curious and competent colleague with the same dry humour he had. Initially, she had been part of a partner organisation working together on a project with the agency Milo worked for. She had successfully set up a foster program for disabled children when everyone thought it impossible. As soon as he saw her work, he knew he wanted her on his team and despite bureaucratic interruptions, he made it happen. Gia had been asked to rewrite a program guideline and hired as a consultant. While she was solution focused, she had always been the first to speak up when something was complete bollocks.

As his body wafted in and out of consciousness, he leaned into the memory and remembered how, after their first meeting, her charisma and capability had made Gia stand out professionally as well as personally.

"We don't have a position to offer you straight away," he had told her. "But I'd love it if you could work as a consultant and get the program guidelines written."

"I don't think I could make it worse, so sure, I should be able to do that, though I will need some guidance on it," she had said.

"Of course. I need someone who isn't going to write a bunch of BS; that's why I asked you," he said.

As she had perused the file, her head tilted to the side, and she let out a light laugh of air and said, "What's the worst that can happen?"

He had left that question unanswered.

When she had asked him to take a look at the first draft, he had been blown away at how incredibly detailed it was. Her first draft had shown she could outwrite the experts. Finally, he had been able to get her working with them full-time, and she had been amazing in every capacity because she could assimilate vast amounts of information and make it understandable and logical to even the most inept reader.

Even when his brother had visited him in Cambodia on an extended holiday from London, she had jumped right in. Milo had been concerned about how he'd keep William occupied and unruffled. Gia had insisted on being part of the solution. At first, she and her wife Celeste had met Milo and William for lunch.

William had only been in the country a few days, and

9

jet lag had taken a toll, so they went to a small restaurant Milo knew well. It had a cosy, plant-filled patio and a great menu. The two brothers had arrived first, and William was a bit out of his element in the tropical environment.

"There they are." Milo pointed to the two women weaving among the busy tables.

"Do you think they'll want to move? They'll have the sun in their eyes," William asked.

"No, it'll be fine. They're used to it, and the food's worth it." Milo had waved off the concern as he got up and wrapped Gia in a one-arm hug. Her hair flipped out like rays from the sun, and she hugged him back, then reached down to pull out the chair beside her for Celeste. Gia sank into the chair beside him with a flourish, simultaneously finishing a conversation with Celeste as she greeted Milo and William.

"I was just telling Celeste how you are the master of getting out of boring meetings." Gia nudged him playfully.

"Yes, avoiding unnecessary meetings is my specialty," Milo said.

"So is ordering the perfect wine for the occasion," Gia added.

"Sounds like it was more of a hard drink day from what you were telling me," Celeste said.

"I won't argue with that." Gia pulled out the drinks menu. "You missed a good one, Milo. We had regional management come in to tell us about how we'll be doing a feasibility study to determine if we're maximising the cutting edge of program implementation." Pushing her sunglasses back up her nose, Gia stretched back and let out a quick breath. "Of course, that means nothing, so it's just an excuse to set up another pointless committee instead of actually getting shit done."

"Undoubtedly, the three days I spent working on the statistical analysis of the findings will be shoved in a drawer somewhere, never to see the light of day," Milo said.

"Not necessarily. They might take your work to their bloody committee and decide your findings are theirs." Gia said.

"The scary thing is that's accurate." Milo had signalled the waitress to bring another round before their meals came.

"I don't like meetings at the best of times, but the whole thing was nonsense," Gia said.

"No more talking shop," Celeste said. She looked over at William and smiled. "Once you get Gia started, she'll never stop."

"Milo is the same way," William replied. "Once, we were returning home after sailing all day. He was getting tired, but as soon as I got him talking about care reform, it worked better than caffeine."

"Gia is exactly like that," Celeste nodded towards her newfound ally and lowered her eyes at Milo and Gia.

"To be fair, I am just catching Milo up on what's been going on since he's been off for a few days," Gia said.

"Is it true you get used to the heat here?" William asked, effectively neutralising the conversation.

"I didn't say you get used to it. I said you learn how to adapt to it," Milo replied.

"I didn't ask you," William said.

"You do get used to it." Gia leaned in. "What you don't get used to is the traffic."

"It is a bit intense," William said, though that was putting it mildly. They fell into chatting about the traffic and adjusting to the local lifestyle. A waitress appeared with their drink order, and the conversation switched to food, family, and travel.

As they were taking their first few bites, Gia dropped her fork and looked up. "I forgot to tell you the worst part. We're halting any new cases until the committee makes recommendations."

Milo stopped eating, irritation creeping across his face. "You must be mistaken. What about the children we're meeting with this week? We've been working on this for months?"

"It makes no sense, I know. But come on, you're the one who told me to expect the stupid decisions to come from the top. Unfortunately, it's the kids who suffer for it," Gia said.

"That's shit," Milo said, pushing his plate away and finishing his half glass of wine in one long draw.

"Back to talking about work again," Celeste joked.

"I think it's kind of funny," William had said, voice flat. Milo raised his eyebrow at his brother, wondering where he was planning on taking this line of dialogue. "Both of you are so crass and jaded, but all you care about is fixing families."

A moment of silence had been interrupted by Gia and Milo laughing together at that specific, hilariously accurate connection. Leave it to his brother to point out the glaringly obvious. His comment had set the tone for the rest of the lunch, and work talk was left behind in a flourish of funny anecdotes.

Milo stopped fighting the pain and urgency and let his memories lull him into a sleepy contemplation. He mused about how certain friends you connect with end up being more comfortable than family. Gia had grown to fit that definition. Her family was also in the UK, and she delighted in introducing Celeste to her three nephews and her sister Ava. She had compared the antics of the three brothers to what William and Milo got up to as children and insisted that she and her sister were much better behaved.

During the duration of his stay, Gia and Celeste had taken William under their wing and made him feel comfortable in Cambodia. He had also visited them while he was in Siem Reap, and they showed him the sights. After they had welcomed him in Cambodia, they had kept in touch. Later, when Gia and Celeste visited the UK, they had a great time catching up with his brother.

Weighed down by memory, he fell deeper into a thick and cloudy sleep, thinking about finding Gia and his brother in London, who would be unlikely to visit again. Or was he already dreaming? Probably it was irrelevant as dreams and memories whirred by at random, including glimpses of his first memories of his brother. Their dad had been posted to Aberdeen, Scotland, and William had trapped his finger in their huge oak door. He couldn't have been more than six, and Milo was around three. Considering his conservative demeanour now as a judge, William had been a rambunctious sibling, and they had gotten up to all sorts of shenanigans. Once, William had somehow managed to start the house on fire while trying to cook frozen peas. The sofa had also been set on fire after they rearranged the living room and put it a little too close to the radiator.

When he awoke again, he felt the hard metal bed below him. Pain still permeated his whole being, with another sensation creeping alongside. Dread. With a deep breath and an unintentional grunt, he forced his eye open enough to get a sense of his surroundings. He strained against the stabbing in his chest that dulled that pain in the rest of his body and focused intently so he could look down without moving his neck. His clothes were soaked in blood from head to toe. At least he looked fabulous in brown!

On the downside, Milo realised he had to get out of there. There were better ways to dye his clothes, and now wasn't the time to think about it. If he could only find his friends, his phone, or some semblance of what was going on here. It was obvious, even in his state, that the blood he was covered in was his own, at least some of it.

As he built up the energy to move, he tried to take time to triage himself to get an idea of what he was faced with. Groaning under the strain and grimacing with pain, he had it in mind to roll onto his side, but he quickly discovered that wasn't going to happen. He'd been bleeding out alone for a while now, which concerned him less than the fact that moving his neck felt wrong. Through the fog, he guided his mind through his medical training.

His airway was controlled though he was unsure he had spinal stability happening. Regardless there was little he could do about that for the moment, so he would have to be careful and hope for the best.

What came next?

Yet again, his awareness shifted, and he saw the hospital full once more as it had been in the aftermath of the accident. And there he was *in medias res,* being pulled in nine directions. Milo had been forced to makeshift body boards, out of whatever was lying around, to support his colleagues' spines as they were prepared for transportation. The speed at which people were searching for suitable materials and begging cars to stop and be used as transportation to the hospital had sent him spinning. Everyone he knew had been on the phone trying to get ambulances, vans, or anything that could help.

In glimpses and jolts, he saw how his colleagues had surrounded him; all but a few requiring urgent medical care that was only available hours away. The resort town by the sea was a gorgeous place to get away, but it was a place to avoid trying to get any sort of emergency handled. The hospital itself was really just a shelter for the desperate. He had to find out if they had all gotten out.

The quiet of his current reality settled in, and something poked Milo from within. And he felt urged forward to find out what happened next. He wondered again where everyone went and tried to search through the haze for what he was forgetting, but it was all cloudy.

If he could only find Gia, they would get things sorted, and she would poke fun at his confusion. His quick flashes of colleagues and chaos brought no images of Gia at his side or with the injured. Now he was still in that referral hospital. The peace he had longed for during the moments of unspeakable uncertainty was an eerie and uncomfortable silence. He had more questions than answers, and Gia wasn't there.

He moaned as he tried to move from his position. Swallowing what seemed like gravel down his throat, he wondered about the likelihood of getting something to drink around here. He somehow remembered having been served tepid tea earlier but had no recollection of where he'd gotten it. He'd love something stronger than tea, and yet he needed to leave here to seek care and find out what was going on. Turning his attention to his immobile body, he sensed himself shaking and felt like he was being refrigerated.

"That's shock setting in." Years of training spoke for him as he seemed between realms of comprehension. That was when the voice of experience started to realise the depth of his current predicament; something terrible had happened to him. With a determination that was unnoticeable in every inch of his broken body, he gave himself an internal talking-to. He warned himself that the cold he felt creeping in was a serious alarm bell from his body. "Fuck me, this is serious," was the last thought he had before he drifted between sleep and unconsciousness again.

# TWO

# DOCTOR DISAGREEABLE

Waking up unclear about where he was or how he got there wasn't new to Milo. He was often more comfortable corked out of his gourd and in an unknown location because that gave him a mystery to solve, and he didn't have to focus on what was really happening in and around him. Baked into his morning routine for many years was solving that self-imposed mystery, as well as discerning whether there were any substances still wreaking havoc on his system. This time it wasn't self-induced as far as he knew, and the cloudy haze he was crawling through to reach consciousness had a sharp edge to it, not the soft high of his favourite chemicals.

Reaching the surface, a sound in the background twinged at his ear. First, he heard the twang of the music bringing him to awareness, and then the voices became more prominent. He could only understand a few words in German, but some sounds are universal. When Milo managed to pry open his eye, he got a face full of naked ass. On-screen rather than live and in the flesh, though there were a few times in his life that the latter might have been a reality. There was a phone less than a foot away. The camera view shifted, and the next scene showed a close-up view of penetration, German porn style. The running commentator inside him, who enjoyed his ability to be ready for a funny quip, wondered where the Hippocratic oath comes into play in this situation. Still, the humour of it got lost in the cloudiness.

"Ffff----" was all Milo managed to say as he shifted his gaze in an attempt to see who was holding the screen in front of him. It was a doctor sewing his head up with one hand and watching porn with a phone in the other hand.

Disoriented and frustrated, Milo didn't want this doctor touching him. He made a frantic grab for the phone with his only good arm, startling the doctor into losing his grip. The doctor made a grunt in disagreement as Milo fumbled the phone and succeeded in ending the show before the doctor took his phone back.

Somehow, he communicated to the doctor that he refused to be further touched at all. There was an ugly oozing aura around the doctor, and it went beyond his porn preferences. Finally, he left Milo to his own devices and ruminations.

Doctor Disagreeable reminded him of all the people in his life who were particularly or purposefully nasty. His ex-husband was probably at the top of that list. Fortunately, that ended years ago.

His most recent difficult encounter had happened at the office only days before the accident. Milo had experienced a confusing and unpleasant run-in with Vanessa, the difficult manager. Everyone at work had called her Ms Vanessa, and he was the only one who could get away with calling her Van. As was typical, once again, she had avoided the difficult work and was probably in her closed-door office avoiding phone calls. Any meeting with her had always necessitated after-work drinks every time. Usually, they had been cordial to one another though her toxicity had permeated the workplace, and he remembered her snarling at him when he had asked about some forms he needed for their trip. No one ever wanted to ask to approach her for anything, but sometimes communication was unavoidable, as it was that day. He had reminded himself to wait until after at least two cups of coffee before approaching her after she bit his head off when he asked to see some forms.

"I've already filed them, and I'm sure you've got something better to do than check up on me." Her words had been needlessly sharp.

He had nodded, bridled his tongue (a rare occurrence, he must have been feeling generous) and walked away. Milo had later discovered she had a personality disorder when certain revelations came to light. This most recent meeting had been the beginning of all of it, and if he hadn't been so irritated by her, he would have seen the warning signs. What had happened next, he wasn't sure. The blank spots were beginning to fill in, and hopefully, they wouldn't always be as unpleasant.

He would have been thankful for an interruption if it wasn't in the form of Doctor Disagreeable, who tried to sew up his head again. Without knowing the extent of his injuries, Milo wasn't capable of consenting, and he could feel the swelling, dull feeling that he had to physically resist, and in his limited capacity, he insisted the doctor back off. When the doctor finally left, probably figuring it wasn't worth the bother, Milo passed out again (from blood loss or pain, it didn't matter), considering the way to deal with horrible toxic people and the things they do. He had long ago learned it's best to only do what you can and avoid contributing to those that make it worse.

There had been a particularly cruel nurse at his first school. The whole system had been abusive, from the way the teachers treated the students to how the older boys were allowed to bully and abuse the younger ones, but Mrs Holmes had seemed to take pleasure in it. She also happened to be the school nurse who had assumed every child who entered the sanitorium was a hypochondriac.

Milo remembered how boarding school had been so bad. An emergency trip to the hospital was like a holiday. At the age of ten years old, he hadn't felt well in class and had been dismissed to go see Mrs Holmes. As usual, she had been leaning back in her chair, primping at her beehive hairstyle that sat half a metre above her head. She had groaned when she saw him enter the room, and her eyes narrowed.

"What's wrong with you then?" she had bellowed.

Milo had been having sharp stomach pains and an urge to lie down and curl up. He was flushed and answered slowly. "I'm feeling sick."

"Well, if you can't be more specific than that, you're

likely just trying to get out of class." She still hadn't yet lumbered to her feet.

What happened next sprang her into action. Feeling dizzy, hot, and queasy all at once, Milo had puked on the floor in front of him. The liquid had steamed and started running down the uneven floor. His mouth tasted foul, and he had felt no better.

"Argh, will you look at that mess." Mrs Holmes had launched towards the small boy as Milo coughed on the bile at the back of his throat. When she reached him, she had grabbed hold of him and immediately felt he was burning with fever. Her mothball smell had made him gag. "Don't you dare," she had practically dragged him to the nearest sick bay and thrust a bedpan at him in case he needed to be sick again.

Milo had miserably watched from where he was sat as she swore under her breath and threw herself around the room looking for cleaning supplies. Every few minutes, she had glanced in his direction and scowled. He had lost track of how long it took her as she seemed to go by with a blur and a growl as the room spun around him.

The school doctor came in once a week, and he had arrived by the time the clean-up was almost finished. Mrs Holmes's countenance changed, and she had politely welcomed the doctor and described the poor boy who had gotten sick all over the floor. As the doctor came and checked him over, Milo remembered a clear, quick shift in the doctor's mood and body language.

The doctor got quite tense, and his face turned purple. He had sprayed saliva at the nurse as he practically shouted at her to "Get him an ambulance now!" And before he knew it, Milo had been rushed to John Radcliffe Hospital in Oxford for emergency surgery to remove his appendix.

There were worse people than Mrs Holmes, however, she had been simply disagreeable rather than purposefully nasty or overly violent like Mr Hewitt, the terrible housemaster who had been the cause of both Milo's fear of short people and his dislike for birthdays. A few years before his appendicitis, he had been writing out the names of six people who would be allowed to have cake with him the following day at lunch. A birthday was one of the high points of every boy's school year, and choosing who else to share in a rare treat was no easy feat.

He had it down to eight and had to cut two more from his list. It would have been so much easier if everyone could have had cake, but he hadn't been the one who made the rules. Once the list was made, there were no changes allowed, and Milo had dreaded the thought of having to disappoint anyone. It hadn't even been that good of a cake, but it was his. He had been all scrunched up considering his choices, so he didn't even hear the footsteps approaching him.

Having the light on after hours was another rule, and Milo had lost track of time. As a result of his transgression, he had been dragged out of bed by his hair by Mr Hewitt, who scooped him up over his knee and beat him for daring to disobey. It had happened so fast Milo was shocked into silence. In his terror, he urinated all over the housemaster, who was so repulsed he threw the boy across the room and then stormed out, leaving Milo to be tormented by the older boys who were left in charge. He couldn't remember if he had his birthday cake that year or not. What he never forgot was the look of disgust as Mr Hewitt tossed him aside like a rag.

The eyes of the housemaster, withering contempt at Milo's audacity to exist, morphed into his ex, the master of that glare. He had a unique talent to make you feel minuscule without a word. All the truly nasty people could do that. Even the gorgeous ones, who would go out of their way to make it appear like you wanted it that way. How many people fell for that deadly look, thinking it meant the allure of a good time? Milo counted himself one of the many, all too often.

Doctor Disagreeable came back, shaking him from his memory. Milo reached for the doctor's phone so he could call someone to get him out of there, but he came empty-handed. He tried to articulate that he wanted to know how he got there and where everyone else was. The doctor said no to every request. Did he misinterpret what Milo was trying to say, or was he just being obstinate?

Milo moaned, knowing he was getting nowhere. Then as the doctor spoke again, something in his body language twinged a recognition. He would have realised it right away if he hadn't been so smashed up. You don't have to know the local language to recognise when you're being asked for money; you only have to be cognizant of the signs. No, spoken firmly is also understood almost universally and finally, the doctor backed off again.

Feeling agitated at the assumption he would be accosted again at any moment added to the urgency, and Milo wanted to run away if only his legs would allow it. Running away wouldn't find his friends or answer how he had gotten so broken, so fast. Running away was rarely the answer to anything, but it was a catalyst for change of some kind. Milo had run away for so long; he was proficient at it in all forms.

Physically he started running in university along with kickboxing to keep in shape and challenge himself. Once he and his ex-husband Roger had been married, becoming healthy was one more thing to argue about. After years of toxicity, Milo had started going for a run to get away from Roger and avoid any unpleasantness. It was a small escape. He had tapered off his drinking at that point because he knew he had to be clear-headed to get away. Roger had been spiteful and would stay out even later simply to make a point. Going for a run in the morning had worked great as an avoidance tool.

Milo would gear up and leave the house as Roger was returning home from a night out. Since they had been on different health paths, they didn't discuss it. And since Milo had not been able to push himself out of his toxic marriage yet, he first pushed himself to run; harder, faster, and longer. He was running away from his own thoughts and his own life choices. It was much easier to train for something new than deal with old problems.

Every morning like clockwork, in the drizzle or overcast day, he had run for self-improvement, and he ran for his life. Though even then, he had no idea what would come of it. On those cold British mornings, he had no inclination that he would end up in the desert after he had left Roger behind in search of a more peaceful adventure.

After getting a time of 3:45 in the London marathon, he had decided to prove to himself more than anyone else that he could handle an even bigger challenge. Fresh from a new bout of leaving the heavy drinking and focusing on his health, he had heard about the Marathon des Sables. Running 250 km over the course of six days in the northern Sahara Desert was a step up from his morning run and just extreme enough that he had hoped it would quell the whispers he was beginning to hear from deep within. He had to prove to himself he wasn't an addict; he could quit anytime, and he would prove he was fit enough to take on one of the most extreme foot races on earth.

Originally his brother had planned to join him, but a scheduling conflict cancelled those plans. So, Milo had headed off to Morocco to face the sand alone.

Endurance running is so much more mental than physical. Well-trained, daily runners often do poorly in events like the Marathon des Sables. The first year Milo ran it, he had started out going quite easy on himself. While other racers were quite seriously preparing for the race ahead, he happily collected up their small sample bottles of wine and drank them down. He had enjoyed a light-hearted evening and slept deep and hard.

Climbing dune after dune, knee-deep in sand had been psychologically difficult. Blinking back tiny grains that got into everything, Milo had felt the air thick as sandpaper scratching his skin. It had been a struggle against himself. The hundreds of other runners had been a backdrop to his own journey, as he was a face in the crowd to them. When he felt like he couldn't go on, Milo had reminded himself that this was what he signed up for. Physical exertion had lost its meaning after the third day. As he reached the precipice, all matter outside him had blurred into the background, and people were like multi-coloured flags strung together and waving in the wind.

He had stuck with his motto, 'Start slow, finish slower'. Pushing through to the last day required plumbing the depth of endurance that he had never expected. Milo remembered the grind at the height of the Marathon des Sables, where he had found something inside himself. When he had been at his most miserable, exhausted and in pain beyond belief, he found compassion for himself but also compassion for all the other miserable people in his life. He realised they could be in the middle of their own marathon. Being hurt is no excuse to abuse others, but when we are faced with our own consuming pain, we often can't see past it. After three days of relentless heat, Milo had been focused on his own pain in the desert, blinded by sand and with visibility reduced to no more than a few feet in front of him.

Over the years, he had always returned to running as an integral part of his healing. To think he had gone from running to get away from Roger, to running with the sun burning down as he waded through hot sand, to now seeking solace in the rhythm as he ran for inner peace. Roger and the other miserable people had failed to take that from him.

One gorgeous devil, who was worse than Roger, had tried to take everything from him, but that wasn't a memory he was willing to visit, so he pushed away from that period of his life.

*You won't be running for a while.* An inner voice reminded him. Some semblance of conscious thought interrupted his reverie, but he still had miles to go on his march down misery lane. The unpleasantness continued as he left his body on the hard hospital bed and was whisked away in his delirium to his childhood. As with most of his memories from when he was young, it came in fits and starts. Purposefully forgotten, probably.

Any child who has had to stay with a spiteful grandmother who doesn't like them can probably relate. Milo's grandmother had been a proud Victorian matriarch and a particularly viperous woman. Whenever she was around, no one had a good time. She had made sure of that.

On one visit, she had been particularly nit-picky. For whatever reason, she had sent Milo to the shops for some groceries she needed. When he got back, she had checked the change.

Almost immediately, she looked at him accusingly, "You've stolen two pence off me!"

In a bored tone, he had half muttered his reply, "Uh, no."

"Yes, you have. I know how much there should be here," she had insisted.

"I haven't stolen two P," he repeated.

"It's not P; it's pence." She had corrected him.

That had been enough for Milo. He was unwilling to sit there and argue semantics with her, so he turned sharply and headed for the room he was staying in. As he reached the stairs, he turned to see his grandmother following him across the creaking oak floor. For her, the argument wasn't over. She had set herself on the stairlift and started up after him, shouting at him all the while. Milo had been shaking his head when he spotted the main switch for the lift on the wall beside him. He hadn't been able to resist switching it off and watching the shock on his grandmother's face turn to outrage.

At the bottom of the stairs, his grandfather had arrived on the scene, duty-bound to see what all the commotion was about. He had looked up, given an almost imperceivable smile, and then walked out of the room. He had always seemed to suffer through the viciousness of his wife silently. That time he had taken the opportunity to walk away unseen without coming to her rescue. Milo had turned away and stifled a giggle while his grandmother's shouts of "Come back here right this minute, young man" and "Get me down from here" bounced down the echoey hall. When he got into the paisley-patterned spare room, he had flopped down on the bed and buried his laughter in his pillow for more than a few minutes.

Sometime later, he had still been chuckling as he creaked open the door. All was quiet. After letting her stew, his grandfather had eventually come to the rescue. When his dad had heard about it, he had given Milo a stern talking to. Of course, he had been in another country, so the effect wasn't nearly as intimidating as intended. The whole thing still made Milo grin decades later. The way the old dear was poking her cane at him while shrieking over his use of language was a vision he brought up if he happened to be carrying on about something trivial. He had avoided visiting their house again, a fact for which he was grateful.

The echo of approaching footsteps interrupted the memories. As Milo fought to gain an awareness of his surroundings, the doctor entered the room, holding his phone in one hand, and carrying a bottle of something in the other. Milo knew it would most likely be a sedative, so he wouldn't feel himself bleed out and die. As the doctor approached, he guarded the phone, fearing Milo would make another grab for it.

"Back off," Milo hollered as he finally found his voice. He didn't understand the doctor's reply. "I'm leaving," he said with conviction, trying to convince himself that he could.

Doctor Disagreeable stepped back and scurried away.

# THREE

# HOW TO HAIL A TUK-TUK WITH A BLEEDING FACE

Alone in the room with the fan whirring above him, he worked his way towards the slowest escape ever. After several hours of fighting off doctors and memories, with a sheer force of will, he pushed himself off the metal slab and got seated. When both feet touched the smooth floor, the electric jolt through his body brought blackness to the corner of his eye. All he wanted to do was lie down again. The stabbing agony of putting weight on broken bones radiated out from deep inside him. One small miracle, the first of many, was a drip pole directly in front of him. He grasped it and wrapped his one good arm around it, bracing himself. More like he leaned into it, finding an awkward balance, on the verge of collapse.

"This is shit." He spoke aloud, though the words did not reach the depths of what he currently felt. Pain encircled him so that he could not distinguish where it originated. Standing up was merely the beginning of the long journey before him, which felt hysterically out of reach. Dragging himself across the floor, he was out of breath at the door to the hall. His head hung unnaturally to the side as he glanced around the space outside his room.

The light hung from dim bulbs that cast shadows on the checkerboard floor. In his blurry delirium, the hospital hall looked like a funhouse, and he was the creepy clown.

Milo heard himself laugh before he really realised where the sound came from. He shuffled a few more steps that felt like a marathon. He wobbled, wondering if this attempted escape was a dream. But it couldn't be; the pain was blaring compared to the blur of the dreams and memories passing through. Now he needed to pass through the hallway before he passed on.

Impressed with his own good humour considering the circumstances, he considered how much he would appreciate it if he had someone to banter with, to take the edge off the horror that was today. He continued pushing himself step by slow, screeching step, first pushing the rickety drip pole in front of him, then dragging his broken body towards it.

At the end of the hall, there was a ramp. It was nothing more than a slight incline and then a sharp turn to the right. It might as well have been Mount Kilimanjaro. Once more, he marvelled at the emptiness around him. In his mind's eye, he could still picture the unsettling disarray with people pushing past each other, the hallway packed, and no one coordinating care. He was confronted with the cloudiness of the circumstances and couldn't make the connection. The sharp pain of his body shrieking while he dripped along was a signal to his conscious self, insisting that this nightmare was based in reality.

The sparse hospital staff were about as helpful as a garden gnome at a fashion show. They were overwhelmed, under-resourced, and only spoke basic English. After his experience with Doctor Disagreeable and earlier, while trying to help the others, he had little confidence in getting any assistance. As he was making his way down the hall, a female doctor came around the corner. Her gaze was steady, her demeanour lacking empathy. Milo had lived there long enough to know that in Cambodia, locals often assume that if you've been in an accident as a foreigner, then it must be your fault. All of that was written plainly in the gaze on the doctor's face, underlined by an exhaustion that Milo had learned to recognise as a result of trying to work with too few resources. Milo felt like he was underdressed at a fancy party, and the host didn't approve.

Her mouth was moving, but it didn't register. Milo felt her body language from down the hall and tried to hobble faster. She followed him, and he suddenly saw himself years ago at home when he was a teenager. He had been as out of it then as he felt now, wobbling down the hall, but then it was on purpose and for fun.

It had been approaching evening, and Milo was leaning into a park bench.

The smell of smoke had burned his nostrils and awakened a desire to inhale more. He slurred his speech and staggered to stand as a stranger walked toward them, smoking. "Have you got a cigarette, man?" Milo had asked.

In response, the stranger had glowered and picked up his pace, striding quickly towards the group of friends. "You little fucker, fuck you for even talking to me." His mouth kept moving, pushing out obscenities. Then, this stranger, with a similar scowl as the doctor following him, had punched him in the nose.

One of the drawbacks to being stoned and out of it is the lack of spatial awareness. Having polished off the last of whatever alcohol three seventeen-year-olds could pull together for an evening (which is often a copious quantity), Milo was wrapped in a shroud of bubbly numbness. The space and time reality of this random violent stranger was so out of touch with where Milo had been, he didn't have the time to react. That night, he found the effects of his altered state had been especially beneficial, but he had felt it the next day.

He turned to his friends, "Man, that was a bit unfriendly. Why'd he just do that?"

When Milo had glanced over to ensure they witnessed what happened, those around him had started laughing. "There's a cigarette on the end of your nose."

The lit cigarette in the stranger's hand had burned onto Milo's nose, where it stayed poking straight out like Pinocchio. At least he had gotten what he asked for. He had shrugged, pulled the cigarette off his nose, and relit it.

He could surely use a cigarette now. The craving jolted him out of his memory back to the hospital hall, where he was still scraping forward, progressing at an insect's pace. Behind him, the female doctor was waving him down. He wanted to get out of there without further interruptions. As she got closer, Milo saw she was carrying the same receipt book he had been threatened with earlier. Annoyance crept in through the pain and awakened his irritated inner self. What was with these doctors, and more importantly, what was with these flashbacks? Milo tried to shake his head for clarity, which was immediately a bad idea as the bolts of pain shot through him, and he had to cling to the pole so he wasn't knocked off his feet by it.

When the doctor caught up to him, he had had enough. The look in her eye was utter disgust, and he knew he was another useless foreigner to her, so she was trying to find out how deep his pockets were. She told him he had to pay before he could go. Apparently, Doctor Disagreeable had sent back up. Ignoring her entirely was impossible as she blocked him from progressing down the hall, and he was in no position to be making evasive manoeuvres. He gestured to his ripped, blood-soaked clothes.

"Look, I've got nothing; you've done nothing. I'm leaving," he insisted.

"No, you will pay first," the doctor insisted. Then she looked down and noticed blood dripping off of him right in front of her, so she stepped to the side.

Milo followed her gaze and saw the slow drip off his shirt cuff. He was hesitant to check where it came from. He supposed it didn't matter much if he didn't get on with it, so he started to move forward again. As he continued pulling himself along, the doctor protested without making a move to stop him.

"You need to pay," she said again.

"Fuck off," Milo spoke without turning back. Feeling her eyes burning into his back was a small boost that pushed him forward at slightly faster than a crawl. There was no way he was paying for whatever they had done to him here, even if he had a means of doing so. As it was, it was going to be near impossible to get help of any kind in his state.

When he realised she had finally gone, he stopped, positioned his walking aid against the wall for added support and worked on breathing in hollow gasps. There was no sign of other patients and no one he recognised throughout the entire building. There was no sense of urgency among anyone he passed. There were no curtains or privacy in the bare-shelter hospital. Overall, nothing much was happening around him as he tried to drag his body forward—confusion mounted with every agonising step.

Rounding the corner and seeing what he faced next was almost too much. There were four steps to go up before he could make it outside. His knees threatened to buckle, and his body begged for a rest as he still clung desperately to his drip pole anchor. As he looked down at the base of the stairwell and his crudely slippered feet, he knew he didn't want to collapse there amidst a mix of unidentifiable refuse. He'd had his share of rude awakenings, but the forbidding stairwell propelled him to move elsewhere for his imminent collapse.

He had once awoken in a janitor's closet, wrapped around a commercial garbage can, feeling worse than trash. It had been close to midday when he pulled himself up, still wearing the wardrobe of a proud Scot, complete with kilt and seal-skin sporran. The outfit had been fantastic at the wedding the previous evening, but the next morning among commuters in business suits, it was a tad awkward, especially with the accompanying fragrance of too much whiskey. Milo had blamed the whole night on the Irish granny, who kept slipping him more drinks.

While he wavered on the hospital railing, positioning his drip pole as a lever and prying himself up one dreadful stair at a time, he considered there were worse things than being unaware of where you are, like being unable to remember where everyone else was.

To avoid feeling what he was doing, he concentrated on those he was looking for. Rith was a close colleague who also wouldn't have left him there injured and alone, but then again, they had their hands full with six colleagues in varying states of medical distress. It was conceivable that Milo could have fallen and been overlooked in the fray. He still hadn't heard from Gia and the others. That was one of the major reasons he knew he wouldn't have left his phone willingly, waiting to hear from everyone and communicating a response to the accident coming from across the continent. No, definitely not. He should have his phone on hand. Could he have been robbed?

That was one explanation for his injuries and empty pockets. It still didn't explain what seemed like a time warp where he shifted from a full, frantic night into an empty hospital with daylight creeping in. His husband and friends had been right outside. Could they still be there waiting for him? With that optimistic thought in mind, he carried on, pushing himself with great effort to the top of the few short steps.

The morning light tried to push through the grubby glass doors and beckoned him forward. Now Milo faced a new problem. If he brought the drip pole with him, he'd be stealing, and someone would likely chase him down. It wouldn't be much of a chase. However, he was more than concerned that if he left the drip pole inside the hospital, he wouldn't make it more than a few steps. It was a heavy choice. Neither option was pleasing.

There was no way he was turning back to face the stairs or the doctors. And the uncertainty of what his pain meant wasn't going to stop him. Considering the strangeness of it all, he leaned heavily on the drip pole for a moment and then heaved his way forward away from the hospital without it. Shaking all over, he slid out the door and held his breath. He took another step embodying the mindset that he was fully in control of his body. At this stage, ignorance allowed him the pretence of being capable, despite grievous injury.

No one was waiting for him.

The hospital complex contained four identical white buildings, two on each side of the road that ran down the middle. White buildings, with red roofs and a white wall surrounding the whole place: the effect was disorienting, and Milo prayed he was heading in the right direction. There was only one way out.

Walking past grey and white pillar after grey and white pillar, the vertical disco posts also served as a place to lean when he wanted to fall over. He became aware of the sound of traffic ahead of him, and it propelled him forward out of hope he was headed in the right direction. He kept on.

Down the dimly lit path, more than a dozen steps in front of him, a tuk-tuk driver was parked at the curb. While he still couldn't move his left hand, he lifted his right arm to about mid-torso and waved with as much enthusiasm as he could muster. He realised he must have looked rather scary and bedraggled. That wasn't quite strong enough for how he was feeling like death warmed up and dragged behind a truck.

Looking around, he saw no signs of the disaster that occurred, no vehicles he recognised and a quiet morning stirring. He knew his husband would never have left him there for anything. Neither would his friends, come to think of it. In his mind, he had just spoken to them briefly, almost in this exact spot.

He had asked them to search the outskirts of the dark parking lot where they were waiting for anything they could use to help move people. Then he had to get back inside.

"We'll see what we can find," Kali had said. Nathan and Piper had been on the phone, working to get additional vehicles and support.

His husband had locked eyes with him before Milo turned away and spoke softly. "It'll be alright." From his smile, Milo had known he meant it and had allowed himself to be comforted by the illusion for a nano-second before getting back to the trauma and calamity inside.

Now, the light of day was brightening on an empty parking lot, and he was really confused. Had he relapsed? That didn't make sense. It had been years since he had woken up, still drunk and uncertain as to his current location. He had a recollection of getting sober for himself.

Though he had contemplated it and even dried up a few times in his life, was recovery an illusion?

Drinking had been a quiet companion when he felt alone at school and alone at home. Life was one long transition from one place of loneliness to another. He'd go from home to school, flying internationally as a child, being passed from responsible adult to responsible adult until he was dropped off at the appointed location by friendly strangers. It had been his reality growing up, so while he felt the sting of being on his own, there seemed nothing strange about it.

In fact, he was often reassured he had the privilege of a prestigious education and that he must be thankful for his life. That bit was confusing. He and his brother had talked about it whenever they were together.

In Oslo, they had often gone sailing during school breaks, or they'd hang out at home while their parents were working or busy. It had always been an exciting occasion when they got to see their father, especially because he was in the special forces and away for work a lot. When he had been home from school, they'd often go on holiday, and that was when the adventurous stuff happened.

Home life had always been a constant shuffle between school, grandparents, and wherever dad was stationed, moving in quick succession from England, to Germany, to Scotland, and then Norway. It didn't really matter where they ended up; they spent most of their time in boarding school.

One of the first times he had been buzzed around his brother, they had talked about it. A lot of their discussions revolved around their childhood, piecing together how it happened through collective memories. His brother had been jealous of a friend of his who got to stay home year-round instead of having to travel for school as they did. They had been talking about what it must be like to be able to stay home, go out with friends, and explore without so many restrictions. William was sitting on the sofa while Milo had folded himself into the adjacent armchair. Every ten minutes or so, he had nipped off to the kitchen mid-conversation to refill his cup.

"I can't believe Mum hasn't noticed how much you're drinking," William had told him.

"You're supposed to be the smart brother. I'd be more surprised if she did notice, wouldn't you?" Milo asked.

"That's fair," William said, his face had scrunched up as though the conversation had a foul odour. "We're rarely home enough for our parents to pay attention to."

"Are you saying you want to be home more, or have our parents pay more attention? Because I'd say there are some definite advantages to the lack of attention." Milo had smiled and finished his drink. Then he poured himself another one as the warm numbness blanketed him. "In fact, I plan to take full advantage of it."

"Just imagine what you'd get yourself into if we didn't have to leave for school," William said, and he went on to describe how his friend Sylvia talked about coming home after school, relaxing, and hanging out with friends around town. Their parents were alike in many respects. The only thing was, she didn't have to leave for school. She stayed in her own room and was free to come and go as she pleased.

The conversation had ended quite soon after that because, quite frankly, William was ruining Milo's buzz. They were still young at the time; both had been at home on a break of some sort. And while William didn't share Milo's affinity for experimentation, he was definitely not a snitch. The two brothers, total opposites, were always there for each other when no one else was.

Milo's insatiable appetite for the power of a drink to bring him peace of mind, or more rightly, blur his mind, became a constant companion. As he got older and no longer had to hide his drinking, he had leaned into society's embrace of alcohol and endeavoured to indulge whenever possible, and it was always possible; he went to great lengths to ensure that.

An internal joke that went around in his head was how many times he remembered waking up folded in half with no recollection of the previous night's events. That had been a persistent issue. The concern was that he often didn't know what country he was in, which complicated things. Heavy drinking and travelling for work and pleasure can lead to destination confusion. All airports have similarities, and all airport bars taste the same.

If getting fucked up wasn't fun, most people wouldn't get addicted in the first place. He loved the feeling of having his brain knocked offline so he could no longer feel the memories he worked so hard to repress.

Milo had noticed there are at least two sides to every person who struggles with substance use and their never-ending pull towards losing control and getting stuck in paradoxes where the drug of choice is both the cure and the cause of unease. For Milo, it had always been an intimate balance of the joy of wine with friends and whiskey as a desperate shadow friend urging him to take one more sip. Getting drinks after work with friends was good for the soul, and he had built his network on being able to tell a cheeky story.

With Gia, it had been the good times of shared learning and finding things hysterical over drinks. That was where they had gotten to know each other and understand similar and shared experiences. It often started with after-work beverages to take the edge off a complicated case or a particularly unreasonable management request.

From somewhere, he could hear her laugh as if across dimensions and with him in the same moment.

"Or maybe you're haemorrhaging from internal injuries." Her voice and his were mixing as one in his blurry mind. He seemed to be bleeding memories as well.

# FOUR

# SMELL OF NOSTALGIA

In the outside air, Milo felt the fluorescent haze lift, and his senses returned. Really it was just a fourth wave of energy reinforced by new air and the ambition to put as much distance between himself and the hospital behind him as soon as possible.

Gingerly sliding along, he progressed down the slope of a ramp on his continued snail's pace escape. Turning his feet towards the road, he stumbled on every crack in the narrow path. Getting through the gate felt like an epic journey of the unprepared. It was going to take an incredible amount of time. Then what? Would the tuk-tuk driver give him a ride? Where should he go? Back to the accident site?

No. He couldn't think about more than one journey at a time. Following the path to the curb wasn't going to answer any questions. Milo inched himself along anyway.

The smells of the small coastal town mixed together, and he wondered if he was hungry or nauseous. He figured he must be delirious as he noticed the scent of the sea, the nearby fishery, and a restaurant. His nose stung with the smells of traffic and people. Above all the mingling aromas, one pushed through on a platform of nostalgia.

At the end of the path, he could see the blurry outline of the tuk-tuk driver he had waved at, and it seemed like he was waiting a long way off. Setting the expectation that he'd still be there when Milo reached the curb, he fixed his mind on finding answers. The tuk-tuk would be the fastest way to do that, though the vehicle still seemed like a mile away. What were the chances this driver would take him anywhere looking like he did?

There was that smell again that was both out of place and intensely comforting. It was interrupting all other cognitive reasoning. There was no connection for that combination of scents to be where he was. It wasn't unusual that a smell brought to mind a visceral experience; it was the sense of confusion surrounding it. It was as out of place as the smell of fresh pine in the desert.

Was having a heightened sense of smell a sign of blood loss or something? A strong nose for odours was not on his talent list. It was quite the opposite, really, so why was he smelling everything now? Usually, he was able to ignore anything particularly odorous, which came in handy in some of the places he found himself. Whether it was dredging a river of sludge, including decaying organics, walking through a goat herd in the rain, or changing unlimited diapers, he could usually handle himself without a clothespin on his nose. There were plenty of times when friends and co-workers went off gagging at an offending smell while Milo wasn't bothered.

He supposed he could have been imagining it, but if that were the case, he would imagine something tangible as he was desperately seeking security and comfort. If it were up to him, he would smell a meal he had cooked hundreds of times and could almost see himself serving up in front of him: a plate of veggies and rice, whatever was in season, mixed with the right combination of spices. Through the memory of a simple meal, he could imagine his husband sitting across from him in the warm glow of their dining room, sneaking some food to their dogs with a cheeky smile. More often than not, cooking a meal at home meant a few of his close friends who were family coming just in time to eat.

Sliding into memory, he marvelled at how far he had come from the frustrated little boy with no sense of security and a confusion about what to make of this life he was handed. At home with his mum, he had input about what he got to eat, and eventually, he taught himself to make pretty much anything. His first memory of cooking was about seven years old, when he learned to cook a fried egg. The quick shift from solid oval to leaking mess fascinated him. He loved the moment between when the egg was cracked and when the yolk came out, where time seemed suspended. The faster he got, the less likely he was to drip.

Then he began to grill bacon in the oven. As he got better at it, breakfast for tea was what they had, especially in later years when his mum had been working multiple jobs. His bacon and egg breakfasts had been legendary while he was in university, and everyone was impressed that the private schoolboy knew how to cook.

That made it seem like he had an idyllic childhood full of warm hearth moments, but the reality was much more convoluted.

On those rare weekends home during holidays, he remembered experimenting in the kitchen and how it had been the one thing his mum didn't call him stupid for. He wasn't sure why she had to say such mean and cutting words, but that was how she had been. For as long as he could remember, Milo was stupid, and his older brother, William, was ugly. It was only in the kitchen where they had found common ground, which was fascinating because her favourite story to tell was about how he had been kidnapped from right beside her in the grocery store when he was only an infant. It was a true story, and his mother always sounded aghast when she described the feeling of realising her baby boy was missing. Milo didn't enjoy hearing the story, which created a feeling of discomfort because it didn't match the mum he knew. She had always seemed to prefer it if he was out of sight, and he couldn't imagine going to the grocery store with his mum. It seemed it was something his mum had made up or had happened to some other family.

Still, she had encouraged his cooking and allowed him to experiment. It was right up his alley, as he was interested in the science of what he was putting together. He had only ever got the chance on a Saturday or a Sunday; otherwise, he would have been with the nanny. Having his mum home was rare enough. Having her home and interested was rarer still.

It didn't come to him until much later in life that his interest in cooking had started around the same time he started boarding school, where the food was horrible. It was shocking what they had deemed worthy of feeding children. The cottage pie had been like the water left behind after washing up wall paste. Once a week, they had been served tinned tomatoes that tasted like warmed-up metal, served whole with a side of slimy liver.

Coming home for holiday or summer break had always been a confusing relief from boarding school. His parents were busy with adult stuff, and he was just thankful to be somewhere where he was left alone. Still, he had spent the better part of his home time pissed off that he would have to leave again.

"Why are you so angry, son?" his mum had asked him shortly after he had started cooking.

"I'm hungry." He was always hungry, and it had been the easiest thing to say to appease his mother. He wasn't going to disrupt the apple cart by vomiting all over his privileged education, not at that age, anyway.

"Why don't you cook us something up then?"

"I don't want fried egg and toast."

"Cook up that bacon, and we'll have a nice meal together."

"You'll let me cook the bacon? I've never done that before."

"Sure, it's easy to pop it into the oven."

Without getting up, she had zipped through all the steps he needed to add bacon to his repertoire of cooking skills. Following her instructions closely, he had succeeded in burning the bacon and learning about the projectile sizzling fat that would inevitably burn any unprotected skin in the vicinity.

His mum had given the meal a smirk of approval followed by a frown when he mentioned the burn. Still, she had cleaned her plate and said they'd make a chef out of him yet. As time passed, sharing a meal in their ever-shrinking kitchen became one of the few things Milo and his mother enjoyed together. One of the few times in his life he had seen a look of pride on his mother's face was when he had made reservations for them at The Fat Duck in Bray. As an agent to celebrity chefs, there were some perks he had received, and his mum loved them. It became tradition for them to experience two and three Michelin Star restaurants together.

Though they both loved the food and presumably the company, Milo knew his mum truly relished being able to talk up all the places he took her and share every luxurious detail with anyone who would listen, describing everything from the placement of each course to the fact the rosettes on the ceiling were dust-free.

As an adult, putting on a big spread was his favourite way of showing people he cared about them. Since he was so interested in the art and science of cooking, he more deeply appreciated a well-prepared meal.

He had made it a goal to try some of the most out-of-the-way and exotic places. One of his dream jobs had been working as a sailing instructor in Turkey. Someone had suggested they take their day off and spend it in Kuşadası, but they misheard the pronunciation as Kushi-dushi, so they spent the day continuously asking for directions to the wrong place. After driving around in circles for twelve hours, they had arrived at the resort town in time to have an ice cream and drive back to the hotel where they were staying.

It was early evening, and they had been stiff and dusty from the long day when they sat down inside a tiny tavern near their hotel. The owner had asked if they were hungry, and they all nodded, road-weary with stomachs growling.

"The boat will be in, in ten minutes, so I'll get started." He had said simply. And he was right on the nose. Ten minutes later, the boat had arrived, and the owner, chef, and tavern operator prepared the fish simply with olive oil to grill and fresh herbs from the garden around back. Then he had gathered fresh ingredients for a salad and a few potatoes. Slicing the potatoes thinly, he had fried them crispy in oil and served them hot as soon as the fish was cooked tender and flaky. It was the most flavourful, local, and lovingly prepared meal he had tasted.

As they finished up and headed out, they had thanked the man for the delicious meal, and he waved them on like it was no big deal, all the while humming to himself while tidying up for the night. Milo and his colleagues had returned to the hotel feeling satisfied and at ease.

At that same sailing centre, when he had been chief instructor, he ran summer camps for four weeks, which required him to cook breakfast for about seventy kids. Everyone rotated, and the early mornings of his turn had been his favourite time of the week because he loved to get up before everyone. Cooking on a large scale takes some balance, preparation, and specific timing. For Milo, it had been a kind of meditation. It also allowed him to get a perspective on the day. He could see everyone's moods as they came in for breakfast. You could tell who was eager and who was owly just by watching the kids line up to eat.

One morning when they were short-staffed, Luke, the director, had come to help him. They had giant metal serving trays that they stored in the oven. The pans were usually removed before starting the oven for the morning meal, but this morning they had been forgotten, and they came out scorching hot.

Going about his morning routine, Milo had turned around and picked up the pans and burned his hands badly. He had to go to A&E, and the pain of the burn was screaming.

Upon arrival, the nurse had looked at him walking in of his own volition and said, "It will be a two-hour wait." Her eyes had scanned the standing-room-only waiting room. Milo had to speak up for her to hear his reply.

"Please, I can't deal with the pain," he had pleaded.

Another nurse had been watching the interaction, and she came and got him and covered his hands with a spray. The pain had gone away right away. She explained, "The moment you stop oxygen from reaching a burn, it no longer hurts. Remember, if you cover the burn, the pain goes away."

Milo had been so grateful for the relief he never forgot the lesson. He also never forgot the pain and had been much more wary of hot implements after that experience. The searing sizzling pain of a burn was nothing compared to what he felt now, a sharp stabbing feeling radiating from just about everywhere. He wouldn't make it another step if he focused on the pain.

So, he tried to remember when he had his last drink. It had always been incredible to him that he went from hiding his drinking at a young age to the celebrated social/professional drinking that was such an integral part of his work for so long. Indulgence in only the finest wines replaced his earlier years of drinking whatever he could get his hands on with his buddies. Instead of loitering in the parks, looking for a good time, his job was to follow the good time and indulge. He was good at it.

He had spent some time working as an agent in London, where he represented celebrity chefs' cookbooks. At the time, he had been the only agent he knew of checking recipes before publication. He followed them exactly as written, once in a while getting back to the chef and telling them when something wouldn't work. One of his clients would send him recipes on sticky notes, and Milo would type them up, often calling for clarification when something didn't end up as expected.

"Hi, chef. Thanks for calling me back."

"Great to hear from you. How's the book coming?"

"Really well." Milo had embellished. "Just wanted to clarify the last recipe you sent. I must have misread instructions because it turned out . . . inedible."

"That can't be. I just had my smoked salmon parfait not a fortnight ago. Something got lost in the translation for certain. Was something amiss with the flavour?" Talking to Chef Shandro had been an incredible part of his job because everything was described with a flourish. He may have been a bit time-consuming, but he was such a hoot to be around.

"Actually, when I followed the recipe, the whole dish caught on fire," Milo had said with a laugh.

"Yikes! Maybe we better run by it again," the chef had said, then he spoke to someone next to him.

"Sure, I have it right here. Do you have a few minutes?" Milo had asked.

"No, I have to run. Why don't you join me tonight for dinner? I've got reservations. Meet me there." Chef Shandro had hung up without waiting for a response.

One of the highlights of working as an agent had been that he also got to indulge in the luxury lifestyle of celebrity chefs, which had included a top-of-the-line menu and expensive bottles to go with it. That night he had gone to get a recipe edited for a book and had ended up with a five-course meal, £10,000 bottles of wine, as well as endless stories about food and flavours.

Startled out of his memories by the thudding of footsteps coming toward him, Milo came back to his present reality in a rush. Still peeking out through one eye, he saw the tuk-tuk driver a few steps in front of him. Milo nodded, answering an unasked question, and the driver took him by his one good arm and helped him along. There was no telling why he was offered help at that moment, but it felt like a godsend. In reality, the driver probably just wanted to get going, so he could earn his fare. It was likely that he was used to helping drunk tourists home in this small resort town. He definitely knew that a foreigner was going to be willing to pay without haggling. None of this mattered to Milo, who was touched by the driver's kindness and overwhelmed by the empathy of the driver to not only accept a bleeding and broken man but to take him by the blood-soaked arm and help him along.

As they moved more steadily now towards the curb, Milo wanted to engage in conversation, to let the driver know how much he was appreciated. All he could manage was a few grunts. Instead of trying to get his point across, he allowed himself to be led along and recalled learning for himself how good it feels to help people. It had always been in his nature to stand up to bullies, and he was protective over those most vulnerable.

When he was thirteen, he had switched schools. It was a turning point away from some of his darkest moments and a chance to regain his footing in a new place. Still, the food had the same poor qualities and was far from appetising. After a time, Milo had decided that he intended to do something about it.

After a few months of observation, Milo had the idea to set up a catering committee to discuss food issues in the institution. He took on a role he had seen his father take when having to reprimand someone for an error or accident. With military precision, his dad would describe the issue at hand, first focusing on what went well and then politely bringing up the most pertinent changes that were required.

Up until then, everyone had treated the catering staff horribly. Instead of criticising, Milo had told them what was good about the food, and it was the first time they heard anything positive. Showing empathy for people cooking for ungrateful private schoolchildren had made a big difference in the taste of what they were served. For Milo, it had been the first time he had experienced the internal satisfaction of treating others well all on his own. Simply by showing the people who made their food some respect, everyone was happier, and the atmosphere in the whole school improved. That had been the start of Milo realising his ability to see things from a broader perspective. The catering manager likely hadn't dreamt of being a chef for schoolchildren. Encouraging the staff had turned out to be a lot nicer than suffering meal after meal of dread and diarrhoea.

The driver, steps ahead, likely had little indication about the impact of his actions. Milo was probably just another fare to him. There are so many people like that driver who have no idea about the difference they make in their simple actions or the difference the small things in life make; they are just regular people going about doing the same thing day in and day out.

As these thoughts crossed his mixed-up mind, it dawned on him what the smell reminded him of. The realisation propelled a wave of nostalgia and lurching homesickness for a place that was intangible. The unique food revolution Milo experienced in the UK was wrapped up in the smell of fresh fruit and pub food. The latter was something Milo had yet to find replicated no matter where he travelled to. As a university student, he had worked at a pub, and once a month, his closest friends had made the drive from London to ensure his Saturdays were more entertaining. Like clockwork, Milo had found Jay waiting for Milo under the awning before he opened. They'd catch up as they walked together to the bar. Milo had always poured Jay a pint of cider, then went to do his opening work in the cellar. David and Phil would arrive twenty minutes later after first going out for a proper meal. Then they would walk in, each putting a hand on Jay's shoulder and nodding at Milo. Now, all those years later, in this tropical paradise, he smelled pub food, and he thought of the ease with which he and his friends slipped in and out of each other's lives, never too far away and eager to offer advice or a laugh.

As realisation brought a sense of clarity that he was leaving his life behind, he found himself still moving slowly along the path away from the hospital and away from the physical. Finally through the gate, he wondered how pub food could permeate the scents of the ocean, and the remnants on the breeze led him to believe it was all in his head. Hallucinating smell was new to him, and at least, in the past, any hallucinations had been usually welcomed under the guise of a delicious drug-induced delirium. Now as he swooned, he recognised it was from blood loss, internal injuries, and who knew what else.

# FIVE

# FINDING HOME

Standing in the early morning light, Milo was overcome with a feeling that overshadowed all his body was battling. When you lose something, and you can see in your mind's eye where you put it, but it's not there, you feel like you've lost your mind. Then, you go scrambling around, looking everywhere, always returning to where you left it, and when it turns up somewhere completely random, it's a small betrayal of reality. It's almost as though your mind skipped the now and replaced it with a memory that didn't happen.

Milo was facing something similar, but the reality that was missing was much bigger than lost keys. The horror in the hospital had happened, and he had obviously been in an accident. But why wasn't everyone where he left them? His husband anchored outside with his friends were no longer there, and it was shaking Milo's tenuous hold on the situation.

Getting out of the hospital had been powered by a hope and certainty that those he loved most would be where he left them.

If he didn't move now, he would stay where he stopped and be done. Leveraging the driver's aid and syphoning all his remaining effort, he hurled himself into the tuk-tuk waiting for him.

From his half-seated position, he mumbled, "Take me home."

And for a moment, he was home washing up and hearing Ra and friends laughing and glasses clinking in the other room. His dog at his feet or traipsing back and forth between the kitchen and living room depending on who was getting the most attention and who wanted to find a warm corner for a nap. Dogs outnumbered humans only when they didn't have people over, which was rare. Dinner at their house was an every Wednesday kind of thing for all their friends and most other days for the ones who lived closest. They even shared a dog with Kali, their nearest neighbour and dear friend.

Wherever he was, even now floating along, he could put himself in his kitchen and be surrounded by a filling warmth that, to Milo, after decades of running, finally felt like belonging. Then he was gone again, floating past the idea of how he had only recently found his true home.

Still drifting, unaware of where he was headed, he had a flashback to a time he was stuck in Northern Ghana, where he didn't speak the language. The gearbox on his vehicle fell out in its entirety. As he rolled to a stop, he had noticed it was in the middle of the road, 100 yards behind him, and he was 200 miles from the nearest town.

Laughing at himself while he dragged the broken part back to his vehicle, he had told himself that at least he wouldn't be bored. There were only two things he had found to do in Ghana, pay some money to throw a chicken at a crocodile or run across the border to Burkina Faso when no one was looking. That was it. It was a place of crushing poverty, and he had spent some time sitting on the side of the road wondering, "For fuck's sake, how did I get myself into this?"

How did he get out of that mess? He had just kept walking.

The people who had found Milo could hear him miles away and had watched him curiously long before he was aware of their presence. They had stayed out of view and kept about their business, so when he arrived on the outskirts of their village, Milo had been quite pleased with himself for finding them. Dusty and ragged from his ten-mile walk, he had been a flourish of English obscenities until he saw them up ahead, shook off the negativity and pressed on with a smile.

"Good day! Any chance you have a phone?" He had asked the first person he saw.

The amused man didn't understand a word this foreigner was saying, but he could tell Milo was looking for help. From his dishevelled appearance and slow creaky pace, Milo hadn't been an intimidating presence.

In any rural location, when something out of the ordinary happens, it doesn't take long before a crowd gathers. One person will get involved when they stop and check in on someone who is in a bind or out of place. With a language barrier, Milo had noticed simple things become overly complicated as the locals tried to figure out what was required. From a distance and from the perspective of the person walking onto the scene, it was quite funny to witness a frustrated foreigner swearing and kicking a tyre, or looking around in disbelief, or in this case, walking dejectedly miles from nowhere. It doesn't happen so much in the city because people needing help become a nuisance and are largely ignored.

Milo had wanted to communicate as effectively as possible instead of starting a shouting match, so he began to pantomime his experience. He had opened the door to his imaginary car, got in and put his hands where they would be on a steering wheel. With an exaggerated smile, he pretended to drive on until his expression turned to horror, and he had started waggling his arms in the air in a dramatic silent interpretation of all he had been through.

The villager, who had figured out what Milo was getting at as soon as he made the steering wheel motion, found the ongoing performance hilarious. There was movement behind him, and it amused him when his fellow villagers began to take notice and moved towards them to catch the end of the show.

When he had finished a very literal physical representation of his day, Milo looked hopeful that it was easily translated. He had also felt a bit like a clown, and he was certain the villager was chuckling as he beckoned Milo to follow him. Happy to be among people again, and with no other option, he had obliged.

They had walked alongside each other for another mile or more, with Milo dusty, sweaty and grunting from exhaustion. People began to join them in ones and twos, and each time Milo had asked if anyone spoke English. Eventually, they had come to the hut of a man who did speak English and his son, who was fluent. With father and son translating between Milo and the rest of the crowd, they had been able to find Milo the part he needed for his vehicle and the mechanic and tools required to make the repair. It may not have been a smooth or expedient transaction, but it had got the job done.

A similar situation had happened when his steering wheel snapped in northern Uganda. He had to walk six miles up the road past elephants and giraffes and then wait six hours for someone to return his call. What had there been to do but take a step back, pull his socks up, come up with a plan, roll with it, and let it happen?

Milo had learned that when he relied on human kindness because he had no other choice, ninety-nine times out of a hundred people would help. No matter what situation he found himself in, he was amazed at people's ability to lend what was needed to a stranger. Long ago, he had made it a habit to thank people, keep phone numbers, and give back to those who had assisted him.

In the tuk-tuk, the driver spoke, but it was clear his passenger was somewhere else, delirious with fever and in rough shape. Milo was aware in a disjointed way that his memories weren't happening in the present, but he vividly remembered how it felt to be so far from help and how far he had come. From a luxury-filled James Bond life to post-genocide and war zones, he had travelled a lot and got by with only a few scrapes and a lot of laughs. Maybe this was a warning he was running out of lives.

Milo realised the tuk-tuk was moving, but where did he tell the driver to go? At least he'd get there instead of sitting in traffic for hours. A tuk-tuk, remorque, moto or other motorbike-based transportation was his first choice, not because it was the cheapest—it was the fastest, especially in crowded, busy places. Many places in South East Asia were known for crazy traffic, and Cambodia confirmed that stereotype. Vehicles, mostly motorcycles, streamed through the roadways like water gliding into the nearest available open space.

He was a member of a private gym, and while other members pulled up in their Mercedes, he regularly arrived by tuk-tuk. Even when he flew into Bangkok and stayed at the five-star Kempinski hotel, he dumped his bags in his room and ordered a moto. Then he walked back through the lobby, bright marble-reflecting water, drivers lined up under the canopy outside for other guests, and he smiled at the concierge from the back of the motorbike.

This ride was a little different; he felt every jarring bump, bone on bone. Passing out would be a privilege, yet Milo learned long ago that privilege itself was often a cover for unrealistic ideologies at best and systematic abuse at worst. The privilege to have flown around the world from a young age, but also to have nowhere to land. Growing from that place, he had a transient lifestyle and had found places to call home around the world.

The diversity of the planet had driven him to explore as he was pushed away from certain situations and into others. As a child, nowhere had felt like home, except maybe when visiting grandparents. At the age of seven, he had started flying solo to boarding school from Germany (or whatever country his parents were in at the time) back to the UK. Short holidays and family days had been spent with the grandparents nearest to him, and for Milo's good fortune, that was his Granny and Grandad. They had never let him feel like a guest in their house, and they were his one safe spot over decades of misfortune, joyful moments, and poor choices. Still, it wasn't his home; it was theirs.

He once had a penthouse apartment in London in a fast-paced alcohol and drug-fuelled previous life. Who was he kidding? He was drugging heavily everywhere he could get away with it in the UK, Uganda, and Cape Town. The penthouse and luxury life had been exhilarating, but the penthouse he shared with his ex-husband hadn't been home either.

For a large part of his life, he was most at home when he had a nip of whiskey tucked away for emergencies. Alcohol was home, and the satisfying weight of a drink in hand with the warm liquid of a previous one or two spreading from his belly was comfort.

Some of his homes were much more peaceful, like living in a cottage on the south shore. There he was much more chilled out and was able to relax away the edginess he always had felt for a time, at least. His most peaceful feeling of being at home happened when he held his son for the first time. Although he came to parenthood in an untraditional way, both he and Ella had wanted to have children, and they decided to co-parent as friends. Becoming a father had been such a gift, and Milo felt at home in the UK only when he was with Ella and his son.

Time was lost on Milo as each bump in the road bounced him from memory to memory as he tried to get home in different parts of the world. Following nomadic tribes and reuniting children with families who lived in sparse huts reminded him that home is what you make of it and who you are with. There had been a time in his recent past when he had built his dream home and lived by the lake in what felt like paradise, only to lose it in the blink of an eye. If he thought about injustice, he could rant about it for hours. But that home, like most places he encountered, had been built on a false foundation.

Milo felt most at home on the sea and respected her unpredictable nature. He grew up going sailing with his dad and went to a sailing club in Norway. There he learned to feel at ease on the cold, northern waters. The stark beauty of being in nature, combined with the challenge of commanding a vessel through uncertain waters, brought a deep sense of peace in the pure and unfettered aspect of being at the mercy of his understanding of the sea.

Being at the helm with the sails out full in the wind had an exhilaration that was unmatched. Milo couldn't find the same feeling driving any other vehicle, and he had tried most options known to man. Yes, she could be a fatal bitch, but the sea was home in the way that it settled his startled heart and made him find his footing. The ongoing undulations of the waves and the predictable unpredictability of a massive moving body of water was somewhere he felt thrilled to be alive.

He was basically brought up on a boat for all the sailing he did with his dad. Being on the open ocean was in his blood. Stepping from the dock to the sailboat was crossing the threshold to rejuvenation. They were just a short drive to the sailing club when they moved to Norway. In the right season, they would stop for fresh strawberries on the way. After securing their supplies and checking that they had everything, his dad would ask him to untie the rope and push off. From his earliest memories, he could see his reflection in the water as the space between him and shore expanded. It was a feeling of being pulled away into a new world where anything could happen.

Even in the most familiar waters, a rogue wave could take you by surprise if you don't know how to handle your craft. Milo's dad taught him how to act quickly and what to look for. Being light on his feet and moving with the water was something that came naturally to him and comforted his hyperactive nature.

He was ten when they spent two and a half weeks on the water on an epic sailing adventure. After the first few days of settling, they had set a routine and enjoyed the clear sunny sky and calm ocean.

"Always remember: Don't get caught unaware in calm weather." His dad reclined next to him as they shared lunch. "With weather this hot, we're likely to see storms tonight. I'm aiming to stop at Haugesund for supplies; then, we'll find a quiet cove and hunker down."

"Can't we go through it? I want to get further away, and you said we'd be going through some storms."

"We'll meet enough bad weather, no need to go looking for it. Besides, it's better to go through a storm during the day. Let's not borrow trouble." A stern look crossed his face, and then his dad turned toward the wind, squinting at the water around them.

They were a couple of hours from their destination, and his dad was guiding him to take command of the vessel, adding on from lessons in the past. Slowly they noticed the wind changing directions.

"We're coming about to a narrowing in the channel," his dad started.

"I know. It means we're nearing Haugesund. I want to go somewhere exciting, someplace I've never been." Milo felt the shift in the weather, and it prickled his skin with excitement.

"Soon enough. But for now, we have to keep a sharp eye on the wind direction so we will have an idea of where we'll end up when we take another tack. It might seem like an easy run out in the open. It can become much stickier when it narrows out." His dad made adjustments as he spoke.

"Does that mean we might get to go through the storm after all?" Milo smiled up at his dad.

"Maybe, but don't look so excited about it," his dad replied, though Milo could sense a hint of a smile and a lightness of anticipation in his step, and he thought his dad was just as excited as he was. Calm sunny days were incredible, but the exhilaration of an impending challenge ignited an eagerness in father and son.

When they arrived at the public dock, his dad suggested a hot meal; they had earned it. Milo remembered that leg of the trip more than anything he saw after, even though they explored new waters. He learned how to read the water by the vibration of the boat and that the unexpected can happen wherever you are. Most of all, he experienced the control and precision of being at the helm in a profound way.

Times like now, when he was in and out of consciousness, he was so glad he wasn't driving. He was out of control and knew someone else needed to steer him home. There had been times when he had been so out of it, he shouldn't be conscious, but he had the presence of mind to get home safe, even if he didn't always remember the trip home.

Once, during the worst rainstorm he had ever experienced, he saw a car float past him. The expression on the driver's face summed up what he was feeling right now; a total lack of control. It was in Kampala, and he was coming out of the supermarket. The rainfall was about a metre deep, which was fine because he had a snorkel on his beast of a car.

Not everyone was as equipped, and as he turned down Ggaba Road, which was rapidly washing away into the river, a woman in a Toyota Corolla rushed by, hands on her steering wheel and motions doing nothing to control her car in the ever-rising current. He locked eyes with her and could feel the frantic desperation from one human to another in the midst of a storm.

At the same time, he was creating a wake but couldn't slow down too much, or he would stall. He could still see the expression on her face all these years later and thought about it most often when his methods of transportation seemed chaotic.

That's the trouble with most land vehicles. They don't always respond the way you want them to. He much preferred his odds on the water. In a sailboat, you must be aware of your own body as you move along in response to the conditions.

Slumped in the back of the tuk-tuk, he was aware his own body wasn't doing so well and felt pulled to float away from it. His soul was weighed down by broken flesh, repugnant in its limitations, ready to wear his next life, and weary of fighting. Tired of the endlessness of trying to stop the flood and find calm waters, he started to willingly ebb into blackness to allow the world to go on without him. Maybe he could just sleep it off, as he had so many times before.

## SIX

# HIS TESTICLES TRIED TO KILL HIM BUT ENDED UP SAVING HIS LIFE

As the strange morning went on, the tuk-tuk driver tried to rouse his passenger.

"I'm taking you to your hotel, okay?" He had heard about the foreigner who had been hit from behind. It was a David and Goliath accident with the foreigner on a small motorcycle, and the other driver, who apparently hit him like a speed bump and kept going, was in a massive SUV with everyone talking. That's how the driver knew where Milo was staying. Things were ghostly quiet at the time, so anything new or noteworthy drew people's attention and was spread widely.

Things had suddenly gotten livelier for this driver. He also knew enough to get Milo's attention. If he had a passenger die en route, he was less likely to get paid. He turned slightly and nudged Milo as he spoke again. "Wake up, you want to see this. We're coming up to the place you were hit. Parts of your bike are still there."

Milo had barely felt the nudge as he was numb to the pain, but he felt the intention of the words urging him to come back from the blackness. The words echoed around before stirring him, pushing himself to move his mouth and his body. In his mind, he realised the driver was talking about an accident, but it was a bike, not a bus. He managed to moan, "Whh--" unsure if he wanted to know where, or what, or why.

The driver, urged on by the sign of life, slowed as they came to a curve in the road. "Look there on the left. You'll see where the accident happened. Look at what's left of your little bike. Surprised you made it."

As the words sunk in, with rubble from the accident still visible at the side of the road, the horrible realisation came to him:

*The bus accident was two years ago.*

Gia had died on that bus.

Dreading the memories even as they flooded through his incoherence, he realised the aftermath at the hospital he was remembering was almost exactly two years to the day. Confusion untangling into concerned consideration brought Milo through the buzzing and back into what was now in front of him—the remains of the motorcycle he had been driving after he had gone to Kep to heal by the sea. Two years after the horrific bus crash led to the loss of Gia and a cascade calamity, Milo was trying to get on with his life, as one does, when he suffered a stroke. The stroke had cascaded into a run of health struggles that started in his brain and ended at his balls.

In a flash of recognition, Milo remembered the bus accident as it happened. How he avoided going on the trip because he was recovering from surgery. He wasn't on the bus; his testicles saved him! The real events as they transpired came back to him with an intensity that broke through his pain-induced incoherence.

Finding a growth on your testicle is easily ignored for as long as possible while still niggling at the back of your mind. Milo found something was off on his wedding day, and he had kept it to himself because there was so much joy surrounding them. Getting married in New York was a true celebration. It was also just another day in the city. They could just be two men who loved each other, promising to share their lives. Having had to previously lie, hide who he was, or leave a country under threat of death, the freshness of the atmosphere in New York added an additional pulse of hope to the union.

Being in New York with the man he loved and special friends Melinda and Evan, who were honoured to host them, was something he would not spoil by bringing up his balls. Yes, the growth was concerning, and it niggled at the back of his mind.

Still, Melinda made him promise to get it checked out as soon as possible. If he didn't, she'd harass him about it until he did. She reminded him that it mattered. When they were back home in Cambodia, he got it checked out and found out he had to have his testicles removed, which sounded horrifying at the time, until he realised he'd likely have died if he hadn't needed that operation. He was scheduled to join the team retreat but stayed back to be near the hospital. Milo was supposed to be on the bus, and

Gia and the others gave him a hard time for his reason for staying behind. It wasn't an excuse; they knew he was still healing and preferred to stay nearby for medical care. And to stay far away from a four-hour bus ride for multiple days that would have done a number on his still sensitive bits.

There were twelve-fourteen colleagues that had left together that day. The bus they were taking should have failed inspection, and by all accounts, the driver was grumpy and difficult from the outset.

He had said goodbye to his colleagues on Wednesday, and Milo went to work at home since nothing would be going on in the office. After they left, he had found out they were moving forward in the process for a huge EU grant, which was a wonderful surprise. The day progressed quietly, and Milo had been content about avoiding a team-building retreat, thanks to his testicles.

He heard about the accident that afternoon just as he had been checking emails and finishing his third coffee of the day.

"There has been an accident" can have so many different connotations. It's something you might say when you finish the last of the wine for the night or, more seriously, spill a stain on your outfit moments before going on to do a massive presentation. It is also something you might say to explain why a road is closed. The words carry urgency; however, our minds go directly to how we will be inconvenienced, not the life-changing implications.

Milo was so accident-prone he was usually involved in some fray, often of his own making. When he had received the call, he was frustratingly distant, and the reality of his quiet work-from-home day was shattered before he had even responded to the panicked terror in Bora's voice on the other end of the phone.

"I'll be right there." He hadn't known what he was saying, just responding out of reflex and the understanding that they would need help fast. He had stayed on the phone with Bora as he floated around his apartment, gestured to his husband that he had to go, and drove to the office. It had been like one of those dreams where you are in one place, then you are somewhere else. He hadn't remembered driving there. Somehow, he had arrived, and he immediately wished he hadn't forgotten his cigarettes.

He had arrived to find the office turned upside-down with chaos and decisions having to be made quickly. Someone had to go to the crash site. More people were needed at the referral hospital where the injured were being brought. At that time, there was word of some fatalities, but they hadn't known who or what really transpired.

Milo had hopped into a work vehicle with colleagues, including a co-worker who was married to one of the people on the bus. Inside the vehicle, everyone's phones had been going off as they raced to the referral hospital where the victims of the accident were, unsure of who they would find when they got there.

Of all his times travelling, this one trip had seemed like the longest. The 3.5-hour drive had been an eternity of interruptions, and it felt like everything was moving in slow motion. Milo couldn't get to the hospital in Kep fast enough, and yet everything had seemed to be undermining their progress. First, they had to stop for petrol.

As they headed out on the road again, Milo sent an

update to his husband and friends about where he was and what had happened. Simultaneously, he had been answering phone calls and messages from people trying to find out specifics about who was on the bus.

While Milo was fielding phone calls, Rith had been by his side, usually so quiet and reserved, getting louder as information had come in and screaming when he had received confirmation of those who had not made it.

"Oh no, not Lida. Please, not Lida."

And then, too soon after, "Not Pola, no, not Pola too!"

The echoes of those screams have stayed with him ever since. All the while, Milo had been searching for Gia, and he was frustrated by how little information he was getting. Celeste was driving down from the provinces where she worked for another NGO. She called Milo while she was on her way and asked if he knew anything about what happened to her wife.

"I've just had a phone call from someone in your office. When I asked if Gia had died, she just said yes and put the phone down. There must be some mistake." Celeste told him. The panic in her voice was being held back by sheer hope.

"No one would give you news like that on purpose." He had responded, trying to keep the shakiness out of his voice. "The phones were going off, and it was sheer madness when I left the office. I'll see what I can find out and get back to you."

After waiting for a response, the afternoon turned into evening. Then for some reason, Veha decided they needed to stop for bread and other snacks to bring to the hospital for those who had been in the accident.

"Really, do you think that's necessary?" Milo said through clenched teeth. He was screaming on the inside at the urgency he felt to get to the referral hospital immediately, but he knew there was nothing he could do about it. "This isn't a time to stop for snacks."

"They might need them," Veha insisted. Milo was overruled by his travelling companions and sat and stewed while they went into a little shop for snacks. Nothing happens in Cambodia without snacks, even apparently in an emergency situation.

Then he sent a message to his friends: *I think Gia is dead.* Did he really type that? Even with confirmation from multiple people, it didn't seem that it could possibly be true. She was the utter definition of alive and filled everything she did with life. He stared at the words he typed, incapable of comprehending the new reality he was facing.

Ra and their friends were coming together in Phnom Penh to follow after him as he had been updating them on a group chat. Finally, Milo got a hold of the country office, who confirmed what he had heard from those at the referral hospital; Gia had died.

Reaching nearer the hospital where the victims were still in need of help, Milo had to call Celeste and tell her that Gia was gone. Celeste just screamed.

Night encroached when they had finally arrived at the small referral hospital a short while later. He walked into carnage. People were bleeding out on metal beds, and Milo had switched into medic mode from training earlier in his life. There was no first response system in the country, so they had to triage people and get them to another hospital.

The referral hospital was a simple building with a tin roof, few rooms, and metal beds. There was no lifesaving equipment and no-one with trauma training.

The first step was pinpointing the members of his team who needed the most help. Ranging from the most severe to less life-threatening, it was difficult to assess. One of them had a punctured lung and internal bleeding, so they sent him out with the first available ambulance. Calling it an ambulance was a stretch. It was a van with a light on it, but there were no supplies inside.

Heng, an incredibly kind and patient child protection worker, had the top of his head sawn off due to a brain haemorrhage, and there were doctors trying to glue and stitch his head back together.

Milo was pulled away to the petite body of his assistant Maly who had just died. He let his mind consider the bottle that was waiting for him when this was all done, then he carried on. He took Maly's body and wrapped it up and put it in an out-of-the-way corner until her family could come claim her. He watched carefully to ensure she wasn't bumped or disturbed and kept everyone with cameras away from her and the rest of his staff. Always delicate and effective like a fragrant flower, her fragility was profoundly evident in her death as she left her body behind.

That was when he, Rith, and Veha decided they had to move quickly to get the rest of their co-workers out of there and to the Royal Phnom Penh Hospital, where they could receive life-saving procedures. There were three that had obvious internal injuries, and Milo prioritised who should be moved first.

The doctor on duty didn't want to release anyone, so Milo had to be quite firm.

"They need to go now," he insisted.

"No, they don't," the doctor replied, and his calm demeanour irritated Milo to no end. How could anyone be so uninterested, given the life and death struggle all around him? Walking away with an air of authority, the doctor apparently had nothing else to say.

Milo followed him into his small corner office that doubled as a supply room. The only thing on the shelf was a box of paracetamol. The rest of the room was empty, and Milo let the doctor know in no uncertain terms what he thought of the place and emphasised he would be orchestrating the departure of everyone involved in the bus accident. He must have gotten his point across because the rest of the staff retreated to far corners of the hospital, and Milo, Rith, and Veha resumed the arduous process of commandeering vehicles and somehow transporting critically injured individuals into the hands of the medical professionals in Phnom Penh.

Hours to the north in Phnom Penh, they had to arrange with staff to get to the hospital to receive patients and pay for whatever was needed. Meanwhile, he was still keeping Maly's body out of the way while everything started to quiet down. It was a few hours later that her mum and sisters arrived. Reverently, he lifted her into the back of her family's car.

Things took a turn to the strange as he reflected on the cultural differences surrounding death. In Cambodia, they have a much different view about privacy than Milo did, so when someone's grandmother dies, people post pictures of her dead body on Facebook. It's culturally acceptable to post pictures of dead bodies. It's how they do things, and Milo saw the humour in him spending so much time protecting Maly's body from people who were trying to take photos of her, only to have her mum arrive and whip back the sheet that had been covering her and start taking pictures of her and immediately post them online. At the crash site, people were taking images of his co-workers hanging upside-down, dead on the bus. Milo was being sent pictures of their dead bodies from other co-workers who thought it was fine to share. It was traumatising, and the organisation Milo worked for had to hire someone who worked full-time for three days finding and reporting images of their dead colleagues.

Driving back to Phnom Penh with his friends in stony silence, after hours and hours of total chaos, Milo thought about the four they lost and the many more who were injured. On the way to the hospital, he got a message from the country director asking if he was going to go see Celeste. He replied that he was headed to the hospital and then would go see Celeste afterwards. The director asked to clarify that he would go see her. He typed, "Yes, I will go and see Celeste," but autocorrect changed it to, "Yes, I will go shoot Celeste."

An exhausted breathy laugh escaped his mouth, and he said, "I just told the country director I will go shoot Celeste." The ridiculousness of the image of going to murder her after she just learned her wife died, combined with Piper's bemused reaction, burst into a bubble of laughter between them. Milo had tears in his eyes, and his stomach hurt when the giggles finally stopped, as long as he didn't look at Piper, or they'd both start up again. The rest of their friends looked at them like they had lost their minds. As he settled down, he realised it was something Gia would have found incredibly funny.

The bright lights of the city approaching brought renewed hope and energy. The massive structure was solid in front of them, and Milo stepped out into the warm night. Once inside the hospital, he found there was only one surgeon, so even though multiple people needed immediate help, they were forced to wait. On top of that, the hospital administration required payment upfront. Milo knew his organisation would cover the fees, but that didn't help at the moment. Every available member of staff took out large amounts of cash to cover the expenses. Fortunately, in Cambodia, it's possible to withdraw $10,000 out of the bank at once, so Milo was contacting everyone he knew, asking, "Hey, can I borrow $5,000."

His friend Simone had six phones and was always on the go. She was working with his husband and other friends to ensure he was supported and to get cash to the hospital so they would do the required surgery. In a strange turn of fortune, the accident happened just after the elections, during which time a lot of people take their money out of banks. So, coincidently, people were able to quickly gather a network of funds to get the ball rolling on everything that was medically required.

The intensity of the night, along with funny, strange moments, came flooding back to him while he sat in the back of a tuk-tuk. Alone now, he considered how he had left the hospital when there was nothing else that could be done, and then, after all the night entailed, he ended up at Simone's bar at 2 am, where he said, "I need a bottle of wine now."

They had some drinks sitting in near silence while Milo sent Simone's daughter to go get some Temazepam from the pharmacy that he could bring Celeste. He sat for about half an hour, calming his nerves glass by glass, then went to see Celeste. The funny thing was that Gia's wife initially disliked him; she thought he was a bit of a prick. But there he was at her door with a Temazepam to help her sleep when nothing else would help.

When he got home, he probably drank three bottles of wine in two minutes flat. He wanted to sleep through it all and forget it all, and now he was reliving it again, physically going through his own similar medical emergency, and he wasn't sure how much more he could take. Reliving those deaths and revelling in how much loss of life he had seen pushed Milo with a heaviness that lingered.

He had a flashback to the first person he saw die. He was well trained in first aid, but in some instances, there wasn't anything that could be done. As a young adult, he had been walking back to his grandparents' home one evening. It was a familiar street; the lights were coming on as the sun dwindled. Typical of a day that begins so mundane and ends etched on your mind forever. Milo was just rounding the last corner when a man walking towards him fell flat on the pavement in front of him.

Milo knelt down to check his vitals and potentially resuscitate the man while he called 999. When the paramedics arrived, they assured him there was nothing he could have done. The man had had a massive heart attack and died on the spot. Anytime he faced death since

Milo remembered the immense freedom and sorrow of the fleeting nature of life. He was the last person to see that stranger alive on another normal day. The man had probably been walking towards some mundane errand and left behind loved ones who would count the minutes they missed him.

Making sense of it would drive him mad. Many times it should have been him and so many absurd situations he'd survived. Soon enough, it would be his turn, maybe even more shortly than that.

The tuk-tuk driver had trouble rousing Milo and was unable to get a response out of him for a few moments. Then, one eye opened wide, and he asked, "Are we there then?"

The driver stepped back and cried out in surprise at Milo, suddenly becoming animated. Coming back into the present, Milo still felt on the edge of a dream that was falling into a nightmare. He felt himself being helped out of the vehicle by the driver, shaking and unsure and eager to hand off the responsibility.

Walking again, Milo felt like he was on the edge of two realities. He could feel the fullness of the bus accident so vividly in his mind in this sleepy seaside town. Now facing a walk back to his hotel, picturesque at any other time took on a grotesque humour as he considered the risks of living life. The comedic timing of his own health issues that saved him from getting on the bus with the rest of his colleagues led him to be run down two years later in the same stunning location.

Hobbling along in the early morning, no longer dripping blood, just coagulating in matching splotches, he was chuckling internally somehow. He entered the lobby like part of a zombie fashion show, limping and dragging his body along. As he approached the front desk, he attempted a smile, but his usual dashing good looks and charm were lost under his current costume of blood and gore.

The front desk agent gasped mostly because she wasn't sure how someone in his state could still be standing.

"I seem to have lost my room key. Could you help me get into my room?" Milo managed to ask, his polite manners an ingrained first reaction, even as his whole body was shaking in shock.

"You're a mess. You need to go to Phnom Penh and get to the hospital straight away," the agent replied, stepping back and looking around like she'd love for a manager to step in.

"I'd rather just go pop in the shower. Thank you very much," he said, realising he wouldn't have the strength for it. His head throbbed, and he contemplated resting right on the spot, the hotel floor gleaming an invitation.

"Oh no, it looks much worse than that. Let's get you in a taxi. Does your husband know where you are?" She asked.

"No, I need a phone," he said, stubbornly trying to regain control of his faculties and the situation.

"I'll do it. You need to go." Her tone changed, and she insisted he go to the hospital. She called a cab and also informed the hotel owner, who called his husband. Milo hadn't noticed the driver who walked up beside him until he touched his shoulder. Milo winced.

The cab driver also knew what happened to him. "You're the foreigner that got run over. We all thought you were dead."

Milo's sudden laughter perplexed the driver, who didn't know the number of times Milo had avoided death. He was past his nine lives for sure. It was a funny irony that the times he wanted to die, he lived, and now he wanted to live … well, who knew what would happen next? He had gotten this far already. He needed to get out of his own way and stop trying to do everything himself. He accepted that the international hospital in Phnom Penh was the best place for him and, in his weakened state, wondered if he would live to tell this tale.

Musing on the continued hilarity of the whole situation, Milo started to realise he was his own worst enemy.

# SEVEN

# ACCEPTING UNCERTAINTY

The driver led him on through the haze he was surrounded by, and for a moment, Milo thought he did die. He was unable to appreciate the view of the old colonial houses, lush vegetation, and views of the Gulf of Thailand. He caught a glimpse of his reflection in the window of the hotel and didn't recognise what he saw. The image glimmered, and in the clear glass surrounded by pale blue walls, it looked like he was trapped in ice.

He was transported to a long-ago acid trip with arctic animals after taking pills laced with acid at Bestival on the Isle of Wight. He got separated from his friends. One part of the group went off to drink, and Milo was sticking to pills at that stage in his life. He and his friend David went off to explore, and shared some ecstasy, so he was taking drugs and having a good time. Eventually, David went back to the tent to sleep. Milo went to his tent, and he was joined by a polar bear. At first, he thought it was too much ecstasy, which would have been a first. Normally E wasn't quite so intense, so he thought it wouldn't last long.

He was confused about why it was happening because he hadn't taken any drug that warranted having a conversation with a polar bear. Even when politely asked, the polar bear wouldn't go away. Milo tried to reason himself out of it and put his head into the pillow so the visions would stop. Alas, in the darkness, every shape morphed into an arctic animal. The tent was an igloo. An arctic fox came out of nowhere, and then a rabbit. Apparently, his subconscious was having an exceptionally realistic polar experience.

The next morning, he felt a little skittish, worried that every shadow would once again transform into a talking animal. When his friends asked if he was all right, he told them what he saw. They all laughed at him.

"Come on, I'm no lightweight. It was seriously intense. I had the feeling the polar bear was quite bothered about being there as well." Milo looked around to see if anyone else had visited the Arctic via hallucination.

"We all had a normal Bestival experience. If you didn't want to get fucked up, why'd you bother coming?" Roger mocked him, and the rest of the group joined in.

Even Jacob, who was fairly new to the group, added his two cents. "You're being a bit dramatic about it, really."

His comment brought a chorus of agreement from everyone else, and Milo was about to tell them to piss off when David spoke up. "Sorry, I'm with Milo on this one. Unexpected hallucinations are one way to ruin a good trip. If I saw a polar bear in my tent, I'd be terrified."

"It was very intense. It was not a cute and cuddly cartoon; I could see its teeth!" Milo shivered at the memory.

Talking to the polar bear felt as real as talking to the driver did now. Even if it was a hallucination, it had been a harrowing experience, and he could feel the surge of adrenaline and the shiver of the cool arctic air. Now was he remembering it or dreaming it? Was he conscious, or was this part of another, wilder trip?

The driver stopped him as he started to meander off course, then took his arm and guided him to the vehicle. He told Milo that he had seen the accident and the police chief of Kep also witnessed the accident, took his possessions, and brought him to the hospital. Milo had no recollection of any of it though later, he was astonished at the timing of it all. If ever anyone was in the right place at the right time, it was the police chief witnessing Milo being run over.

Thank God for the police chief of Kep. He was one of the good ones. When he saw the accident, he had the foresight to stop and help Milo rather than chase down the perpetrator. While it meant the person who ran Milo down got away, it also meant the police chief likely saved his life. If he had been left on the side of the road, he would have been left for dead.

Whenever Milo was asked about law enforcement, he cringed a little inside. It's such a tough, usually thankless job. A lot of what they have to do is shit. Maybe that's why it attracts some of the worst people. There are probably ten or more bad ones for each good one. His close friend, Jim, was an officer in the international paedophile department, and he emphasised the challenges inherent in law enforcement.

As the driver was talking and leading him down the sidewalk, other police encounters that were strange and humorous came to Milo's recollection.

In Uganda, he spent the night in jail after getting stopped for intoxication. He ended up having beers with his cell mates by bribing his jailer, only to be called into the head officer's office early the next morning. Terrified, he walked into an officer welcoming him over to his computer to help him find a flat for his daughter a thousand kilometres away in Birmingham. The officer had heard there was an Englishman staying the night and recruited help to ensure his daughter would have a safe neighbourhood to live in. That wasn't so bad.

Brazil was a bit worse. He and his ex had been kidnapped by police while walking along Le Blanc beach in Rio De Janeiro. That was one incident that led to Milo distrusting the police. He was quite angry about it and told the officers they should be ashamed of themselves. Later, when they lived to fight about it, Roger had said, "Only a private school-educated boy would get moral when being kidnapped."

At the time, it had been annoyance, not fear, that had propelled him. Milo had been indignant at the audacity of the officers. Upholding the respectability of the uniform was important, and Milo had felt it was his duty to inform them of his outrage; his bravado might have been amplified by a lingering buzz. His husband had found nothing humorous about it.

Some incidents were funny rather than hair-raising. One trip to Tanzania became a source of amusement when he had the police following him around for ten days. He had been in Arusha, near Kilimanjaro, checking on potential organisations they could work with on voluntourism visits. Everywhere he had stopped, the police would visit just after he left and ask about what he was up to. Since it is a popular tourist destination, many people work without visas, and the police worked hard to stop it. The night before he was set to leave, the police had arrived at his door to arrest him. They had assumed he didn't have a permit to work in the country and had sent four officers who were clearly eager to take him away. What they didn't know was that Uganda was part of the East African community, so he was legally allowed to work there, and he ended up telling them how to do their job. Milo chuckled to himself as they walked away sheepish and empty-handed.

At an organisation earlier in his career that had programs in Uganda and Kenya, he had helped discover that one of the volunteers was a paedophile who had infiltrated the system, gained access to vulnerable children, and was abusing the children they were supposed to be helping. Milo heard from someone who claimed to have been a victim, and the organisation didn't want to report it. They brushed it off as an excuse for the victim to get money.

Appalled by their lack of compassion, Milo insisted they help her. Even though the organisation promptly removed him from existence because of it, Milo knew it needed to be done. It was ridiculous that they would no longer acknowledge his contribution to the growth of the organisation, but to Milo, his integrity was too important, and the health and well-being of the victim were paramount.

When he had received a call from London that the paedophile had been arrested, he had jumped on a plane to talk to the police. The questioning detective was Jim. At their first meeting, Milo had been eager to provide any information that would be helpful. Jim had been investigating the organisation to see if anyone else was involved. Within the first few minutes of their meeting, it had become less of an interrogation and more of a conversation.

After their meeting, they had exchanged numbers. Then they met for a drink after the investigation had closed because the pilot killed himself.

Jim explained that he had been trying to establish if Milo facilitated the volunteer and realised within one minute that Milo only had an interest in protecting children.

They had a lot in common and found they shared the same dark humour that came with working on the pointy edges of child protection. Over the years, they had worked together to stop British people from going to other countries to exploit children. Milo had been well connected internationally with different organisations and would pass on info for Jim to take action on.

Both of them had similar ways of decompressing by obliterating all emotion with whatever illicit substances were available. More than once, they had found themselves sharing a weekend, losing count of the lines until the horror of what happened had been blasted away.

Dropping out of memory and back at the street, wavering on unsteady feet, he was starting to think this really was all just one bad drug trip. His feet still refused to function. It didn't make sense, and yet his body somehow continued to propel forward. This journey seemed endless, and he was stuck in a cycle of unknowing. Had he ever made it out of South Africa?

The driver guided him gently into the back of the cab and asked if he was ready or needed anything.

Milo thanked him and said he'd love to go sailing, the effects of shock setting in, causing him to forget his peril. He hadn't been sailing for so long, and yet it had always been such a crucial part of who he was. He remembered the sailing club in Norway and then spending summers teaching sailing in Greece. The sea was a cruel mistress, untameable and uncertain, and fit his unsettled heart like a well-worn tool in the hands of a craftsman. He loved the rugged uncertainty of a place like the tumultuous waters of the Gulf of Corryvreckan.

He had sailed all over the world, and he loved the challenge of the strong Atlantic currents. It was a region of intense tidal changes known for whirlpools and standing waves. As the tide moved through the narrow channel between two islands, it sped up and rushed over the sharp topography below. Navigation required a steady hand and a keen understanding of how his boat moved through the water. It was such a harsh climate and a challenging and unforgiving course that tested him to his limits and got him out of his own mind. Off the coast of Scotland, it was also close to his heart and part of his home. It was that strong Scotsman in him that he leaned into when life's seas got rough.

In his dazed remembrance, he compared the tempestuous nature of the sea to the uncertainty of life and his current circumstances and decided to just ride the tide and see where he ended up.

The changeable nature of his experiences taught him to be exceedingly adaptable. For a long time, he had really struggled as he tried to be excellent at everything. One of the best things Buddhism brought into his life was to accept mediocrity. Previously, he always had to be the last person standing at the party. At work, he was unstoppable. He would work sixteen hours a day, then party all night, and still get up at 6 am after getting three hours of sleep. It was ridiculous how relentless he was no matter what he sought.

In Milo's mind dictionary, beside the word relentless was an image of ants swarming the tent as he and a friend had camped out during a trek through the Chyulu Hills in Kenya. In the middle of the night, amidst a deluge, millions of minuscule insects had taken refuge in their tent from their flooded nests. With headlamps blinding one another, Milo and his travelling companion had fought the ants for a tiny corner and waited out the night. That unpleasant lesson was a visual reminder that ants work incredibly well together and don't stop no matter what obstacle they face. The relentless ants were an unwelcome surprise and had proved to be a difficult life form to share shelter with. They had made it through the night with bites all over, as well as the gnawing memory ants, adamant in their drive to escape.

Why was he thinking of ants while he was dying? Oh yes, the inevitability of a cockup. You will be minding your own business, even sleeping in your own bed, when an army of ants will literally or proverbially throw you backwards until you're huddled in the corner getting bitten.

It was a hard lesson that always brought out an intense curiosity in Milo. He wondered why accepting the uncertainty of life was less of a focus in school rather than leaving people to figure it out on their own. No one knows what they will be doing tomorrow or even later the same day. There are too many surprises in life, both good and bad, and death rarely arrives when expected.

When he was a teenager, maybe sixteen years old, in great shape physically because he had been in military training at the time, he had gone night skiing and taken off over a ravine careening down the hill. He had landed way down in an off-limits zone and had missed some sharp boulders to his left by only a few metres. He stood up, steadied himself and took a look around. The temperature was dropping fast, and he knew no one would find him where he was. Even when his dad and brother reported him missing, the search would be limited until daylight. He had known he was on his own, and as his gaze moved up the cliff he'd be climbing, he felt loneliness spreading like ice over his skin.

He grabbed his skis and poles and had found a foothold. Tentatively and without reassurance, he had made a slow ascension. Midway up, he had slipped and lost a few feet before catching himself. He thought better of leaving his equipment behind and kept going. Even out of breath while sitting, still the cold had started to creep in. It was taking him longer than he expected, and a sliver of fear pulled at him.

He had heard the chairlift above him shut down, and the light he was climbing towards went dark. The park was closed. Now when he reached the top, he'd get to ski down to the chalet in the dark. The panic and dropping temperature had combined to freeze Milo in terror as the thought of being stuck out there crossed his mind. He wouldn't live until morning; he had known that much. No. He wasn't going to be a Milo-icicle for them to find in the morning. He had forced himself to trudge on.

When he had reached the top, utterly exhausted, he lifted himself up to the crest of the hill into the blinding light of a rescuer's torch. It had been rather anticlimactic, but he was too relieved to care and accepted a ride back to the chalet in a sled full of warm blankets where his father, brother, and the ski resort staff were waiting. They had all been in a state of elation, his family eager to see him in one piece and the staff eager to close up and head out without further issues.

He had arrived home feeling silly at how relieved he was.

"You gave us all a good scare. Scared yourself most of all, I bet." His dad had hung around the room. "Even Bogle won't leave you alone."

Milo had ruffled the fur on the Scottish deerhound's neck as the dog pressed into his side. Bogle had been following them around since they got back. Usually out of the way of any commotion, he had planted himself next to Milo and refused to leave. After his close call, Milo had been thankful for the extra warmth and comfort of having this furry companion with him. "Yes, there were a few times I was a bit nervous. Mostly though, I was thinking about what an embarrassing death that would have been."

William, who had been quieter than normal during the whole ordeal, finally laughed, and his face lightened. "You're right. It would've become a family joke. Watch out for that ravine there. You don't want to end up like Milo."

He had tried to grab a pillow and throw it at his brother, but Bogle was on top of it and wouldn't budge.

"No need to make jokes about dying. You faced a serious situation, and you got yourself out of it. Shows you used your training." Their dad had brought the mood back to a sombre one.

"Yeah, mostly I was lucky not to have broken anything when I fell. I knew how cold it was supposed to get tonight," Milo had said, considering the negative double digits outside and sinking further into the blanket wrapped around him.

His father had nodded, which was his version of approval, and walked out of the room.

Living in all different weather conditions helped his adaptability. One thing more, it allowed him to talk about the weather to anyone in any part of the world. The weather was one of those cultural universals that connected Milo to other humans. We can all be miserable in the rain, shivering in the cold, and sharing the shade of the only tree in the vicinity during a sweltering afternoon.

Milo noticed how humans adapted to the weather in all but words. Life would go on as usual, and the temperature and change in the seasons was like a constant. In the UK, "it's been very rainy lately" is a comforting blanket to be lathered on any awkward social interaction. Drinking was as certain as the weather to create a buffer of liquid courage. Humans put an awful lot of effort into the perception of security—we thrive unhealthily on it. Milo could see in others better than he could pinpoint in his own life how we set ourselves up for inevitable failure by expecting more of the same.

It would become a lifelong pursuit to embrace groundlessness rather than clinging to the illusion of comfort. In his life, he had found solace in his career with the understanding that at the pointy end of child protection, everyone is relentless and slightly crazy—they had to be as they worked to help children who faced unimaginable hardship. Every organisation was different, but the individuals on the front lines brought incredible empathy and passion for what they did.

The social workers that stick by children and families are heroes. Milo had learned that from years of working with some incredible people. They are the ones who get up at 2 am and make the tough calls. Milo had noticed the women were especially relentless in improving the lives of children, no matter how difficult the situation. Joyce had worked with him in the Uganda slums, where she insisted on wearing high heels. One of her children had gone missing, and as they were walking up a rough path full of faeces and other refuse, she saw him and called his name. The young boy was spry; he had heard her and took off running.

"Wait, Joyce, don't chase him. We'll catch up with him later," Milo had yelled as her heels slapped the worn path.

She hadn't looked back or paused long enough to respond. She had just kept going, determined to find the boy and make sure he was safe. Milo laughed at her audacity in a business suit and heels. When she had turned up thirty-six hours later with the boy safely in tow, Milo had known he'd never question her again.

In that same slum, some months later, he had been cornered by a group of social workers because their manager had been ignoring the case of an orphan who lived on the floodplain with her grandmother. Their house had been constructed of a few rough pieces of wood with a tin roof. The workers had been concerned because the girl's grandmother had died, and she was sleeping next to the body. Their manager had known about the situation and did nothing. Since the other workers had spoken up, Milo was able to help the girl and fire the useless manager.

Trekking through shit-filled streets, trying to help children and families that don't want help, and interfering in situations like an attempted child beheading take a toll on even the most prepared-for-anything veteran. The uncertainty and precariousness of every individual was visceral, and a dark humour often developed as a coping strategy. For many, it was a means of survival. For Milo, the dark humour came first as a coping strategy for life.

The dark humour was a connection he shared with others who had seen the horrific circumstances that are, unfortunately, a part of child protection.

It all went backwards to that first line that took the pain offline like fireworks compared to the low lull drinking offered. He wondered if he really was ready to feel the pain that he had been running from and drugging into oblivion his whole life. If it was his time, so be it. He had considered death's welcoming arms many times. Through the glint in the window, he saw Gia's smile reflected in the sunlight. Breath paused. He half wondered if she was there to take him home.

He had a memory of them standing on the edge of the pier, water blending into the shiny sky. Stars glittering with the milky way blurring through the night, he had tried to impress Gia with his astrological knowledge. She had looked at him, whipped out her phone and then said, "Yeah, you're right, but most people just use the Stargazer app since it's verified."

"Well, thanks for taking me down a peg. I was anticipating teaching my son how to pinpoint certain constellations," Milo had remarked.

"One more dream dashed by modern technology," Gia had replied. "There is something to be said for having a skill with no app required, however."

"I suppose so, but it takes some of the awe out of it, doesn't it?" Milo asked.

"Yes, though I've always thought that the constellations do the same thing. By naming them something of the earth, it takes away from what those stars are unto themselves," Gia said in the way she had of breathing new life into an old concept.

"That makes sense. Humans have a tendency to name things we don't understand," Milo said.

"Yes, and now when we look up, we see the stars in a manmade pattern," Gia said.

"We do the same things with each other, don't we? I was sitting here thinking about how to impress my son with my knowledge. We all want to construct what we are remembered by," Milo had said.

"You took that deeper than I intended," Gia said with a smile. "You're right, though. We see that with our donors daily."

"That's the perfect example of the altruism of leaving a legacy, one might call it. In a more universal way, I suppose, it all comes down to humans being scared," Milo said.

"Scared of what they can't control, right?" Gia had added. "We spend so much time creating constructs because we don't want to experience the uncertainty of being unable to know for sure what tomorrow might bring."

"Totally, then we get stuck in the what-ifs of life," Milo said.

"Like, what if it was Artemis instead of Orion?" Gia suggested.

*What if I stopped the bus driver from taking you on that trip?*

The loudness of that thought caused an abrupt shift. The spell was broken as the cab screeched to a start and bounced down the rutted red road.

# EIGHT

# FIRST AID

Driving the road to Phnom Penh from Kep takes 3.5 hours minimum. That's with no accidents or interruptions. Having traversed Cambodia for years, Milo didn't like his odds. As they left the coast behind, he stared ahead at the road being lit by the new day with dark trees on both sides. The effect was like rushing through a lighted tunnel. In that moment, a hollow dread started to press him, a sinking feeling that the experience was a premonition of what was to come. He could sense that death was imminent.

After all he had been through that night, there was still a long road ahead of him. They passed through the trees and wound down the road through farmland and villages. Milo rested, admitting to himself that his body was beginning to show signs of shutting down. His vision blurred and he focused inward, past the point of pain. Thoughts were staccato in his mind. He had faced the end of his life so many times it had become as familiar to Milo as the bottom of an empty bottle.

Now it seemed good, old, dependable death was sticking around, and Milo felt to the depth of his being that this would be his last day.

There were worse things than death. His work showed him that little nugget was true in all corners of the world. Life was constantly shifting in an ebb and flow that brought incredible highs and also miserable lows. In those low places of suffering, abuse and violence, death can feel like a merciful release. Milo had seen people living with mental illness that were bleeding out emotionally, which could sometimes be worse because it was less discernible. When you have a physical injury or worse, it is noticeable, and people can see how to help. Like Milo was now, with his new brown ensemble, looking like a horror show. The real wounds no one could see, and those most wounded learned to hide them well and early.

It wasn't that he was scared of death. In fact, as the minutes ticked on, he was starting to seep towards acceptance. He realised he might never see his husband or son again, and tears came to the corners of both eyes. Gently weeping, Milo reached for a phone he didn't have and prayed those he loved would know how much they meant to him. It was difficult to accept not being able to say goodbye, especially to Ra and his boy. They were the two people in the world he didn't want to disappoint or leave grieving.

He had struggled so hard to get his health back after everything he had been through in the last two years. During those challenges, he had the determination to fight and the knowledge about how important it was to get healthy and sober for his son. He was doing it first for himself. He couldn't put the burden of his success or failure on his son. He had fought so hard for his family, and now he felt the fight inside him waning. It was a devastating thought, and the tears blurred what little vision he had left.

The dampness cooled his cheeks, Milo's breath slowed, and he considered the birth of his son as the moment he understood what it meant to love. In his dwindling capacity, he couldn't express it beyond that simple truth. He wasn't weeping for himself; it was nostalgia for the beautiful lessons of a tough life, along with a sadness for time lost. It was more than just a will to live; he wanted more time, especially with his husband and son. Previously, he had such a complex, tortuous relationship with others until he saw that it started with himself.

With agonising clarity, he could see the moment he and his husband had connected, remembering the trepidation of finding peace after multiple toxic relationships. By slowly letting his guard down, he opened himself up to change how he tried to convince himself there was a catch to a good relationship. As they faced their ups and downs, Milo didn't want to wreck the relationship and was worried that his husband might be uninterested in going through the getting clean journey with him. His deeper fear that didn't see the light of admission was that he wouldn't be able to get a handle on addiction and would sabotage the relationship as he had before.

Right now, the outcome was irrelevant. As he was bleeding out on the highway on the way to Phnom Penh, his chances to enjoy the fruits of his relationship were ebbing away. His tender husband had brought a solace that Milo hadn't known he could find in the world. Together, even if they disagreed, they were comfortable and content. Milo cherished the life they built. A few years ago, they were headed to Siem Reap for the weekend when Milo got a call about a dog that needed a home or would be sent to a meat market. They already had four dogs, so he apologised that he wouldn't be able to help.

After he got off the phone, Ra had stared at him until Milo asked what was going on. "You better call back and say we'll take that dog."

"You can't be serious; we already have five," Milo had replied.

"You can't be serious. How can I go back to Fendi, Miu, Louis, and Pierre knowing I let one of their family members be taken to be eaten?" Ra had asked.

"Our dogs won't know. Remember, when Louis was a puppy, we said no more, no matter what," Milo replied.

"We said we wouldn't GET any more. This one came to us; we have to take it," Ra had said.

"That's cute. You're arguing semantics with me," Milo had said.

"You always bring it back to the language when you know I am right. We get it, you're English, and we're getting the dog," Ra had insisted.

And as usual, he had been right. Chanel had been a welcome addition to their family. Though she wasn't as graceful as her name suggested, she was a lumbering rottweiler who fancied herself a ballerina. Milo, in his delirium, began to remember how she had introduced herself to the rest of the fur family by encouraging them all to go for a good tear around the apartment.

Milo was jerked forward by the ceasing momentum of the cab. The driver had to stop for fuel but was kind enough to ask Milo if he needed any snacks. He tried to politely decline, and in the other space he was seeping into, he laughed at the timing of it all, bringing him so close to the day when his team was decimated in another vehicular accident. The irony was funny yet gruesome. A part of him had died when Gia did.

After the bus accident, he had Gia's belongings with him as he went home, where he immediately took some powerful sleeping pills and crashed. A few short hours later, at 5:30 am, the alarm on her phone had gone off, signalling the start of her work day. The sound awoke Milo, and he jolted out of bed in terror, pushing blindly into the dining room where he had placed her personal possessions that he had been given from the crash site. It was still damp and covered in dirt, grime, and spilt fuel from the crash. The smell permeated whatever had been left of his sleepiness. He had tried to silence the phone before his dogs joined in the cacophony. Since her phone was smashed, there had been no way to shut the alarm off. Panic had started to creep in as he couldn't get the phone to respond to his touch. Gia had always gotten up early to go for a walk before work. The morning after she lost her life, her alarm had blared out a loud and unending ode to the unfairness of it all.

His first reaction had been to fling it into the wall, but of course, he knew the memories on the phone would be irreplaceable for Celeste. Somehow, by the grace of

God, Milo had eventually managed to stop the alarm. Afterwards, he ended up sobbing in a heap as the physical loss of Gia started to sink in.

That had been day one of his awareness of the gravity of the situation. From there, he had been faced with a massive volume of calls with different members of the organisation taking a lead on different aspects. As part of the Cambodian mourning period, he had needed to find traditional white clothing and black and white kramas worn by those grieving a loss. Returning to the office, the first thing he had seen was the four pictures of the colleagues they had lost, surrounded by flowers. It had been momentous to be confronted by both the survivors and those left behind: what was left of the team.

Milo had reeled from the gut punch of the massive holes left in the organisation. Meanwhile, some of the victims were still in hospital, and he had been concerned about their recovery. He had also coordinated with Gia's family to return her body to the UK and ensure Celeste was recognised as next of kin. It was incredible how close he had felt to Gia in those days of chaos when he was trying to write her eulogy. He had talked with her a lot, still does, but then it was so clear he had been able to hear her and feel her with all his senses.

She had been able to write circles around him, and he had struggled trying to capture her bright light taken too soon, but it all sounded so trite. In his head, he had heard her say, "Fuck off, Milo, you're making me sound like a saviour."

Those days, as they happened, were a blur of travel and responsibilities. He had spent some time in the UK and then back home in Cambodia. It was incredible how far he had fallen and how far he had come, only to circle back and bleed out himself on the long road to the hospital.

Milo was aware that when you get run over, most often, whoever hit you will back up and make sure you are dead. It's bad luck to drive a car that has been involved in an accident in Cambodia. Did that mean he was twice lucky?

He found it funny that he had been driving a little motorbike when a drunk driver hit him from behind and drove over him in a big Lexus 4X4 because he had a tendency to be an aggressive driver. He was taught to drive by his dad, who had reinforced the lesson that it was often the best choice to accelerate out of problems instead of applying the brake. Moving around a lot as a boy had its drawbacks, though, as it turned out, they seemed to be in the right place at the right time for some good adventures and life lessons. When he had been around the age of thirteen, they lived in the UK briefly, and there was a defunct army base nearby.

There had been an entire village that was completely empty, where he could go from shop to imaginary shop, practising driving along the way. There was no better place to learn and no better teacher than his dad. Battle tough, his dad had been able to handle the jerky uncertainty of a brand-new driver. He was patient and had explained in his simple gruff way the essentials of staying safe on the road.

"That's right. You're getting the hang of it quickly. You want to be in command of the vehicle but also aware of what everyone else is doing on the road. We'll get to that later." His dad was encouraged that he had seemed to catch on quickly.

"Too bad I'm starting on this little car; I'd love to drive something bigger and faster!" Milo had been young and excited to be barrelling down the empty road behind the steering wheel with his dad to the left of him.

"Don't get ahead of yourself. Learn the rules first," his dad had said.

"You said I was learning quickly," Milo retorted.

"I did, but you were fifteen minutes late for our lesson. You know …"

"I know! To be early is on time, to be on time is to be late, and to be late is unacceptable." Milo had spoken in a tone trying to emulate his father's deep Scottish voice and a phrase he'd heard often.

His dad had turned away to hide a trace of a smile, not bothering to ask Milo to watch his tone. After a pause, he had told Milo to take the next right and practise what he'd learned. Later, in Norway, they continued the lessons.

Milo had worked on honing those skills by driving himself wherever possible in different countries, road conditions, and with different vehicles. As a point, Milo felt safer if he drove himself. Over the course of his life, he had taken driving tests all over the world. In Thailand, where they were cracking down on fraudulent international licences, it took three days. The parallel park was made deliberately hard with a specific indentation in the pavement, so it had to be perfect. The examiner had been a young guy who was more interested in practising English and was definitely not a driving expert. At one point in the lesson, Milo had admonished him light-heartedly, telling him, "I've been driving longer than you've been alive."

In Cambodia, lots of people drive without licences for the simple fact it is quite difficult to get a licence. Milo had to go back twenty times. Each time he had to guess the answers to nonsensical questions. Some of the places he had operated a vehicle were a free for all, and he had to drive aggressively just to survive. Those congested and chaotic situations helped him put into good use the driving skills he had learned from his dad, and he was grateful.

As the last bit of energy seemed to drain from him, he remembered more difficult times with his dad when he wanted to die. At the time, he hadn't spoken with his father in over a year when he travelled to Norway because he had nowhere else to go.

It was there in the remote north where Milo had felt so low he didn't want to go on. He had yet to recognise the trauma he had been through. Still, it coursed through him, pushing him to a depth of devastation he was unsure how to climb out of. It had felt like every option had been taken from him, and he was too broken to go on. He had composed a letter saying goodbye to his loved ones and attempted to take his own life.

He had survived. His father had taken an emergency flight home to be with him and ended up sleeping with his arms around his son. For Milo, it had been both weird and wonderful; he was already a grown man himself and couldn't remember the last time his father had embraced him. And still, somehow, it had been a powerful gesture of unconditional love that was new to Milo.

Afterwards, the two of them had taken a drive through the mountains. It was a crisp, sunny, blue-sky day, and Milo had been able to see the sharp edges of the world again. The ride had been filled with silence. When they had reached the peak, they parked and sat together, overlooking the expansive valley below. Every moment or two, his dad had made a sound like he was about to speak, but he said nothing. Eventually, they had headed home, the space between them ripe with new understanding. Milo had known then that his dad loved him, needed him in his life, and accepted him as he was.

He had chosen life then. Could Milo do it again?

He wasn't sure yet. He had faced so much death and learned that it was not always a choice. Too often, he had seen people he loved, people he was close with, and people he had never known suffer and die through no fault of their own. No one escapes death, and we can't all die peacefully in bed of old age.

He started losing all awareness of the physical and saying goodbye to his body. In a way, it was all too hilarious for him to live through it. The timing was so close to the accident where he lost Gia and so many close co-workers. It made him chuckle to think he would be remembered alongside them.

As he laughed at himself, he found peace about the death that was claiming him. After all the close calls, terrifying roads, and driving practice around the world, it was funny that he was finally run over. Milo remembered that he had been on the way to pick up a first aid kit—which would come in really handy at the moment.

He couldn't get over the irony of dying in the back of a cab. As the world whizzed past unnoticed, wells of emotion sprang from Milo as hilarity and sorrow concurrently. The intensity of his love for the people he was leaving behind was nearly overcome with the staggering disappointment that no one was there to joke about the ridiculousness of it with him.

Body beyond pain, he experienced a separation that he once sought line by line or pill by pill. This time, instead of injecting or ingesting a substance into his body to get jacked up, his life force was leaving his body, seemingly leaking out through a thousand cuts. Dying certainly this time, a fate he avoided and embraced in different places and times, was now in front of him as the driver continued the long lonely drive to the hospital.

At that moment, he saw himself from a loving distance as a boy around ten years old. Feeling old anguish arising, he tried to reach beyond time through to his younger self, imagining how young Milo would be shocked into disbelief about this beautiful life he had made for himself. Then, he saw himself simultaneously with his son. Both unreachable, both innocent, both loved beyond measure. Milo, in the midst of his trauma, with experiences yet to come, was only just beginning to comprehend the boundlessness of what he didn't yet know. He felt attached to his son by a glistening thread.

# NINE

# CLUB FREEDOM

When the vehicle bounced to a stop, Milo was stirred back into the physical under a thickness he could hear like the left behind buzzing when the lights came on after a concert. He had arrived at the hospital. However, in his state, it looked like a glowing blue bowtie enticing him to a good time. From the outside, he thought this was where the party must be; perhaps he could float there. Though his awareness was fleeting, he hadn't met death yet; he could hear the cold whispers of it.

The hospital staff recognised him from his recent stay and wondered why he was back so soon. He quipped that he couldn't stay away; the food was good enough to get run over just so he could have more. Half of the staff laughed at his joke; the others looked on in horror, unable to comprehend how this living dead guy could be making jokes in his condition.

He was only half conscious of it, the other half still back outside in the street, wondering how he'd gotten from the back of the cab onto a comfy hospital bed in an environment that enveloped him with the unmistakable antiseptic smell of life-or-death cleanliness. His defence mechanism of humour was on the maximum setting, and what came across as light-hearted to the staff was simply a wave of relief crashing into the lighthouse of hope he had clung to.

He had a vague sense of sinking into morphine, and pain relief washed him with the familiar feeling of how drugs initially swept him up into a lifestyle of partying and escapism. The memories were bursting through Milo with last-chance urgency.

His early days in London had felt like freedom. He didn't see the need to drink away any problem. Instead, alcohol had lubricated his liberation. Finally, he wasn't being asked to hide who he was.

As the debacle that was his boarding school experience had ended, London had all the allure of a tropical island in a society that was still very much conservative. Coming from a place where people equate homosexuality with immorality, London had been his first taste of the freedom that coexists with acceptance.

In the UK, it had been legal to fire someone for being gay. HIV and homophobia were still raging. London and New York were the two prominent havens for people to be themselves. Milo had started to be used to coming out and was enamoured with the idea of embracing self and moving away from expectations. It had been a haven of acceptance, a relief from the pressure of his parents. His mum had joined a support group for parents of gay children, focusing on how her life would be affected, and his dad didn't know how to get his head around it, so they didn't speak for over a year until he was low enough to consider suicide.

The scene in London couldn't have been more opposite and was exploding into a positive and inclusive place to be. As he had soaked in the partying atmosphere of the popular gay nightclubs, he had relished finally feeling and seeing people who were confident in their sexuality and inclusive. Ready to shake off disappointment and fully embrace his identity, he had been fascinated with other people's coming out stories and read voraciously.

It had taken him a while to get his feet under him when he got to London. It had not been an immediate walk down easy street. There was a time he was so broke he had shoplifted to feed himself. That didn't last long because he had gotten food poisoning from a stolen lasagne, which he had taken as a sign to find food another way. He didn't steal again. He had slept on a park bench for a few nights. He had also ended up sleeping with older men because it gave him a bed for the night.

He had worked at Ku Bar, at the heart of the party scene. Everyone had wanted to date the Ku boys, so he had used that to his advantage. It was a busy club with a packed crowd from Thursday to Sunday night. Chest to chest, they'd weave and dance through the club, serving up glittering glasses of whatever was on order. Milo had loved the high energy, and the neurons of his high-seeking brain loved every inch of the place.

Eventually, he got a one-bed studio apartment though he was rarely there. He had to be the last one standing at the party, and the partying would usually start at work. After some time getting to know the place, he was let in on the under-the-table recreational activities that kept the party blasting on much longer.

One night as he was clearing tables in the back corner of the bar, Kevin, the manager, had walked past with a wink and a smile, "What the hell are you doing down here? I've left you something upstairs. Check the loo."

Milo had been on the periphery for a few weeks, and he had noticed without word the change in demeanour of some of the other Ku boys after coming back from upstairs. Eyes wider than jaws, feet fast and free, it had made them ready for more drinks like a shot of concentrated, rainbow caffeine. If alcohol is liquid courage, cocaine is the asshole cherry on top.

Later, he had started to notice a quiet nudge between a few of them and a look with the question, "You want to get on it?"

Before long, he had been getting in on it and from the first taste dripping from his nose down the back of his throat, he had craved more. Cocaine produces, for those who sniff its powdery white crystals, an illusion of supreme well-being and a soaring overconfidence in both physical and mental ability.

In his early twenties, he had been alive with the youthful vitality that came with the lightness of finally living in a place where he didn't have to hide who he was, among people who embraced him instead of trying to change him. For the first time, he had felt like just another face in a crowd rather than standing out as different or being told to hide a part of him. Under the strobe lights and heavy rhythms, he could dance, meet people, and breathe in the atmosphere.

It had come as no surprise that he was experimenting with everything he was offered after living a regimented boarding school life. He had been ready to just get knocked offline and let loose. Freedom was what he had craved, and doing lines of cocaine kicked that feeling up a notch and kept it there. Drinking, dancing, flirting, and working in the nightclub scene in London had been a blur of bliss blended with a dark shadow. Coke kept them up, but it had also added a negative charge. He had liked the lift coke gave him until he got introduced to K and other club drugs.

As his friend Jay had so accurately put it, "Coke makes good people shit and shit people shittier." Nothing ruined a club mood faster than a loud, arrogant partier with one too many trips to the bathroom.

When he met Jay at a house party, he had felt an immediate connection, and it wasn't just that they were both gorgeous. They were also both out of it. Jay had found some ketamine and was hiding in a cupboard. Milo had opened the cupboard looking for a glass and found Jay instead. So, he sat beside the cupboard, and they had a lovely chat. As time went on, and their circle rose and shrunk with the tide, it drew them closer.

Right away, Milo thought Jay was really cool, though Jay had likely thought Milo was a bit of an idiot. In his naïve and new-to-the-scene way, Milo had looked up to Jay's confidence, talent, and charisma. While Jay had started the friendship by keeping a suspicious distance, in time they became best friends. The three musketeers, Jay, Milo, and David, or Grandma as they liked to call him.

That night David had been chiding Milo to take it easy when he walked over and met Jay in the cupboard. Later in the night, David had either eased up or accepted defeat and was watching Milo's antics with a bemused smile. David liked to have a good time and would stay up with the best of them. He was simply more reserved and safety aware than the rest of them.

Jay once suggested they start calling him Mr Safety, but by that point, Grandma as a nickname had stuck. In the early days, they were just part of a group enjoying the hedonistic pleasures of clubbing together or at house parties, especially Phil's. Phil was the D'Artagnon of the group. He lived in Kensington and was as generous as he was gullible. He believed everything at face value. That was part of what had made his house parties so fun. They were guaranteed to be as wild as the club because he'd say yes to anything.

"Just a small band in the garden?" One of his friends would ask.

"Ok," he'd reply, more concerned about counting the number of grams and bottles that would be consumed.

"The sound stage and speakers won't take up much space." Someone would add-in.

"If you think it best," he'd reply.

Milo loved watching the individual and group interactions of his friends and, for a long time, counted himself as separated or observing from the outside. When you're in the moment, you're just having a good time with people, unaware until later on about how important they'd become to you.

During those first flushes of freedom in London, it had taken Milo a while before he felt like he could express himself openly. For the first time in his life, he had felt no pressure. Drink, don't drink, no problem. Drug, dance, or dive into deep conversation, it was all on the table. With a lack of inhibition and an influx of attractive partners, Milo was like a kid in a sweets shop. Though he was relatively promiscuous at the time, there was always a deep wound where he wanted to be loved. He did not voraciously sleep around like many of his friends did, partly because he lacked self-confidence. Partly because a piece of him was an old romantic who was looking to be swept off his feet. He would often be disappointed when he'd spend the night with someone and hope to see them again, only to be kicked to the curb quite quickly after they'd gotten what they wanted. It was an uglier part of the club scene. Milo's MO was one of self-destruction, as he had been insatiably attracted to every bottle and an array of gorgeous, superficial, and toxic men.

For a while, he was living with David. One Monday night, he got home late. As usual, he had been out clubbing for four days and five nights straight. He started on a Thursday and stayed out all weekend, moving from one party to another, ignoring the fact that his brother William was staying with him because he had final exams to write that week in London. William woke up when Milo got home and noticed his brother looked more than a little jacked up.

Milo was too out of it to remember, he started at the club on Thursday evening, and it was 72 hours later. The great thing about London was that after the alcohol stopped flowing at 2 or 3 a.m., late-night lounges opened up. Sure, they couldn't serve drinks, but they gave people a place to continue the party until the clubs opened up the next day. The drugging that happened in the witching hours of the morning was unspoken but well-understood. So, a weekend of partying meant full-on getting it on for three days straight.

By the time he got back to his apartment, it was no surprise that William was really worried about him. His brother left a message for David to check on Milo when he got home. When David arrived, he drunkenly came upon the note and phoned Jay in a panic. His anxiety spiked, and he clung to the phone as a lifeline, asking Jay what he should do. Since David wouldn't let him off the phone so he could call an ambulance, they got Phil to call the ambulance. Jay stayed on the phone with David while they waited for help to arrive.

William woke up when the ambulance arrived, and Milo was rushed to A&E. Milo had no recollection at all until the hospital, where he remembered seeing the worried faces of his dad and brother on the outer edges of awareness. After being sedated, Milo woke up surrounded by addicts. One patient directly across the room from him fixated on Milo. She stared at him without moving or saying a word for enough time that he was long since creeped out. After who knows how many minutes, she got up without breaking her gaze and started walking towards him. With no one in the vicinity, he frantically pushed the call button pinned to his bed railing.

The patient was almost at the end of his bed when she reached the end of her catheter. With a slight struggle and a wrenching of the hips, she ripped it out and took another step towards him. Blood dripped on the floor as a nurse stepped into the room. Quick on her feet, she slipped in front of the patient and redirected her back to bed, cooing about getting her comfortable. Milo, frozen in horror, looked around the hospital ward and wondered if he'd arrived at one of the lower levels of hell. His jokes at the time were ruminations on how he got there and where he was going.

When he spoke with the doctor, he was told it would be easier to tell which drugs weren't in his system than list all the ones that were.

He went back to David's for a while to try to get back on his feet. He had a few part-time jobs here and there. He started trying to be more careful, but too many people in his life encouraged him to drink and indulge in club drugs. Not that he ever blamed anyone else for his choices. He wasn't one to say no. It was all part of the social atmosphere around him.

Milo's first job in entertainment was for Eric Clapton's 50th birthday at Earls Court Exhibition Centre in London. Fleetwood Mac and BB King were playing, and he was a runner, part of the team to make sure everyone had what they needed. He was also high as a kite when he got called to a room to fill a request. When he got there, he didn't recognise the band or anyone in the room. They asked for Lady Grey tea.

He started laughing and said, "You'll not get Lady Grey tea at this hour." Then he walked away. A few minutes later, his manager came up and asked if he really laughed at Fleetwood Mac, and Milo said, "Who?" Later, more sober, he realised who they were and what happened. That was an oops that got him fired. At the time, he was so out of it, it didn't register.

After university, London life was flashier as he lived it up with a high-level career and as part of a power couple against his best friends' advice. As he spent time with celebrities and lived the high life, his home life felt more and more like a ruse. He was an agent courting clients and managing celebrity chefs, while his husband worked at the premier ad agency in the country. To anyone who couldn't see that his eyes had lost their glimmer, he had it made.

His cocaine use escalated, and he started doing a few grams of coke every night. Holidays and weekends drowned in a blur of drugs. Slowly as he recognised he was losing himself night after night of partying, he would change it up, and some weekends, he'd get up early, go to the farmer's market and spend the day cooking. It was his attempt to maintain control, to prove it wasn't a problem. By picking up healthy activities and staying active, he convinced himself it was alright.

One night, he remembered clearly, was a time when it was all coming to an end.

"Phil's out of it, considering it's still early." Jay was unusually perceptive, Milo thought, or maybe he was being unusually paranoid. Probably both.

Jay hated when Phil did coke, and Phil definitely liked to indulge. It made for an interesting dynamic between the two. Milo often played the middle, keeping the peace between them with a funny act or raunchy joke. When there was no powder, there was no problem. Jay thought Phil was too sweet to need the extra edge. Milo could see both sides. Phil was so kind and gentle; he felt the high he got from coke balanced him out a little and gave him some bravado. Milo felt the same way to a certain extent.

That night he was feeling extra protective of Phil. In their penthouse, Milo and Roger loved to entertain, and Phil had been arriving early for the past few months. In an unspoken way, Phil had indicated that he understood the negative nature of their relationship and felt like Milo could use the company. He was right, and Milo was so thankful for the gesture of friendship.

"He's been here a while, and I've been enjoying his antics," Milo said.

"You haven't been joining him, have you?" Jay asked warily, still standing at the entrance with his coat on.

"Looks like you're going to be the life of the party tonight. The answer is no if we're going to play twenty questions," Milo responded saucily. "Now, come in and join the fun, or I'll find a way to put a smile on your face."

"I could tell right away you're too chill. Alright, take my coat. I swear you just have parties to show off the view." Jay stared across the open-concept penthouse to the floor-to-ceiling windows showing London lit up for the party. Then he glanced back at Milo like he had more to say but thought better of it. A look passed between them.

Jay had become the kind of friend where words weren't needed, someone you could get pumped up with at the club for two days straight and then sit and talk for twelve hours straight about what he saw, what others were going through, and what mattered in the world. It is a rare blessing to have someone who cares about you, especially when they are both a master of a good time and there for you when it's inconvenient and ugly. Jay was that friend to Milo, and he was quietly encouraging him now. When most people saw Milo's success, Jay was encouraging him to leave an abusive relationship. Both he and David had begged him to do anything other than marry Roger.

Coming to the party that night wasn't just another night of good music with a view. He was one of the few people who knew how Milo was emotionally and was encouraging him to dry out a bit and change his circumstances.

It wasn't just his relationship that was going off the rails. The longer Milo was in the entertainment industry, the less he had the heart for the game. It was a cruel business, and for his clients to succeed, others had to be trashed. It was a popularity contest, and the veneer wore thin.

He had been talked into sitting on the board for a non-profit by Ella, a friend of Roger's who became a close friend of his and an important member of his family. Volunteering for aid organisations, travelling to Africa, and seeing children in poverty made him want to leave the entertainment industry to pursue child welfare full time ... and that's how he ended up in Cambodia, but it had taken him a lot to get there.

In his sedated and unconscious state, his memories replayed like dreams.

# TEN

# COINCIDENCE, A LOVE STORY

Crazy coincidences surround everyone if they just stop and take notice. Life has some surprises and plans, and if you don't see them, you don't know. Coincidences can be inconvenient as well as life-changing. Milo was still swirling through the memories and connections that brought him where he ended up.

It wasn't just surviving the bus accident only to be hit in the same place two years later on a motorbike. Or how he'd gotten the job in Cambodia after a decade of country hopping, working in care reform, and seeing up-close the real faces of child trafficking and worse.

All of those events were triggered by a smaller coincidence, imperceivable until all the pieces came together years later. Weather-related coincidences have a serendipity to them because they seem like an intimate nudge from the universe. A chance meeting while getting caught in a rainstorm sounds like a fictional construction but can often be much more subtle than that.

After a summer spent working as a sailing instructor in the Mediterranean, Milo had been seeking to reconnect with his grandparents because they had been consistent caregivers for him as a child. They lived in Portsmouth, and he got off at the train station, which was about a half-hour walk from his grandparents' house. He had been caught in the rain and took refuge in a little shop which happened to be a Portsmouth University information shop.

A lovely woman with a broad smile had walked up to him. "Hello, dear, are you interested in Portsmouth University?"

He had definitely not been looking to commit to something like university, and his immediate response was: *No, I have no intention to go to university at all.* But being brought up in the British way, of course, he wasn't going to actually tell her what he thought.

He had replied, "Yes, I would love to hear more about it," when what he had meant was the opposite. It was quite a cultural quirk, really; the ability to be polite and interested while seething with disinterest.

"Oh, so what are you interested in?" she had asked.

Since he had been reading a lot of psychology books, that seemed like a good enough answer.

She had been reinvigorated by his response. "Well, we do have a new course, psychology with criminology. Would you be interested in that?"

He had acquiesced to taking a pamphlet and reading it over. When the rain stopped, he had headed out and brought the pamphlet with him to lunch with his grandparents. Right away, his granny had noticed the university logo because she had worked there, and she pushed him to attend. He had spoken with a few other people who encouraged him, yet it was her support and encouragement that had cemented his enrolment, which had led to an eventual career as a child advocate and mental health writer. All of what was to come had been initiated by an attempt to escape an unexpected rainstorm.

He had wanted his grandparents to be proud of him. Yet there was more to it than that. Milo had always known that when you are getting advice from a friend or family member, they always seemed to have an agenda, even if they were unaware of it. But he hadn't felt that way with his grandparents. They seemed to want what was best for him regardless of everything else. They were his only visitors when he had been rushed to the hospital with appendicitis as a child. No matter what he faced, Milo knew Granny had just wanted him to be happy.

Granny and Grandad had been through a lot together and had been there for him and his brother William, come what may. The presence of his grandparents was a positive influence in his life and the stability he had longed for, even though they had all experienced past traumas. While Milo and William attended separate boarding schools, quite often, their breaks would overlap. So, the brothers had spent a lot of time at their grandparents' house during half terms, seeing as both their parents lived abroad. Their personalities had been opposites in many ways, and that helped them share perspectives on their similar life experiences.

One day they had been poking through some old family pictures when William asked, "How'd Granny become the second wife anyway? Was she the nanny or something?"

"Don't you know their story?" He had asked his brother.

"Nobody tells me anything," he had replied.

"Not true, I do." Milo had smiled in the silly way that always made his brother laugh.

William had cast a sideways smile back at him. "Well, you're an outcast like me, so what do you know?"

"Ah yes, the black sheep brothers of the Portsmouth waterfront," Milo had remarked, and they both laughed at the fitting insult.

"Are you going to tell me or what? I can't see Grandad being involved in an epic love story."

"In WWII, he was twenty-one. Shit, that's the same age as we'll be in a couple years. His lieutenant, a guy called Mad Jack, was playing the bagpipes calling them to attack up a steep hill on the island of Brac."

"Yeah, in Croatia, I've heard this story. What's it got to do with the love story? Granny wasn't there. When did he get to South Africa?"

"Stop interrupting. He was injured and taken prisoner, and forced to march to Germany from Belgrade in the winter. If he didn't try to escape, he would have died," Milo had continued.

"Was he married then? Not to Granny, you know what I mean" William had asked.

"Yeah, to his first wife, our step-uncle's mum," Milo had said. He pushed his hand through his hair and went on. "He won the military cross."

"I've heard about his military history. No one has ever mentioned the epic love story?" William had cut him off again. Though they were brothers, no one usually guessed they were related.

"You've got the patience of an angry rhino." He had smiled and nudged his brother good-naturedly. "Right. So, he's majorly known for his courage and stalwartness in the face of danger. Then, later he goes to South Africa and meets Granny, and they fall in love. They had both been called there out of duty, and they found an undeniable connection. But they both already have families, so they could not be together. Eventually, he sailed for home back to his wife and family in the UK."

"That's the worst love story I've ever heard."

"It's not done. Are you sure you haven't heard this already, and you're just having me on!"

"I have no idea what you're talking about."

"Well, you know, with Dad being away all the time and Mum being in and out of treatment facilities, this was our fallback place. And unlike you, I don't spend my time hiding in a book. Granny and Grandad have always been my go-to place, where I felt comfortable. So, I've heard a lot."

"Yeah, that's the one thing I know for sure about them. They love all of us, no matter what. I shouldn't be that surprised they have a romantic story, but it's Grandad. He's all military."

"Some of the bravest humans have the softest hearts. Strength requires compassion. I think it makes perfect sense."

"Of course you do. Will you get to the story now?"

"Now you've taken all the suspense and romance out of it, haven't you?"

William had given Milo a look. "Well, I never asked for it to begin with, did I?"

"Well, after they were pulled back to their lives, Granny got a letter from him. Imagine how she felt, thinking she'd never see him again and then getting a letter filled with love, sorrow, and hope. Grandad had just lost his wife, and he had three children she had left behind. He was writing to Granny broken-hearted yet determined to make a life with someone he had an intense connection with. She immediately came by boat to join him in England, her own children already grown. From the moment she arrived, they considered their two families one and became the power couple we know and love." Milo had beamed as he concluded the story, though he hadn't been convinced his words expressed the elegant intricacies of their relationship.

The love and acceptance of a couple a world apart, coming together to form a mixed family, had inspired Milo. And he got to watch, from his vantage point as their grandson, as they had spent their lives keeping everybody together and overcoming adversity as a united front. They were the only example of a healthy married couple he had, and they had given him hope in the possibility of relationships that are real partnerships. Spending as much time in their house and lives had instilled in him a more positive outlook on the family dynamics that cut through the dysfunction.

Granny could come across as stoic, but Milo had seen her deep capacity to love. What many didn't know was how Granny and Grandad had saved Milo's life just by being there for him. When he had been struggling in school, Granny knew. She hadn't known what was going on, and she didn't try to pry, but she did offer an outlet to talk or just help him forget about it and go do something else.

One thing Milo had in common with his granny was being known for liking a little nip of alcohol here and there. When he was old enough, they had shared afternoon drinks often. On one occasion, they'd had a few too many, and he had reminded her about it the next day.

"Milo, a gentleman never remembers," she had told him.

He had loved her for it and took that phrase as his own to keep her close to his heart. The two of them had made it clear, over and over, the beauty that can come from great adversity. And early on in his own life, he had seen that come true.

He had seen great beauty. In fact, he prided himself on having seen some of the most beautiful places in the world. Still, he wasn't done. He was rooted serenely in the still place of remembering where he grieved for what had yet to come. Fighting so hard to live just for today, Milo was on the brink of the unknown. Was it purposeful forgetting or part of the process?

After the first year without Gia, he had experienced loss after loss that set him on a path to self-destruction. Since alcohol is so socially acceptable, it can become a vice so simply. It's slippery that way, and Milo had found himself standing at the sink with his husband looking at him with eyes that said, "You're opening the second bottle already?"

Milo had grinned at Ra and shrugged. What he didn't say out loud was, "Actually, it's my third." And because it went unspoken, it remained hilarious – a funny joke between a married couple. What had been less amusing was how quickly it was going to spiral into something darker. He didn't want to live through that, and he had come close to the edge, drowning tedious office days in funny cat videos, especially ones involving cats pissing off dogs. He had felt an affinity towards cats because, for such a small and adorable animal, they didn't take shit from anyone.

He had struggled with the extreme heights and depths of his emotion as he cherished life but also railed against the ugliness he couldn't control. Finding many things to be thankful for, he had strived to live a good life regardless of the pitfalls, accepting that uncertainty was something he was tackling day by day. He had long been aware of and felt the ethereal fabric that connects all of us. Sometimes it's stretched over miles, sometimes, it is soiled, but it has always existed. Milo felt it as a spiritual hug, like a warm jumper. He had become more connected in the last few years since he had chosen recovery.

While his sedated body was being repaired, his mind was in a free fall of memories. It was as though they were seeping out of his fractured bones and whisking him into a different time.

In a flash, he was in Uganda, and the spiritual hug was replaced by the arms of his dear friend around him. He had met Melinda's husband Evan first, up in the mountains amid the crater lakes. Then at dinner that night at a resort where everyone had shared the meal together, they sat beside each other and were friends that moment. Milo had felt immediately at ease with the native New Yorker.

She had challenged him intellectually though in a nurturing way.

"You remind me of Evan when he was younger. Your work in care reform, as you know, gets to the heart of a desperate problem. But since you don't want to take the stage, no one can hear you." She had looked at him deeply and with smiling eyes. "My Evan did the same thing for years."

"Did?" Her husband had cut in from the other side of her. He had put his arm around his wife and leaned in to include Milo in the conversation. "Still do. That's why I'm here."

"I am definitely no fan of the spotlight, to say the least," Milo said, and they had clinked their glasses in agreement and looked over the wilderness spread out in front of them. They had shared a jaded view of the world and an affinity for belly laughs. As they connected deeply, they had both extended their holiday to be together a little longer. After that, they had stayed in touch and visited each other throughout the years.

When Ra and Milo were married, they had been invited to stay and have their wedding in New York at Melinda and Evan's gorgeous guest house. Usually, his husband was quite shy, but he had taken to them right away, and they enjoyed the apartment and garden as a quiet break in the bustling city. David had flown to New York to celebrate with them, and Milo's mind settled on a memory of lunch they had together before David went home. He could see it like a photo even though no physical image existed of that moment. His new husband by his side, they had enjoyed a fresh meal in the garden of the guest house Melinda had prepared for them. David had been seated across from them, at ease and content with Milo and Ra's happiness.

The image of that afternoon was a memory he cherished as he had grown so much from the younger version of himself, getting married the first time. When Milo had been with his ex-husband, David had begged him to get out of the marriage and was one of the most vocal supporters he had in his attempt to leave the abusive relationship. All of that was water under the bridge to Milo now.

Gaining awareness through the cloud of pain, it came to him that his life was flashing before his eyes in the wrong order. Was that how it was supposed to happen?

"I can't even get dying straight!" He mocked himself for the muddled way that he was sifting through the events and important people in his life.

Of course, he wouldn't have a smooth transition. He wasn't one to take the paved path, preferring the road less travelled. Was there order to it anyway? As a Buddhist, he practised mindfulness of death in his regular meditation. Now that he seemed to have reached the end, it was an onslaught of self-driven memories happening to him rather than the calm transition he had intended.

He had to be dying. He knew for sure now, as the people who had the biggest effect on him were close to him in memory, and each conversation and situation felt visceral, as though he was reaching through time to relive them. Clarity before he lost consciousness for good? Milo wasn't sure. Although he'd been surrounded by death in different ways, he had never spent enough time really considering the final transition until it was happening to him.

## ELEVEN

# RUNNING TOWARDS RECOVERY

The white light of the hospital room permeated all of his other senses. Milo wasn't dead yet. He floated on a cloud of light, aware of movement and himself. Eyes closed, his breathing steadied, and it felt like a long time ago that he took a deep breath. Chest expanding as he inhaled, his broken bones groaned against the task and the pain threatened to take him back into darkness.

He started to wake up to his surroundings, body numbed by narcotics, mind groggy and just outside of the here and now. It was almost as though he could push off from his body and be released from the physical altogether. The strangeness of it was different than any high he had experienced, and he wondered if he was dying in slow motion.

There were moments of lucidity, like a transmission making it through static for a few minutes at a time. He was sometimes aware that other people were around him. Doctors. Nurses. Familiar voices that reverberated through him with sharp real sound, but further away and vague, from a distance, rather than the up-close, detailed conversations of his memories. In those snippets of reality, he found an anchor of optimism as he fought himself back to life.

Over time unmeasured, the whispers of the white blurs of medical staff become less hushed and rushed. Milo would find out later that he should have been medically evacuated to Thailand, but because of the global pandemic, he was stuck. With whispered panic, he was carefully watched over. The hospital in Phnom Penh was keeping him alive but didn't have the equipment or services to rehabilitate someone with such immense brain trauma. Still, bit by bit, thanks to their professional medical care, he edged away from death.

In his isolated awareness from an overmedicated haze of nothingness, he had glimpses of optimism on each exhale. Even though he was still touch and go, he was feeling the possibility of recovery, and slowly he moved his compass towards healing instead of saying goodbye. The mindset shift clicked inside him and connected him to a previous recovery from substance abuse. Then, he had required help and chose to fight for his life. Now, in a different way, he was doing the same thing.

After the tragedy and fallout of the bus accident, he had been struggling with inner turmoil over the responsibility of continuing to work for World Children's Services in the aftermath of the team being decimated. From coming to understand individuals and the corporate mindset that lacked compassion to trying to figure out how to serve the families as the program intended, the impact of loss had reverberated beyond comprehension. All the while, he had been helping with the care of the survivors and families of the deceased, which remained priority. Instead of following the overwhelm towards an inevitable breakdown, he had done his best and drowned the rest in drink.

After work drinks had no longer been a way to relax but a lifeline and an attempt to obliterate all the death and trauma in his life. He had also started drinking a bottle of vodka before he went out for the night, finishing the night off with two bottles of wine before passing out for the remaining few hours until he got up to do it again. Things had started getting darker as he struggled to maintain everything he felt responsible for, entirely ignoring his own grief, trauma, and immense loss. He also began taking uppers and downers; to help him sleep, he told himself.

His years of working as a high-functioning addict had helped him ease his way into survival mode. Whatever was stressful at the moment, he could drink away at the end of the day. His friend, Simone, owned a bar; his husband and friends were always up for a good time, so it had been easy to keep up the veneer of acceptability.

Inside, the storm had been churning out of control. One Friday night, he had been out drinking with his husband, and he had an increasingly demanding urge to seek something more, falling to old habits. From an acquaintance of a friend, he had obtained the number for Bob, the only connection to crystal meth and cocaine he had in Phnom Penh.

When they arrived home, he had been sitting on the sofa looking at the phone number on his phone, ready to pick up. A tiny part of him had known where this road would take him. He'd been down that way before. He hadn't wanted to throw it all away and dive back into hard drugs. Instead of choosing release through crystal, he had called a friend, got the phone number for the rehab centre she had stayed at and chosen that road instead.

He had called the centre that night and got the details, booking himself in for the following day. It had to be immediate and he was shaking as the call ended. It had to be better than the cycle he had kept finding himself in. Ra had been supportive from the moment Milo spoke the words:

"I need to go to rehab."

In his loving way, Ra had replied without pausing, "Okay."

And that was that. He had continued to drink wine as he packed, not daring to think what the next few months would bring or even the next day. It had seemed like a shocking and abrupt decision, but it was a long time coming, and Milo quietly contemplated the potential for changing his mind. This time though, his stubbornness and refusal to quit had provided enough incentive to get himself there even as a large part of him wanted to go fast and far in the opposite direction.

The flight the next day hadn't been early, and the airport bar was open. He had a few drinks to calm his nerves before he left. Partaking in as much substance as you can before rehab is normally how it is done, as the person with addiction seeks one final fix before the work begins. Milo had figured since he was going to rehab anyway, he might as well get his money's worth. It was flawed logic, but he had gone with it.

He had a small stopover in Bangkok, but there was no time for drinks. Then, much to his dismay, they hadn't served alcohol on the flight to Chiang Mai, so his last drink had been the shitty white wine they gave out for free in the business lounge in the Phnom Penh airport.

Walking into rehab had been an interesting experience because Milo somewhat felt like he was escorting himself there. The part of him that had called and made his reservation was dragging his drunk ass in. He watched himself drink at every opportunity before he got to the centre and once there, he had felt the pull to go in another direction.

Ra had taken him to the airport and was the only one who knew where he was going and why. Milo had known he had to take care of himself first and worry about explanations to everyone else later, or not, he'd figure it out. Right at that moment, it couldn't matter to him what other people would think or do.

Upon arrival, his credit card hadn't worked. That wasn't a great thing to deal with when he had already been on edge and in a new place. Milo hadn't wanted to cope. It had been a long day, and he was tired. The little voice that knew all the tricks to get him had begun to get much louder; he could easily say fuck it and find the nearest bar. Drugs wouldn't be hard to find from there. Or check into a hotel, where his credit card would work, and those lovely little bottles would be close at hand.

As he stood there for a nano-second, he had considered it to be a sign from the universe that he should leave. A hotel and spa would have had the same amenities without the sobriety. It wasn't much of an internal struggle. He had been committed when he made the phone call the previous day. It just took his ego longer to accept it.

Instead of fleeing, he had dialled Kali's number.

"Hi?" Her greeting had been a question. Milo had known a conversation would be simpler than back-and-forth texting. There were few people Milo knew who would agree to a $10,000 loan at the drop of a hat. Kali had been the obvious choice, but he still had to admit where he was and why.

"Could you transfer money to an account for me?" Milo had asked and provided Kali with the details.

"Sure, I'll do it right now." She hadn't hesitated or asked questions even when the name of the rehab came up.

"Thanks, you're a lifesaver," Milo had said, oblivious to the depth of truth to his words. She wished him well, and her voice was a reassuring balm, quieting down the jitteriness of his quick decision.

It was one thing to make the call and get on the plane. It was another world completely arriving, being shown to his room and told all the rules. There had been a period of strangeness as he settled into a strict and regimented situation. During the first ten days to two weeks of being alcohol-free, his body was in survival mode.

Milo had always been able to clown around about the copious amount of alcohol he could consume and still appear relatively sober with it. What wasn't so funny was the damage being done to his liver. His timing for rehab was another coincidence, as his physical health had been in bad shape, and he wouldn't have been able to push it much further. Was it blind luck that he had gotten there just in time before the damage was irreversible? Milo didn't believe in luck and had thought there must be something more to his sudden decision to go.

Getting clean had been an ultimate gift to self. While he loved the life he had, including drinks with cherished friends, he had wanted a life beyond that. When Gia's life had been cut short so quickly, Milo had started a slow march towards taking his own life. Still, he hadn't gone to rehab for Gia.

When he had considered her influence on his life, he could hear her say, "Don't be a dick; change has to come from within."

And that's where many people struggled. Getting sober had to be for yourself. If anyone else is your reason, they will be your reason to relapse when you have a problem in your relationship with them. Milo had known that from a clinical perspective, yet here he was, listing all the external reasons sobriety was required of him.

Milo had noticed that as soon as you say, "I am an addict", people write you off as a person. Addiction can be weaponised, and people with decades of recovery are still often labelled as nothing more than a junkie. Substance use issues bleed into all aspects of life, especially once it becomes prolonged and excessive. Some people don't see it as a disease, and for a long time, Milo had separated himself from the addict label because he separated business and pleasure so well. Working in social work protection, there was no room for error, and Milo had never let his extracurricular activities risk harm to anyone but himself. Since he had held that distinction, he thought he was fine.

For a long time, *I'll try anything once*, had been Milo's motto. After his first line, he had been introduced to new party drugs directly. His inquisitive nature had encouraged him to partake in most things offered, and, after university, he liked to joke that it was field research. Simply thinking of the smell of cocaine, an unmistakable mix of petrol and chemical, made his mouth water and his nose sniff with a tingle of anticipation he could taste at the back of his throat. For K, E, and MDMA, it had been more of a full-body reaction that tingled with world tilting expectation.

He was generally opposed to needle drugs, but that didn't mean he never did them. Injecting himself had given him a higher hit for drugs like meth, though when that had become an issue, he had multiple alarm bells telling him death was imminent.

One morning while in rehab, lying in bed waiting for the appointed breakfast time and antsy for the day to begin, Milo had made the connection between the institutional nature of recovery with scheduled group meals and the lack of control that was the trauma of his boarding school years. As a natural early riser, it had been difficult to wait until he was allowed to start the day. He knew the purpose for the strict schedule, and he allowed himself to work through his emotional reaction knowing the purpose of his current situation.

After getting through the initial weeks of drying out, Milo had begun to see the gravity of his problems and how it may have manifested as a substance use issue, but it was an effective coping mechanism after years of trauma and abuse. Initially, he had thought it was just about being sober, but quickly he realised he'd need to stay longer than he first anticipated.

There was no medical detox though it was highly structured, and he had been restricted from leaving once the program began. He had to stick with it in spite of an urge to use. Compulsion is a powerful abstract that Milo spent a long time thinking about. For him, his substance use wasn't rational. He had always known what he was doing, he knew why it wasn't healthy, and he even knew the many reasons he wanted to stop. Still, if the opportunity arose, he wouldn't say no. He'd risk it because it felt good or it helped him dissociate from it all. Every other consideration was off the table until he had his after-work drinks.

When he worked in entertainment, midday drinks to toast a success or a boozy lunch to woo a client had been the norm. Changing careers had altered his ease of slipping into drink mode. Making life-changing decisions for children and families in agonising situations was a high-pressure job, and he wasn't willing to risk their future. Still, he knew everyone working in social work, or for children and families in any area, suffered from the extreme stress of the job, and many of them turned to substances to blunt the trauma.

Milo and Gia had often spoken of the implications of their line of work and the level of dark humour required to process it all. It had drawn them together. At one meeting, there had been a huge uproar made by one of the donors about how reports were being handled.

Finally, fed up with the nonsense, Milo had exclaimed, "Chill out. No one's murdered a baby."

As the room fell silent, he caught Gia's eye as she was

suppressing a giggle. Everyone else had looked shocked by his words. Milo had calmly explained he was simply drawing their attention to the fact that they were getting all wound up over nothing.

In rehab, with nothing to blunt the emotion, thinking of Gia and the rest of the people he loved in life had caused his eyes to sting with tears. He had felt precarious and fragile while somewhat grateful for a chance to hide away while he dried out. The program had worked well for Milo's rambling heart as it incorporated increasing freedom to travel and explore as time went on.

Attending the NA (Narcotics Anonymous) fellowship meetings had required travelling a short distance into Chiang Mai, and Milo had relished the journey through the city to the community centre where the meeting was held. Milo had felt comfortable in the relaxed and inviting atmosphere of the fellowship compared to the more rigid nature of rehab.

Wherever he was, when he met people who were also living clean or on their journey to becoming sober, it was such a varied mix of people. Whether they had been there for months or years, finding strength in the fellowship of others, supporting each other was a reminder of the severity of their circumstances.

Milo had grown to hear through others about the tragedy of addiction. Nima had been one of the first close friends he made, who was a recovering addict. Milo and Nima shared cigarettes and a sense of humour. Nima had parallel experiences, although he was twqenty years into recovery, and his perspective helped Milo see a clean future for himself.

Milo remembered one conversation with Nima clearly because it resonated through every day and brought him to a new place of intentionality. He had met Nima for coffee, though he had been in a pensive mood. His usual greeting had sounded a little flat as he was replaying something he had learned recently, and it was eating at him. It had been a long day, and he hadn't been paying attention until Nima repeated, "More than half of all recovering addicts relapse and die."

It was a harsh statistic and a true one. Milo had been replaying it in his mind ever since. The first time it registered, he had stared into his cup and stirred the milk around again and again.

"Something got to you?" Nima had noticed the change from his friend's usual light-hearted demeanour.

"Yeah, the reality of how many addicts don't make it," Milo had admitted.

"That's a tough one. It's all you can do to not dwell on it. You don't want to make friends because you know you will lose them," Nima had replied, nodding from personal experience.

"You were hesitant with me the first few weeks," Milo said.

"Exactly." Nima had pointed and winked.

Death after rehab seemed inevitable for more than half of those who recovered. Part of Milo already counted himself out of life, assuming he would be in that category inevitably. As time in rehab went on, Milo slowly became aware that he might make it; he felt like he was coming back into himself.

Those initial trips had sparked a love of Chiang Mai

and an eagerness to explore. Slowly his yearning and the thrill of new experiences had begun to reach his deadened senses. Each passing week he had the opportunity to earn free time before or after fellowship meetings and, eventually, as day passes.

These small forays into the world, bustling on while they recovered, had been therapeutic. He also began to explore and love the diversity of Thailand as he learned the difficulty of choosing sober life, combined with the realisation of the power of addiction and how it takes control of you. When you have a reason to get sober, it's easy to make excuses.

He had been able to consume huge quantities of alcohol without getting ill, but he got to rehab just in time. His liver had been severely diseased, and he had to face his health dead on. He didn't have control and saw that once he let go of his ego, he could do the work and heal. Letting go of ego, he had realised, was separate from surrender.

One Sunday afternoon, he had been delaying his return to the rehab centre, strolling without a destination in mind. In his thoughts, he had been considering the energy of Chiang Mai and a rejuvenation he was starting to feel growing within. Walking past an unassuming door, he had gotten a whiff of incense that had a hint of citrus. There had been an air of familiarity to the place, though Milo had never been there before. What he had seen in front of him was serendipitous as he had recently been speaking to Nima about sound bowl healing and now he had stumbled upon a shop with a stunning collection of bowls. Milo had felt drawn to one wall, but the shop was busy. A couple of tourists were having a conversation in front of the bowls he had wanted to look at. He had a look around and then patiently waited before deciding to come back another time.

He had left empty-handed and empty-feeling like there was something he was missing. On the bus ride back, after resolving to ask Nima if he knew the place, he had watched the vivid, mountainous jungles interspersed with tall modern buildings, temples, and traditional architecture. The energy of the city promoted healing and connection with nature with an abundance of parks and green space.

Later, when he had asked Nima about the shop, he had been surprised to find out it was part of a healing centre where Nima and his friend Kanshin practised sound healing. Before long, Nima introduced them. Milo had relished the opportunity to get to know Kanshin and learn more about the frequencies and artistry of sound bowls.

He had started out planning to stay five weeks in rehab and realised quickly it would take longer. Initially, he hadn't realised he needed to address other issues rather than just getting sober. Slowly he had come to terms with the gravity of the situation. Previously he had heard stories of high-level execs and CEOs only spending four or five weeks to dry out, but what he learned was that then they keep having to come back.

The standard twenty-eight days for rehab is surprisingly unrelated in any way to human response to recovery. Back in the day, sailors were given twenty-eight days of shore leave, so rehab was set up for them to dry out and head back to sea. That might have worked for convenience's sake, though Milo hadn't wanted to rush it. He had taken his time in his journey to recovery and had slowly found sobriety.

# TWELVE

# HAPPILY EVER AFTER

When Milo's eyes opened, he was still and present in his body, in the hospital bed that had become like an extension of him. For a moment, he took in the stillness of his breath and the concrete sensation of his physical body. He noticed he was peeing, becoming uncomfortably aware of the catheter working as intended. There was still a medicated edge to the world, but he was in it. He hadn't yet moved, eyes still adjusting to the light, while body and mind became reacquainted. Before looking to his bedside, he could feel Ra's presence. It felt like he had been gone a lifetime.

In that instant, he knew he was alive and right next to his husband, who was sitting beside him in the hospital room. Shifting his gaze, he could see Ra looking down at his phone, one hand resting on Milo's chest. Ra's eyes moved around the screen, and Milo could tell he was considering the lighting or other detail on some images or perusing a fashion exhibit. A feeling of contentment and gratitude that he was given a happy ending began to spread.

Over the next few hours, he was to learn that the aftermath of the accident left him with twenty broken bones, a broken neck, three skull fractures, and a brain haemorrhage. After being unconscious for fifteen hours minimum, then waking up and escaping the referral hospital in Kep, he had almost been out of time when he'd finally arrived in Phnom Penh. Fighting off Doctor Disagreeable had likely saved his life as sewing him up without stopping the internal bleeding would have been a mistake Milo would not have recovered from.

Now, he was content in the quiet solitude and started to have an urge to go home, his one true home where he felt safest. There, his husband kept him grounded and wasn't afraid of making fun of him. They called their home Wednesday because that's where everyone gathered on that day. Their life in Cambodia was centred around their apartment. They lived and worked within a two-kilometre radius, happy to walk, shop, and live locally. Above all, Milo felt an urge to get back in the kitchen even before he was mobile.

That first Wednesday in the hospital was an example of how he could ride out any storm with Ra and their friends. Getting run over kept him in the hospital longer than he would have liked, but he had no control over that. On Wednesday, when he should have been cooking up incredible aromas, he was feeling sorry for himself, thinking about what he was missing out on. Ra left earlier with a promise to check in before the end of the day. His vagueness was given away by a crooked smile, and Milo figured Ra was headed home to spend time with their friends, where presumably they would talk about how to best manage Milo, who they dubbed *The English Patient* in a social media group they started to keep everyone in the loop regarding his condition.

"I'm not even English. I'm Scottish," he protested when he found out their new nickname for him.

"See, Ra, that's why we didn't want to tell him," Nathan admonished with a teasing voice.

Milo hated to be the cause of their concern and tried to downplay how he was doing, which was difficult when fully immobile. "Well, you've probably just set up the group so you can have a good laugh at my expense. The least you could do is let me in on it."

They surprised him that evening, doing their best to bring Wednesday to Milo's hospital room. Now the room was a vibrant flourish of activity, with everyone circling his bed and settling in. He still wasn't eating much, but of course, they brought snacks. Though they tried to make small talk, they took turns glancing over at him every few minutes with a look of concern or a furrowed eyebrow. He knew he looked like shit but didn't want to be the centre of their depressed attention. There were a few sure-fire ways to lighten the mood. Given his condition, he resorted to taking the piss out of them.

"Why didn't anyone include me in the plans for a matching wardrobe?" Milo made a joking reference to the brightly coloured clothes everyone was wearing. "And Piper, did you wake up this morning and think, well, today is the perfect day to look like a lemon, or is there a fruit theme I am missing?"

"Oh, behave, you cheeky thing." Piper chuckled, looking down at her yellow trousers and matching shirt. Her laughter brought a wave of relief to the room.

"We had a pair of bright red hot pants so you could be the strawberry, but Ra vetoed that idea," Simone put in, joining the silliness.

Since no one wanted to ask how he was doing, they took turns labelling everyone's outfit according to the food item it best matched. When the laughter subsided, his friends seemed less anxious. Milo realised the better he seemed, the more relieved they were.

"Well, what else did you bring?" he asked.

"I know you wanted your face cream. What's it called?" Kali asked.

"Crème de la Mer," Milo said.

"Right, well, when you said you couldn't live without your Crème de la Mer, I went through your vast quantities of toiletries looking for it," she said apologetically. "I'm unsure where you keep it."

"Please tell me you knew I was joking." Milo's laugh was cut short by the pain in his ribs. "Where would I put it, seriously?" He gestured to his bruised and scraped-up face.

"Seriously? We know how particular you are about your morning routine," Kali said.

"That's unfair and untrue. Just recently, I skipped my whole routine and opted to sleep on the side of the road," Milo replied, his voice thick with humour.

"Way too soon for jokes, Milo," Simone inserted.

"Seriously, you haven't even left the hospital yet. Stop being hilarious and heal."

"Yes, and let us know if you change your mind about wanting someone here with you through the night," Kali insisted.

"Absolutely not. It's going to be a quiet night for me and my morphine, and I won't have anyone interrupting that." He might have been exaggerating his excitement for spending the night alone in the hospital. He loved each of them deeply, but he was ready for them to fuck off. He was tired of being fussed over.

Making their departure, they left Milo with instructions to check in, hugs all around, and cheerful words of healing. Then he was alone in his hospital room, assessing his exhaustion after an abundance of love, considering his injuries, and figuring out where he could go from there. It seemed like a huge physical recovery, and he had a long way to go. It was a challenge he was ready for as he wanted to take back his health and go back to the strong life he was living before he was run over.

Before he drifted off to sleep, he considered that challenges were something he excelled at. He remembered starting the Gia Wellness Centre in memory of Gia. Offering ethical mental health services was something they had spoken about many times over. In their roles at World Children's Services, they had been able to affect change to a certain degree, but the agencies and their funders would always have an agenda. By creating a place where the patient outcome was upheld as most important, he could ensure quality care.

Offering free mental health services for children in

crisis had been part of his business plan. The wellness centre was an amalgamation of all he had learned, incorporating Eastern philosophies and contemporary psychology to provide human services for healing. He was so thankful for those conversations with Gia that had cemented his determination to create a centre based on values. He was filled with love that she was such an immense part of the project.

He had laughed thinking about coming up with some of the policies he instated during some downtime with Gia. They had often had long conversations during the traditional two-hour lunch break in Cambodia.

"Why do you think people resort to shaming, especially in the professional setting?" she had asked him during one sweltering afternoon, seemingly out of the blue.

"Where'd that come from?" He had answered her question with a question.

"Something Celeste and I were talking about; she was dealing with an issue at work. The details aren't important. She's stuck in the middle."

"Control likely. Or a passive-aggressive way of dealing with a toxic workplace."

"That happens a lot, doesn't it?"

"It's ridiculous. There are so many simple things people can do to make a more inclusive and healthier place to be. Having an open-door policy would be top of my list," Milo had said.

"And it's so easy to simply leave the door open, right?" Gia had added. "I've always said I would have a mistake of the month award, so we could all learn from each other and stop being afraid of screwing up."

"I love that. It would take away the shaming aspect of mistakes and stop people from hiding when they mess up."

"Exactly."

As he was making future plans for the Gia Wellness Centre, he had incorporated many of those ideas into the policies for the centre, including the mistake of the month. As the centre grew, he had realised that things may come to fruition, though seldom as expected. The reality of a dream come true isn't necessarily as glamorous either. When dreaming up the Gia Wellness Centre, he had his focus on the services they would offer and the people that would be helped. He hadn't daydreamed about the reality of the bureaucracy and mundane business requirements that had taken up much of his time. He knew the balance was worth it, and the work, so far, had paid off.

In his youth, when his mind was preoccupied with sailing, he had a similar experience. He had always dreamed of a life of living and sailing full-time. When he did live on board for one season in Greece, it had been as incredible as he imagined; being rocked gently all night in the hull of the boat, the *Poseidon*, waking to the sunrise on the water, teaching all day in the sun, then kicking back with drinks after work. It had also meant boiling all night in the hot boat, having to clear everything out of the front cabin every morning to make room for clients, and the precise checklist of maintenance that started at 6 am every day.

Once upon a time, it had been his biggest dream to be chief of child protective services for the UN, but he'd rather boil his feet than do that now. That was part of the beauty of uncertainty. Desires can be the opposite of what is best for us. They also evolve. So, when everything went sideways, Milo liked to take a positive perspective that it is precisely what needed to happen to set up for something incredible. He felt that way because he could have never dreamed up his life, but it was perfect for him.

Floating to the surface of reality, he had a flashback to a beach holiday he took with his husband months after the bus accident while he had still been reeling from all that had happened. The warmth of the memory needed no words. Just the two of them walking hand in hand on the beach, phones left on aeroplane mode for days at a time while the sound of the surf sent a vibration of peacefulness. His reflection during that trip had been the first calm spot he had had for many months, and Ra had given quiet assurance that he knew it was what Milo needed.

For so long, he had craved consistency in relationships, and now he had a rock-solid marriage with a man who accepted him. Having a relationship where you are in total partnership and find each other's foibles amusing was a new oasis he had found himself in. That feeling of acceptance had spread to their surrounding friendships. A tight-knit family sharing lives in a neighbourhood in Phnom Penh.

Milo also had that same connection with friends who had been in his life since he was seventeen. Over the years, they had remained close despite being separated by oceans. Wherever he was in the world, he knew he could reach out to any of them. He had called Jay once using their code word meaning, *it's an emergency.* He had been at his breaking point and needed help to see his way through his own misery. What Jay didn't tell Milo at the time was, at that moment, he had been about to start a show. He had been about to rise through the smoke to perform for 30,000 people live, and he had told everyone to hold up while he took a call.

Jay, in his caring, capable way, had managed to reassure Milo and get the show started. The audience had been unaware of the impending crisis, and the show went on. Later, when Jay joked about the impeccable timing, Milo had found it hilarious and horrifying. "You should have told me!"

"I knew it was important," Jay had replied with a grin.

And that was how it was with Jay then, now, always.

He had so many spiralling stories of vacations and adventures they took together. Before he had moved to Cambodia, he went out with his friends; it might have been the last time they went clubbing together. They had ended up at a club called Heaven. He was there with Jay, David, and Phil. The night had stuck out. It was supposed to be an invite-only event though someone had inevitably missed that memo because it was beyond packed. Bodies and coloured drinks strobing to the beat had heightened the intensity.

Jay had been teasing David about his choice of comfortable footwear, and before Milo could add his two cents, they were lost in a crowd. Unwilling to get further separated as they were swept up in the undulating mass of people, Phil and Milo had linked arms and worked their way out of the milieu, eventually finding their way to a corner near the exit.

Even with the nightclub being a bit more raucous than expected and being separated from his friends, Milo had felt at ease. He had enjoyed the ketamine high, smoothing him into the beat of the music. One moment he had been dancing, and the next, he felt himself slipping into a K-hole—too much of a good thing. When taken with E, ketamine can lead to a feeling of paralysis, called a K-hole, causing people to lose the ability to speak or physically control their body, though they are completely cognizant of everything happening to and around them. When it happened to Milo, he hadn't been able to do anything except cling to a nearby pole and wait as even the music seemed to beat in slow motion.

After an unknown passing of time, Phil had realised what was happening, peeled him off the pole, and propped him up in a chair he had managed to wrangle. Milo had marvelled at the feeling of complete loss of control and understood the panic that could happen to users who didn't understand what the substance was capable of.

After the effects of the ketamine wore off and he had regained physical control of his body, they had found Jay and David in a random swell of people. They had both looked like they were over it.

Jay had grabbed his shoulder and tried shouting over the roar of the music. "It's getting claustrophobic. If I don't get out of here, it's going to end up like Valencia." One word was all it took, and Milo knew how Jay was feeling. Nuanced within that word was a wicked shared experience and years of understanding. His friend could go all night at a rave with a wave of revellers. Put him in a crowd of coke fiends, and he was out of there or out of his mind. In Valencia, things had gotten out of hand, and it was a reference none of them needed an explanation for. At once, the four of them pushed towards the door.

Together they had heaved their way outside, holding on to each other as they wove between the undulating masses. It was a tight but easy escape after what seemed like an endless night.

"Weren't you the one who said this was supposed to be low-key?" David had asked as they caught their breath and adjusted to the change in atmosphere.

"That's what I thought," Jay had shrugged. "Usually, I can handle a crowd, but that one had a different energy to it."

"Let's get out of here and then never speak of this again," David had replied. Laughing, they all agreed.

"Wait, what happened in Valencia?" Phil had asked as the three others turned on their heels and headed out.

David, Jay, and Milo had looked at each other until Milo's words came out in a tumult, "It's kind of hard to explain, but basically, David talked us down and saved the day."

"You're misremembering," David had scoffed. "You were fucked up as usual."

"Yeah," Jay had added, sarcasm dripping even before he spoke. "You only saved our lives. No big deal, right?"

"You mates save my life every day by giving me something to hold onto," David said softly.

"Stop being humble and tell us about Valencia," Phil had insisted.

"Not going to happen," Jay cut in. "There are some incidents that will remain for my eyes only, but none of us will forget Valencia."

"So, why the cloak and dagger act?" Phil had replied. "Put up or shut up."

"Aren't you a bit of a bitch tonight," Milo had teased.

"Thank you," Phil had said, then he turned and walked off. The rest of them followed behind. Looking back, they had all thought it was great fun, though everyone they described it to thought it sounded horrendous.

Milo woke from the memory like it happened last night, more real than dream. Under the harsh glare of the hospital lights, it faded, and he was left with the warm glow of gratitude.

As he sat up for the first time, a wave washed over him that he had been spared and would be the friend, partner, and father he knew his loved ones needed. One of the things he had learned from his husband was that what we perceive we want can be the opposite of what we need. Milo had once considered an image of his perfect man, but what is perfection? He had learned that love is laughing at what is irritating and accepting people for who they are. That's how he fell in love with Ra. It wasn't about finding someone who was willing to do the dishes or fill the partner role. It was someone who could fill zero expectations and still be irreplaceable. His love for Gia blossomed from that same compassion and understanding, and helped bring him to a place where it extended into all relationships in his life.

He thought of the different roles he had as important parts that fit to make his life a complete outfit. Contemplating the intricate beauty of his life, Milo watched Ra sitting beside his hospital bed, working on the next fashion week show. A slideshow of images from previous years folded into Milo's mind. In his recollection, he saw the artistry and production behind the scenes as well as how it had played out to the audience. Fashion, as introduced to him by Ra, seemed like a microcosm of what was going on in the world, and it offered a glimpse into ethnography, iconography, and celebration in a gorgeous exhibit. As MC for the second annual Phnom Penh fashion week, Milo had been dressed and directed by Ra and got to feel the energy and excitement of it all coming together amid multiple costume changes.

"You'll do great," Ra had said, after explaining the timing of the show, Milo's first time.

"Watch for your cues." Nathan had placed another outfit on top of the pile Milo was trying on.

"Look fantastic," Kali had added.

"And watch the magic," Simone had finished.

It had been an intricate performance, and any misstep could cascade quite quickly, but watching Ra, Don, and the other designers, make-up and hair artists, models, stage management, and industry professionals working behind the scene, it was incredible to be a cog in that machine. Simone wasn't wrong; it was magic. Since she saw the work her friends put into it beforehand, she had a glimpse into what was to be expected, yet she was still astounded by the energy of the end result. From on stage as MC, he had experienced being between the two worlds. He could see the performance as the audience did, but close up and with the added dimension of taking in the audience's reaction while the whole thing took place all around him. Once he got over his nerves, he had enjoyed taking part and the vantage it gave him.

He might need a cane for the next show; however, he was determined to be there. Milo was sure he could pull off the look.

# THIRTEEN

# ACCEPTING HEALING INFREQUENCY

The better he felt, the more antsy he got. His friends and family encouraged him to rest, heal, and blah, blah, blah. He knew they meant well, but Milo itched to get out of the hospital. They visited him and brought him what he needed. He was an atrocious patient and preferred not to have visitors at all. He didn't want people interfering or getting involved in his healing; it made him feel like a nuisance. He wanted everyone to get on with their lives, and he'd be back soon.

Part of being a boarding school survivor is you tend to hate anything that makes you the centre of attention. Forced jollity was another thing Milo loathed. Birthday parties, Christmas, all of it. He had a reticence to fake happiness.

He was waiting for the results of a final few tests and was becoming an impatient patient; it was exhausting, and so was the drab hospital room he was stuck in. There was something about them that made his skin crawl. He had spent enough time in different hospitals around the world to know they were an in-between place where you could just as easily be confronted with a miracle or tragedy.

Hospitals could feel like that dream where you are lost, and every hallway looks the same. Both dreams and memories held the same sort of etherealness to Milo. Sometimes they run through your hands like water. It could be difficult to tell the difference, especially when you find yourself in a place between a memory and a dream. Milo thought about that often. He dreamt of Gia visiting him in the hospital. It was her turn to sit in the hard place, reassuring the patient while feeling uncertain.

While he was dreaming, it felt like she was really there.

"You forgot about coming to visit Celeste and me in Madrid," Gia reminded him. "You might have got a temporary reprieve, but you can't stay away forever."

"Just try to stop me. I am so ready for a change of scenery," Milo said.

In his dream, the hospital room had lengthened into something closer to a hotel lobby, though the bed remained the same. The walls were curtained with exquisite tapestries with gold embellishments. The tiled floor shone like marble, and there was a sound of rushing water, though Milo could not see where it was coming from.

"I thought I was too, but now it's getting closer to moving day, there's a lot I'm going to miss," Gia said.

In his dream, Milo felt the sadness of their inevitable goodbye, swallowed and chose the light-hearted route instead. "Your family must be excited to see you."

"Yes, it will be nice to be closer. Ava wanted us in the UK, but that wasn't happening. At least Spain is closer to the tropical paradise I am used to."

"And it gives her an excuse for a holiday."

"Exactly. The boys are so excited too. For some reason, they've decided Spain is the perfect place for would-be spies, so they can't wait to visit."

"Weren't they intent on being superheroes last time you talked to them?"

"Yes, apparently, spies are more realistic than superheroes." She started to describe why a spy would beat a superhero in a fight and then stopped herself mid-sentence. "Sorry, not relevant to anyone over twelve."

They both laughed, and Gia reached for his arm. He could feel the warmth of her hand and see the lightness in her smile that reached her eyes. Then he was jolted awake, and Gia's face was replaced with a nurse coming in to check his vitals.

After she left, he was once more alone in his hospital room. His dream conversation with Gia was vivid in his mind.

The echoes of loss were palpable in the coldness of most hospitals. In the quiet moments, he remembered being at that hospital two years earlier, visiting healing friends and coming to terms with the vast hole that was left behind. It had been sitting in a generic plastic chair, waiting to visit one of their colleagues that he had to begin to accept life without her in it. It felt hollow and wrong. He had tied his contempt for the unfairness of it to the discomfort of the hard chair that seemed to put pressure on all the wrong places regardless of his position.

Picking up the pieces and carrying on had seemed impossible and heavy in those early days of grief. Being trapped in the hospital now carried an aura of tragedy still.

He contemplated Gia's loss, and the Gia Wellness Centre built in her memory and called him to return to work. The work they did together was continuing to spread light and help people. Everyone who knew Gia was touched by her energy. It reminded him of the way the warmth of that first drink had put a sparkly hue to his world. With Gia, it was authentic and was imbued with a sense of intense curiosity.

Just as he had to learn to accept her death, he had to accept that life is exceptionally fleeting. In his reflection, he remembered his trip with Celeste to the Andaman Islands, where she had gifted him with a sound bowl and talked about meeting and connecting with Gia. He recalled his first introduction to sound bowl therapy at a retreat he went to with his friend Macy. Then, he met Kanshin and learned from him the ancient history and techniques of using sound bowls for healing.

It was through spirituality and self-discovery that he had been able to stay on track during recovery. He knew it all had to come from within, as everything else could be lost. Moderation wasn't something he learned until he had got clean. Even after rehab, his husband would argue quite strongly that he had put his addiction elsewhere and still worked incredibly hard.

Milo preferred to see it as putting his energy into creating something instead of running away or tearing himself apart. After more than a decade watching the bureaucratic corn maze of international social work, he could wallow in dark humour about the state of the world. When he got in that sort of funk, he realised if he had kept that attitude, he would never have become close with Gia. If he had kept his distance as he was apt to do so, his life would be less because of it.

The way they connected came out of the blue, and Milo hadn't anticipated that at all. In the work environment, Milo usually kept it friendly but professional, and he tried to steer clear of getting invested personally. It came as a surprise to meet someone who brightened his life in such an unexpected way. Everything about the hospital reminded him of the accident and aftermath that rippled with uncertainty. The echoing sounds, whitewashed walls, and beeping machines of a hospital setting reverberated with that loss.

As soon as he was able, he started planning his return home. Even though he would still require time for healing, Milo yearned for a change of scenery, and he was looking forward to being rid of the sight of four walls and a ceiling. More than that, he yearned for a sleep uninterrupted by having his vitals checked every few hours. He started to realise how much his body was worn down compared to after his initial recovery and sobriety. He saw the swirling events that landed him in a hospital with a visceral connection to loss. There with broken bones mending back together, Milo connected his physical pain to the pain of addiction. With trepidation, he had arrived at rehab, ready to confront his substance use issues. His intentionality in healing through it was such a direct contrast to the delicious elation that followed his first drink and his inclination towards mind-altering substances.

Milo remembered his first drink with searing clarity. When he was six, Milo and his family had gone on holiday in the South of France, staying at a country house. They went to a little traditional restaurant, and in France, it's quite typical for children to drink wine mixed with water—so that's when he had his first drink. In Europe and a good many other places in the world, people of all ages drink wine with dinner. Alcohol is part of the celebration and everyday life. Milo didn't remember liking the taste of wine particularly, but he remembered the slight buzz it gave him.

After that, he had been allowed to occasionally drink small amounts, little sips here and there, throughout his younger years. From the age of around thirteen or fourteen, he was allowed to drink a little bit at home. He could have a glass of wine with dinner or for a special occasion, but he had sought it as a way to blur the edges. That's when his secret drinking had started. From the outset, since he couldn't be caught helping himself, drinking had a level of urgency to it. Usually, he had waited until everyone in the house had gone to bed, and then he would sneak some more wine.

By that age, he and William had been sort of left to get on with things themselves. William was Milo's opposite in so many ways, including alcohol. Where Milo didn't know the meaning of moderation, William was allergic and wouldn't touch a drop.

Milo had seen firsthand the after-effects of over-indulgence. He had learned from a young age that usually, a tonne of social pressure makes it tempting to indulge in just one more drink. When he had still lived in London and went through a sober curious period, he had gotten a lot of shit for not drinking, which increased his resolve not to drink. If people told him to do something, Milo's first reaction was not to do it.

The social pressure stopped the temptation for Milo, but for many of his friends in recovery, the temptation was relentless. He had to learn the cold hard truth about losing friends in the recovery journey. When someone close to him relapsed after rehab, his first question was always why. He struggled to get past the why stage.

Milo had learned the hard way that putting distance between people for your own mental health is difficult. When Kathy, a friend from rehab, had chosen to go back to alcohol, he had tried to help her, but eventually, he had to step back. She had sent him a series of nasty messages and accused him of trying to take her things while emotionally attacking him. The sad part was she was such a kind and loving person. He knew it had been the alcohol talking. Unless she made changes in the next few months, she was going to die, and Milo had been powerless to do anything about it, even though he had attempted to help her in every way he could imagine.

The rotting truth was that watching people deteriorate meant accepting they were slowly taking their life. Milo had gotten to a point where he could not condone the behaviour any longer. He had to draw a line when it started impacting his mental health. Having watched the familiar death of Kathy through the ravages of alcohol was his constant reminder of the deep, personal struggle of addiction. He had prepared for her death because he had done everything else he could.

One of the last conversations he had after dragging her alcohol-soaked body out of the apartment she'd just been kicked out of had been as blunt as he could be. "Listen, I have had conversations with your friends and family that they expect me to call them one day to tell them you've died. We expect that I will have to make arrangements to get your body back home to New Zealand."

For a moment, her eyes had flashed in a terror of recognition, and she had started to nod her head slowly. "I know. I am going to get better." The words were hollow, and even then, he had known she was already justifying her next drink, looking for a way out.

Walking away from someone in crisis was against everything he believed in, but there had been nothing else he could do. He had helped her find an apartment to live in, a job, and any other support she needed, but he couldn't force her not to drink.

So, he had to watch her slowly decay, lie to him, and use every trick in the book to hide her drinking.

She had been powerless against the disease—powerless in a more abstract way in that it called back to her no matter where she was. She also hadn't been able to let go of her ego. Milo had learned that as an addict, that's one of the steepest hurdles, you're going to be a cliche, and it's okay.

In his work and among friends, Milo had always tried to encourage people to admit they had a problem and that required letting go of their ego. Only then could they begin the real work. He had made every effort to live the example and found meditation gave him insight into his trauma and how his life unfolded. It took a lot of work to bring peace of mind to his unresolved trauma, which went back decades. And Milo assumed he would continue the practice for whatever decades he had left. Life had thrown him enough lessons that he appreciated his eventual self-acceptance.

In his late adolescence, he had trained as a marksman and was planning on a military career, like his father. He had been an excellent shot and successful in all his training. He had been encouraged to join the military, but he was not permitted to do so if he was gay. They had informed him that he could still join as long as he hid his sexual identity and had no relationships. Milo had declined.

In school, the military had been a natural progression, and it was partly expected because of his family's close ties. Weapons trained at sixteen, he had been delighted over the prospect of pursuing excellence in that role. He had excelled at all aspects of training and took on every task with precision. And yet Milo's excitement for his career path was tempered by his sexuality. It had been a constant lynchpin in his life because it was something he was certain about within himself, but he was not always permitted to express it outwardly. So, during his teenage years, the normal awkwardness of growing up had been made more complex by the mixed messages he was getting in his personal life and from different aspects of society.

As he was coming to self-awareness and working on understanding what that meant for his life, he had found the strength to be who he was, and he had to come out to the Colonel in Chief before even telling his family. Revealing deeply private information in a military setting while he was only just coming to terms with it himself had been daunting. In a stuffy office steeped in tradition, Milo had explained why he would not be pursuing a military career after all.

"I'm gay." The two small words came out of his mouth like bullets, and some of his anxiety had lifted. Now the truth was out. He had felt less choked.

"Don't worry about it." The colonel had been kind and understanding about it and made Milo feel at ease. "Just don't tell anyone."

In a dream state, Milo had listened as his colonel clarified that he could continue his training as long as he stayed in the closet. Though it was painful, Milo had known that wasn't going to work for him. He had recently been introduced to the gay scene in London, and he saw it as a vibrant place that invited him to be who he was with no expectations or rules.

The choice between two stark opposites was a challenge. He had been thinking of joining MI6, and when you do, you can't tell anyone you've applied. The process was completed in secrecy. So, when he had quit the military, his dad got excited and had made comments alluding to the fact that he quite understood the nature of what Milo was doing. While Milo had assured his dad he was not a special intelligence officer, his father had winked, then nodded and said, "Of course not."

When they went sailing together, his dad had told him that he understood the secrecy involved in joining an intelligence unit and that his travel for social work was a good cover.

"It's not a cover, Dad. Sorry to burst your bubble," Milo had insisted, but his dad was having none of it.

"Sure, sure. Look, there is a reason I brought you out this way. See that cliff over there just before the tip of the inlet?" His father had continued pointing as he went on, "It's actually a false front of a bunker. It's camouflaged really well, but it's there alright. There's a lot you'll be learning about things hidden in plain sight."

"Very cool and very cryptic, but please drop it," Milo had said. "Look, there are some whales breaching starboard."

The majestic animals put on a show and stopped all further talk of the military. Milo had gratitude on both accounts.

With his father, most things went unsaid. He hadn't had the capacity to comprehend the possibility of having a gay son. It took father and son a while to get back on track, reaching some dark points in their relationship, but inevitably both came to empathise, love, and support one another. Even though his father had been slow to accept his son, he became an outspoken and supportive Pride dad as time went on.

Milo found the process of coming out was ongoing, and it made him feel vulnerable, especially once he began to traverse the earth. Not everyone perpetuated homophobia, though Milo faced enough of it.

During his last year and a half at school, Milo had developed a close friendship with Richard. They had felt comfortable just being together. Whereas with other people, Milo was worried about what their motives were, with Richard, it had felt natural.

They had thrown caution into the wind by seeing each other every day. Whenever someone commented on the nature of their relationship, his friend had backed off for a while. Growing into yourself and experiencing your sexuality is an uncomfortable time. The nuances of boarding school had made that time more challenging. Towards the end of his school career, he became more comfortable with the idea of starting to come out to his friends and to a few other people.

By his final semester, Milo had been ready for people to know he was gay. A couple of people he told individually. He only had a few close friends. One of them had instigated the conversation and asked him in a polite, gentle way, "Are you bi?"

Milo had trusted him enough to feel like it was non-judgemental, and he replied, "I'm not bisexual. I'm actually gay."

It had been the first time he had spoken those words to another person willingly and without fear. Though it sounded casual, it echoed through him and opened a door that did not want to be closed.

Then at his RA level, he had painted large canvases of Milo and Richard lying naked together. Milo's mother had described the artwork as showing a "post-coital position." It wasn't, and as usual, his mother had been over-dramatising things. It was a sensual painting, and it had been Milo's personal coming out moment.

The result was swift outrage, and there had been moves to ban his work from the exhibition, but his art teacher had fought for him to be exhibited. Eventually, the same art teacher had also taken a couple of pieces and had them exhibited in the Henley gallery nearby.

The headmaster was an incredibly kind human. He

had simply been responding out of pressure from those parents who didn't want their children's eyes besmirched by seeing two men beside each other au naturel on a sofa.

He had select mentors and friends along the way that guided and reassured him. A memorable example was his art teacher, who had supported his final painting. Mr Dylan had been a refreshing whirl of colour in Milo's boxy education. He had been one of the few adults that didn't seem to be full of it. He also wasn't afraid of controversy, especially when it involved the merit of artistic value. It wasn't only that Mr Dylan had insisted Milo's work be exhibited; it was having an ally who had encouraged him to grow rather than hide.

Now, what felt like many lifetimes later, he was an entrepreneur with a team of like-minded individuals who believed in working as a collective for children and families. Even when he had been drinking heavily, he was still up at 6 am and at work on time. He'd taken the long road to get there. Sometimes it wasn't even a road. Sometimes it was driving through the desert to find a nomadic tribe. He'd taken trains across India, travelled by camel, donkey, matatu, and boda boda. He'd also gotten rides from plenty of dodgy potential serial killers.

He was no longer willing to travel by bus, and his husband banned him from getting on a motorcycle. Seeing his current circumstances, he couldn't argue. Once he got up and moved again, it would be a whole other story. The convenience would probably win out. There was still so much to do, and it would be necessary to get where he needed to be. But that was a conversation for another day.

In the meantime, Milo would agree to almost anything if it meant he could go home. While he was making plans and charming the nursing staff to let him out on good behaviour, he got a surprise call from his son.

"Dad, it's me. Mum won't let me come see you. Are you sure you don't need me there?" The loud whisper of his son's voice brought a smile to Milo's face.

"No, son. Your mother is right. Besides, it would be pretty boring for you to visit now and just sit around and watch me rest. Once I'm better, you can come for a proper visit, and then we can have a real adventure." The thought of showing his son the sights of Cambodia and Thailand was a huge motivator in healing for Milo. Though he lived half a world away with his mum in London, Milo had always been present in his son's life in whatever way he was needed.

Their alternative family was becoming less of an anomaly the older his son got, and Milo held hope that the world had become more tolerant, for the most part.

Trying to be the change, Milo was urging himself to be tolerant of the fanfare surrounding his release from the hospital. Ra let it slip that their friends were planning a celebration. Milo made it clear that if he arrived home to any sort of excitement, he would turn around and hop on the nearest bus out of there. Ra rolled his eyes and agreed while his lips betrayed the hint of a smile.

For the sake of his sanity, he wasn't telling anyone else he was home until he had a chance to settle in. The fact that most of his loved ones were scattered and half a world away provided an easy cover. After getting the final clearance from the doctor, with follow-up information and a large supply of pain pills, Milo was ready.

Pushed through the corridors in a wheelchair, with Ra at his side, Milo had a sense of awakening as if from a long meditation. The miracle of each moment felt clear and palpable. It seemed impossible and somehow unfair that, now, he was heading home from the hospital after having been scraped up off the side of the road in Kep.

# FOURTEEN

# FINDING FAMILY

He spent his first night home from the hospital in pain but content. When he got up for the day, which meant hobbling from his bedroom to his living room, he downed some painkillers with his first cup of coffee of the day. Then, he sat down to meditate.

Just as he was settling into calm, he received a frantic call from his mum in London, who was in a state of panic because she had been trying to reach him. She wanted to let him know she was worried about him.

"Isn't it a sign it's time to come home?" she asked.

Purposefully misunderstanding the question, Milo replied, "Yes, I was eager to get out of the hospital and get home to Ra. I left a few days earlier than expected, even though I still struggle to get around."

"No, no, I mean home to the UK. Enough is enough." She tried to sound the stern parent, though both of them knew that ship had sailed years ago.

"The UK hasn't been home in a long time if it ever was. Why would you even suggest it?"

"You know I worry about you. You're so far away, and it's hard for me to reach you because of the time difference. I didn't even hear about your accident until days later. You could be dead, and I'd never know it. Besides, I never get to have you here for Sunday tea," his mum insisted.

"Well, I am in no position to go anywhere for tea for the moment," Milo said. He was suddenly exhausted and didn't want to waste his breath telling his mother for the umpteenth time that he had no intention of moving back to the UK.

During the one-sided conversation, he dry-swallowed a couple of prescription fentanyl pills and recollected another conversation with his mum years ago when he had been informed that they had found his older sister.

Then, as now, his mum had gone on in great detail about her feelings and opinions regarding every aspect of the situation. When it was clear her guilt wasn't working, she added in one last attempt, "Your brother has been very worried about you as well. He's as upset as I am."

"Actually, he's fine. I talked to him earlier," Milo said.

"Well, he wouldn't come right out and say it, but I know he agrees with me about it not being safe there." His mum was an expert in beating a dead horse.

"Statistically speaking, perhaps. It's still not happening. Now can you stop harping on me and let me heal," Milo said.

"Of course, dear," his mum said, then added, "Just think about it."

After saying goodbye, he thought back to the time when they had discovered his sister's whereabouts and met her for the first time. Milo felt a connection to Julia right away and shared the same dark sense of humour. Having her in his life for more than a decade had helped him become thankful for his family in all their dysfunctional glory. She was his connection to South Africa, a place he always thought he would live.

For as long as he could remember, he'd known he had a sister. His mum had been forced to give up her firstborn long before she was married while she still lived in South Africa. The complications resulting from that loss, compounded by the abuse she had also experienced, played a part in his mother's suffering and struggling with her mental health.

As a family, they had been looking for Julia even before Dad left. It took many years, with interruptions like a heated divorce that had slowed them down. Milo remembered the tumultuousness of growing up and coming to grips with the complications of family. His parents had gone through a contentious separation where he felt pulled literally between them physically and emotionally when he was not yet ten. At that tender age, he had not been old enough to cope with being front and centre for the fallout of their relationship.

During that time, his sister had been part of a hopeful future where there would be more love than fighting and family time rather than manipulation. When they had finally been reunited, Milo was a young adult and felt a surge of relief when they got the call. While they were looking for her, Julia had been looking for her birth family, and she tracked them down through their aunt, his Mum's sister.

The look on his mum's face when she heard they found her daughter was one he would never forget. It was part overwhelming joy, part abject terror. Julia had been found and was now just a phone call away.

It had been a bizarre experience to meet his long-lost sister, and he knew he loved her but didn't know her enough to know if he liked his sister yet or not. Straight away, Milo and Julia got on like a house on fire. He met her first in South Africa, and then she had travelled to the UK to meet their mum and brother. She built a reasonable relationship with them, but with Milo, it was much more fraternal. They shared the same mischievous laugh, adventurous side, and light-hearted nature.

He remembered her sombre look when she had stayed with him as she said, "It's so grey here."

Milo had laughed at the obvious.

"Next time, let's meet in Cape Town," she had suggested.

"You don't have to ask me twice," Milo agreed.

And he had been a regular visitor there. South Africa was close to his heart as well as part of his ancestral history. For a long time, he had planned on retiring there after living in Uganda, but life brought him a tropical adventure of another kind.

He hadn't anticipated Cambodia being more than another temporary assignment. Once there, he had learned that home could be found in unexpected people and places. He met Ra on a first and last date with someone else. Milo had reluctantly accepted the date, though the fall guy was only visiting. The visitor had met Ra in the bar and introduced Milo. When Milo had told Ra he had a beautiful smile, his date got pissed off and took it personally.

Right away, he had felt the positive energy and natural ease emanating from Ra. He was like the human form of Valium, and Milo had been drawn to his calm kindness. They became Facebook friends, and Ra asked if he'd like to meet for drinks when they were both in Siem Reap. Milo remembered the moment he was getting ready, and he wondered, "Wait a minute, is this a date? This could be a date!"

He had been oblivious to the idea, and when it came to him, he had a flutter of nervous anticipation while he reconsidered what he should wear. Before long, he snapped himself out of his nervousness, went to meet Ra, and had a wonderful evening.

After getting a little carried away, they had carried on back to Milo's room, where their date continued throughout the night. It was an instant connection that had ended in an awkward moment in the morning as Milo realised his hotel room was connected to the meeting room. He told Ra to stay put while he figured out a plan. If he could distract his colleagues or somehow get them to leave the room, he could sneak Ra out.

He eventually realised it would be futile to attempt anything, and Ra couldn't hole up in his hotel all day, so they had to have a public goodbye as Ra left with a smile in last night's clothes. It had been worth it for Milo to withstand his colleagues' ribbing. After their first date, they had begun to see more of each other, and it wasn't long before their lives were interconnected. It was a slow burn, but as time went on, they started spending more time together than apart.

Their lives became woven together in a natural way, and one morning Milo realised that Ra had moved in. Their comfort with each other had its own rhythm. Right away, Ra had started replacing Milo's clothes, making him more presentable, and securing a permanent spot beside him in life.

There was a tenderness to Ra that had surprised Milo. Though he already had a feel for Ra's mellow nature, the first time Milo had seen his husband around animals, it melted his heart. There are some people, like Ra, who come across as aloof but have a heart of gold, who surprise people with their kindness because it seems to come from a deep sense of love. To Milo, it seemed like a quiet confidence or some sort of awareness that he wanted to achieve for himself. He marvelled at Ra and cherished their time together.

Now home with a recent reminder of the preciousness of life, he relished how far they had come from those first tentative, sweet moments to sharing life. Sitting on the sofa and counting down the minutes until he could take his next dose of painkiller, he focused his reminiscence on memories of his time in Cambodia because that was when his life began to change in a powerful way, and Ra was a big part of what happened to him. Ra was also his future, and he was grateful for the chance to have some new adventures together. It made being stuck at home and immobile for the time more bearable because he had made it out of the back of the tuk-tuk and was getting the chance to heal.

His phone beeped at him for the umpteenth time, and he growled whilst looking at how many unanswered messages he had. Regardless of the love people wanted to share with him, he turned off his phone because he wanted no more well-wishers and just wanted to be left bloody well alone. It was so hard not to get back to work. Sitting still, even when his body demanded, was a challenge. He took two more fentanyl pills without checking to see how much time he was supposed to wait. It was close enough. The numbness washed over him.

It wasn't that he meant to be owly. It was the mundanity of everyone saying *poor you* and he wasn't in the mood. With good intentions, people focus on the bad, dwelling in detail on what happened and why. Milo reflexively did the opposite, skipping the bad, deleting the memory and focusing on the feel-goods of life. Living clean meant feeling good without mind-altering substances, and it put a new perspective on his memories. What amazed Milo to no end was how crystal clear some of his memories were while others were mired in uncertainty. It made sense that some of the more horrific incidents were blocked as a trauma response.

Choosing to remember the highlights instead of the lows, he knew he had done a lot to laugh at. As the numbing euphoria of the fentanyl soaked into his body, his nervous system relaxed. He enjoyed replaying memories of the cities he had fallen in love with. Travelling to every continent other than Antarctica, Milo went out of his way to taste and experience what the world had to offer.

Looking around his cosy condo that he shared with Ra, he felt comforted. While he still travelled for work and to visit family (when he was not peeling himself off the side of the road), Milo's urge to find the next best place was gone. And that was fine with him. He wouldn't be going anywhere for a while, not even popping south for a weekend by the sea.

Just as Milo was appreciating his husband, Ra entered the room, arms draped in wardrobe bags.

"Guess what I found today?" Ra's voice was muffled by his armload.

"That's obvious, clothes," Milo laughed.

"Yes, but vintage clothes, designed by some of the greats." Ra went on in great detail about the luck of finding such a complete collection. When he touched Milo's arm, his demeanour changed in an instant. "You better sit down. You're shaking like a leaf in the wind."

"Yeah, and you are the tree that keeps me grounded." Milo wrapped his arms around his husband, who steadied him and guided him back to his seat.

All talk of fashion design halted. Ra flitted around Milo, reminding him to rest, bringing him tea, cushions, and anything else he thought might help. Milo was only able to convince Ra that he was okay by agreeing to eat something.

While he was picking over his lunch, he felt the security of his life less chaotic. Being sober brought a cloudy sort of clarity so adventures of the past could be understood from a broader perspective. While being high or inebriated was part of many of the moments that brought him a thrill, now, he could feel that connection to the excitement of life and enjoy what he was doing more fully.

A few months before the accident, he had reached his one-year anniversary of sobriety. Typically, he preferred to avoid special attention drawn around key dates; instead, he lived life just for today. One year of sobriety, however, was momentous enough to warrant significant reflection.

Over the course of a year, facing sobriety day in and day out had brought about incredible changes. After the rough few months of physically removing toxins from his body, he had noticed he was sleeping better and had better mental acuity. Facing the upcoming milestone of his second year sober, he had reflected on the gradual shift from surviving the day to appreciating the world in a new way.

At some point in the year, he had gone from merely surviving to enjoying a heightened awareness of the richness of fresh ingredients or the pure enjoyment of a long belly laugh. Then, those moments had become more and more frequent until it was the norm rather than the expectation. It was like a fog had lifted from his consciousness, and a healthy future started to feel possible.

Now he was looking at that time as though through a fog of darkness. The pills rattled in his pocket. He glanced at the clock out of the corner of his eye, a voice in his head telling him he could wait while the urgency inside him disagreed.

# FIFTEEN

# HEART-BREAKING LOSS

Returning to the hospital for physiotherapy and to check on his healing kept him rooted in the past. It wasn't just the pain medication either; it was the never-ending sameness, Milo supposed, that gave ample time for contemplation while healing. He didn't like to sit still at the best of times. In this instance, his body was giving him no other choice.

Milo was physically where he needed to be, but mentally he kept having recurring reminders of his time spent there after the bus accident. Reliving the horrors was hampering the healing process as he felt stuck in time. Events of two years ago were fresh in his mind. After the first raw night gasping to slow the spinning images of all the carnage he had seen, he had to focus on helping those still in the hospital recovering from broken bodies and internal trauma. He had spent an inordinate amount of time in this building before he was a patient.

For weeks, he had visited the Royal Phnom Penh twice a day to be there for Heng and the others, who had a long road of healing. The irony of being in the exact same place, returning for follow-up, and healing from similar injuries was disconcerting. After the bus accident, there was so much happening at once he had sometimes spent more time at the hospital than at work and home. Now, as he limped along the hallway between his physio appointment and the lab, he felt the same sense of having one foot in two realities. At the moment, he found himself thinking he was there, on his way to visit a friend, until the pain of his own body brought him back to the realisation that it was two years previous.

It had all happened in a blur and a flurry as the immediate aftermath of the bus accident had passed. He began helping Celeste and Gia's family, who were home in England. He had worked with them to coordinate moving Gia's body back to the UK and ensuring her personal effects were passed on to Celeste.

The volume of phone calls he had fielded in the first few days was almost unfathomably difficult. There had been staff members still stuck where they had been dropped off by the bus and never picked up. They were also struggling to support the survivors and the families while attempting to maintain programs while missing and managing traumatised team members. Then, right in the thick of it, he had received an email from the US division of World Children's Services reminding Milo that the six-month report was due.

The outright stupidity of the request had almost been enough to push him over the edge. He had been about to tell them to go fuck themselves for their lack of compassion when they lost half their team. Before he had to get colourful, he got an email back saying that in light of everything that happened, he didn't have to complete the report. He had been floored by the audacity to even ask for more work to be completed instead of providing more much-needed support.

The shattered lives of those left behind had been a heavy weight for the rest of the team. The people lost were their colleagues and friends, young, vibrant people working to bring light into dark situations. The survivors and those touched by loss had struggled to carry on. Meanwhile, management seemed ready to get back to work.

After he had collected Gia's bag from the bus company, his agency's logistics manager had flounced up to him soon after he returned to the office.

"I'll need you to hand over Gia's laptop as it is an organisational asset," he had said, holding out his hand, his voice blank.

"Can you just fuck off, please? This is her bag, and it is still full of her possessions," Milo had scolded as he was slowly going through her belongings. The canvas bag had been drenched in water and motor oil and smelled of accident. Milo had methodically taken everything out, drying it off, seeing what could be salvaged. His mood was melancholy, and he had been unwilling to be pushed. "I will give you the computer when I am ready."

"No, I need it now." The manager's face had remained unchanged.

"You need to get the fuck out of my office right now," Milo had said. Fed up with the unnecessary pressure, he had squared off with the guy who was at least a head taller and wider, preventing him from moving an inch further into the room. His office had reeked of motor oil, and it permeated his imagination bringing him to focus on her last moments. The anger he had at that moment for the lack of humanity in considering Gia's belongings nothing more than company property boiled to the surface.

"No, I need it," the logistics manager said again.

"You ask me once more, and I will take your head off," Milo had insisted, finally getting his point across. "A lot more than assets were lost."

Later, Vanessa had stopped by to check in on his progress on the EU grant proposal. It was a technically difficult and time-consuming project that had ramped up right as the accident happened. He had known how important it was. He also knew he didn't need to be checked up on. The added pressure and Vanessa's cold demeanour had made him bristle.

While they had never been friends, Vanessa and Milo had worked professionally together, and he hadn't expected this side of her that lacked humanity or warmth. His earlier argument with her before the accident came to mind. Could he blame her for the accident, or was he projecting? Sometime after he had left the organisation, he had realised the logistics manager had given Vanessa the forms to sign off on the bus before the tragic trip. The two of them had been involved in a cover-up of the accident in a way. The proper steps that were supposed to be taken to ensure safety had been missed, and no accountability was taken.

Why had he stopped looking into negligence? In the end, he knew it would cost more lives. At the time, it wasn't that cut and dry either. The pieces had come together over time, and he connected them more concretely with regular visits to the hospital two years later, with the shadows of his co-workers and the aftermath of the bus accident echoing through the halls.

Sitting in a painful fog after physical therapy, he was unable to manage the menagerie of negativity. He reached for his pill bottle to bring him relief. This time he was medicating for health reasons, as a doctor had prescribed fentanyl to aid in relieving his pain during healing. Since it was doctor-approved, Milo didn't have a second thought when he started to take them more frequently. He had to call his doctor for a refill earlier than expected, which niggled at him a little. Still, it was easy to rationalise the need for the pills. He just counted his injuries. He wasn't ready to admit that more than the pain relief, he was relying on the pills to stop the nightmares he had been having.

In a rush of terror one night, he woke up thinking he was stuck in the morgue. His dream had been a vivid recollection of his conversation with the mortician when he went with Celeste to see Gia's body.

Arriving at the cold door that led to the refrigerated unit in a back corridor of the hospital, he had momentarily mused about how he was well-trained for what he was going through, even though it was heartbreaking. He could compartmentalise his agony and do what needed to be done. That same trait made him an excellent addict.

"Hello," the mortician had said. His quiet voice had made the greeting sound like a question.

"Hello, how are you?" Milo had asked, the question repeated instinctively, part of his proper upbringing he knew by rote.

Startled by the question, or even having someone acknowledge him, the mortician had replied. "Oh, okay, thank you, come in," in a rambling stumble of words.

"You've had a busy night," Milo had noted on the way in, making conversation to fill the silence.

"Yes, a terrible accident, so sad." His lab coat swishing as he turned, the mortician's tone had been conciliatory, and he looked as though he expected Milo to burst into tears at any moment. Milo understood he worked in a place most people didn't choose to visit. A part of him had been sobbing, and internally he was broken, but the rational Milo wanted all the answers, so he had carried on.

"Something you probably deal with all too often," Milo had said sympathetically.

The mortician had breathed out a sigh and relaxed into the truth, "Yes, too often. She was one of the lucky ones." He looked over at Milo and then continued. "What I mean was that she didn't suffer. Her spine was severed, and she died straight away."

"Oh, thanks," Milo had replied, reeling as the words pummelled him. She died immediately. It was equal parts heart-wrenching and relieving. Gia was gone, but she didn't suffer. Milo had been thankful for the information; he was also frozen in the moment of confronting her body and longing for the comfort of his lost friend. Celeste, alongside him the entire time, had been his silent companion.

As he had touched Gia's cold hand, he had spoken words of love to her spirit. All the while, he had kept his composure and then chatted with the mortician as he made the arrangements for her body, and Celeste said goodbye. He had later learned from the survivors that Gia had been sitting at the front of the bus. She must have seen what was coming because she had jumped up and started running toward the back of the bus. What she hadn't seen coming was that the bus turned ninety degrees, and she had ended up in the direct place of impact. Earlier that day, some of their colleagues had been complaining about the erratic driving. Bora had even asked the driver to slow down.

Their office had always had strict protocols for what was required when it came to bus safety, and the waiver should never have been signed. The survivors of the accident had said there were insufficient seat belts. Vanessa had been so eager for everyone to get out for a team-building retreat she had cut corners. When Milo had been asked about the accident later, he didn't mention his suspicions. He had been caught up in the devastation and couldn't cope with more fallout. The trauma of those who had lived through the accident was ongoing, and the families of those they lost had required ongoing support.

After the bus accident, he had left work for two weeks, flew back to the UK, and seriously increased his drinking. By that point, every day, he had been drinking two bottles of vodka, three bottles of wine, and self-medicating benzos. It was Milo's way of keeping it together as he was spending a lot of time with Celeste, comforting her and grieving together. He also had ensured she'd be recognised as next of kin and get Gia's possessions back. Then, he had seen her off to Egypt, where she would be staying with her sister.

After he had submitted the EU proposal and assisted everyone in returning to work, he took two months off and realised he couldn't possibly go back. That's when he had come to the conclusion that Vanessa had a personality disorder. Either that or she was a bitch who was hell-bent on self-promotion, no matter what the cost. Watching her, it had been eerie to see there was no emotional reaction to the loss of members of her team.

Then, as Milo had been trying to make a graceful exit from the World Children's Services, helping his remaining colleagues transition successfully, Vanessa had backstabbed him and badmouthed him, burnt bridges be damned. She had twisted his words and alienated the people he had been close to. Eventually, he had come to realise her culpability played a part in her reaction. There were enough safety issues that the bus shouldn't have been authorised to take the team anywhere.

It was one of those what-ifs that tormented Milo as he played out what could have gone differently. He had intended to be with them, but he would have driven himself instead of taking the bus, and then Gia would have been in his car. Professionally he knew it wasn't healthy to dwell on how he could have changed it; personally, he was stuck in the past for a time. The what-ifs had been loud and repetitive in his ear. He had been fortunate to have his husband and friends beside him to see him through it.

Recovering from his own accident, Milo vividly remembered how hard he had had to push to keep going amid such a tragic loss. After he had left World Children's Services and was beginning to get his head above water, with the help of whatever substances he could find, Milo had lost his surrogate brother, Daniel.

Daniel's parents, Macy and John, had been his roommates in Uganda for the first few years of Milo's time there. Daniel had been attending school abroad. When they came to Cambodia not long after Milo had moved there, they enveloped him into their family. Milo looked out for Daniel, and Daniel confided in Milo. They became close, and Milo thought of him as a younger brother.

Before she returned to the UK, Macy had lunch with Milo one hot afternoon and expressed her concern that Daniel had increased his drinking and was locking himself in his room to binge drink. She loved her son and felt hopeless about helping him. He had recently returned from rehab and still put up a front that he was sober, but his mum had reason to believe otherwise.

One morning, a few weeks later, Daniel's dad, John, had sent a message asking, "Can you spare a few moments to talk?" Milo had been about to jump on a conference call, so he asked if it would be alright to check in later. John replied, "It's kind of urgent."

When Milo had phoned, John blurted, "Daniel died."

*Fuck, not Daniel.* Milo had thought as he listened to what happened.

John had been in Kampot, near Kep and without an internet connection for the night. Daniel lived only two minutes from Milo. His girlfriend had found him passed out and didn't know what to do. She had gotten in touch with Macy, who was back in the UK, and said to put him on his side. Tragically, Macy hadn't been aware that the body of a recovered addict is unable to handle alcohol the same way it used to. A much smaller amount than usual can be deadly.

Daniel had been to rehab and was in recovery when he had relapsed and died in his apartment. One thing many people don't know is that if you don't drink for six months, and then you go back to drinking, your body goes into shock.

Milo had wracked his brain to remember the last time they had been in touch. He had started feeling the old familiar what-ifs creeping in, finding ways to prevent something from happening when it was already done.

To all outward appearances, Milo had stepped back into the same role he played after the bus accident. The experience was déjà vu too soon as he had helped make arrangements for Daniel's body the same way he did for Gia. Not something he ever wanted to become familiar with, he had had to reach his inner depths to find strength for his grieving friends, even when he had also been grieving himself.

Inwardly, even as he had been supporting Daniel's grieving parents, he had felt the crushing weight of the loss. He had felt that if only he had been there in the moment, he could have done more. His young friend had been rebuilding his life, was happy with his girlfriend, and was making strides.

Milo had known something was tormenting Daniel but didn't know what it was. In anguish, he had replayed everything he could remember from what he had thought was the final time they met for coffee a few weeks prior. Milo had been disappointed in himself for missing the warning signs or not doing more for Daniel. Even though he knew it was out of his hands, Milo had been obsessed with the possibilities.

He had continued drinking heavily, sloshing loose the negativity. For a period of nine months, it had felt like death surrounded him, and everyone he loved was facing loss. That had been when he had gone looking for the number of a drug dealer, so he could get his hands on something stronger. The familiar surge of anticipation had terrified him as he saw the steps he had started to take to go back into heavy drugs. With his finger hovering over the phone to make the call, he forced himself to tell Ra he needed to go to rehab instead.

When she lost Daniel, his mum Macy had gone to stay at the rehab he attended in Chiang Mai. She hadn't been looking to get sober, she wanted to connect with her son, and she needed to be isolated from the outside world to find a way to live with her grief.

When Milo realised he needed help, he had gotten the number for the same rehab Macy and Daniel went to, and that's where he started his recovery. As he had time to reflect on the journey to living clean, he realised Daniel had brought him, Macy, and John to Chiang Mai and kept them connected. Chiang Mai had become Milo's second home. Daniel continued to live on in them.

A few weeks after the bitch of a bus accident, before Daniel died, Milo and Ra had gone with their friends to a water blessing at a local Buddhist temple. When they arrived, they had an old monk doing the blessing. While it is a traditional practice, Milo was used to sitting with his back to the monk and then having water dripped over him with a chalice. This monk apparently preferred a different approach, and he began spitting the water onto them.

Ra had been the most outspoken, exclaiming, "Gross."

Milo had stifled a laugh as they cringed through the rest of the blessing, which he had anticipated being serene. Afterwards, sandals squishing, they walked out of the temple. With nowhere to change into dry clothes, they had walked back soggy. Checking his messages on the way, he had found out that one of his friends from rehab had relapsed and lost her life. He felt like he wanted his money back from what had been far from a serene water blessing.

There had been so much sadness over such a short period in his life, but when he had learned to live clean, he had to find peace with it. Addicts die. He had learned early on that making friends at rehab or the fellowship inevitably ends in loss. Successful recovery numbers are low no matter how desperately you love someone and want them to improve. His friend Nancy had been the first recovering friend he lost. Her life remained a stark reminder anytime he became close to another addict and even as he was working on his relationship with himself. The way Nancy had died saddened him and helped him develop a sixth sense of the need for wisdom to know when to walk away. He had watched her slowly wither and succumb to her addiction.

Lying to everyone who loved her, she had hidden her drinking even as she lost weight and had a liver stent inserted to prevent failure. Her parents had eventually capitulated and told her, "If you are going to drink yourself to death, do it at home so we know where you are."

If they hadn't, they would have found her body, who knows where. Milo had held out hope and kept his friend close to his heart, but he hadn't been able to condone her continued addiction. The one thing Milo knew for sure was that staying sober was always an individual choice. Therapy, intervention, love, and support are helpful tools, but each person has their own demons to face and choices to make.

It had been true for Daniel, who had one of the best therapists Milo had ever known and a broad extended family who loved and wanted to help him. It had also been true for Nancy, who had been head of the trauma department in a hospital. She was committed to NA until she wasn't.

Meditation was one way Milo stopped tormenting himself with grief over the light of each individual that was snuffed away by addiction. The sadness stayed briefly as he remembered his daughter born full-term but already passed. When they saw a little girl who shared the name they had given their daughter, he saw Ella's eyes fill with tears, and he shared her sorrow. Their son, born after a sister he would never meet, brought them joy. Both children were loved beyond measure and held a piece of his heart.

Still, his children's mother always told him how optimistic he was. They had known each other for twenty years, and she remarked multiple times on their journey together that he had been able to find humour in things no matter how grim they might appear. Milo thought she might be giving him too much credit. However, it was their son that kept him hopeful. He also didn't think Ella was fully aware of how proud he was of her and how he still mourned the loss of their daughter. Together they had created a beautiful family, and it seemed like a miracle that he was a dad.

# SIXTEEN

# THE LORD OF THE FLY SWATTER

Transitioning back to work while still healing was like hitting fast forward without all his faculties in place. A global pandemic and the uncertainty of healing through a world emergency was the backdrop. Against better judgement and the advice of everyone he talked to, he was ready to get back to it. Working from home had become as common as cocktail hour. He needed to focus on something other than his physicality, and he knew the Gia Wellness Centre needed him.

When he left World Children's Services after the bus accident, he had wanted to focus on his research and start an ethical mental health centre. The mission was to provide trauma-informed care that integrates mind, body, and spirit. It was a gamble to start a business that wasn't focused on being profitable and still make it work. Yet, he had found it fulfilling and, more importantly, much needed. It was also a very personal business, so his clients and employees hadn't appreciated him being run over. Having been in hospital and recovering at home for a few weeks, some clients were angry that he wasn't around. Others left.

As an entrepreneur, you don't get sick days, and if you're doing it right, you want to go to work. The tricky bit was managing to balance the health of his mind, body, and his business. The pandemic was throwing a wrench in the progress of both, as it was for everyone.

Life didn't slow down, and Milo felt himself trying to catch up while he was supposed to be resting. He had help, though he preferred to do things for himself, and nothing would shake his insatiable urge to start cleaning before the cleaner came. That was precisely what he was doing when he was interrupted by his phone. It was probably Ra calling to check on him. He limped over and answered it on the fifth ring, shoving two blue pills into his mouth instead of looking at who was calling.

"Hello," he croaked.

"Milo, glad I caught you. I hate to bother you when you are just home from the hospital, but I need your help." Jim's voice was gentler than usual.

If Jim was asking for help, Milo knew it was important. They had spoken briefly while Milo was in the hospital, so hearing from him was unexpected.

"What can I do for you?" Milo took the call as a message from the universe to rest. He sat down and took a breath.

"Actually, I am headed to Phnom Penh this week and could use some insight from you." Jim refused to go into detail over the phone and said he would be in touch when he arrived. "I'm aware you are still healing, so I won't be too rough on you."

"I can handle it." Milo was glad for the distraction, though by reading Jim's terse tone, he expected a somewhat sticky situation. Contemplating their work together, he hauled himself out of a sitting position. The dark side of their work had created a bond that connected them around the world. While they met in the UK, they had really gotten to know each other in Uganda. Milo's memory was interrupted by a text from Ra reminding him the cleaners were coming that afternoon. He hobbled around the room, tidying as much as he was able.

"Where are you?" He heard his friends enter the apartment.

"In here. I'm cleaning up before the cleaner gets here."

"What? Why? You are supposed to be taking it easy," Kali said.

"Maybe so, but she'll be here any minute," Milo said.

"Oh, shoot, sit down and let me do it." Piper shooed him to a nearby chair and tidied up for him. Their other friends looked on in bewilderment.

"Why have a cleaner if you're just going to clean for her?" Nathan asked.

"It's a British thing, don't ask," Simone laughed.

As they chatted, they surrounded him, sat him down, and brought him some coffee. He knew they were trying to protect him after seeing him so close to death, but he was irritated at the attention. He watched with mixed amusement as they chatted about him like he wasn't there, planning on how to best help him.

He felt an odd detachment from any plans because he knew they were only possibilities and things could change at any time. On the good days, he felt confident he could roll with the uncertainty. Other times Milo learned to lower his expectations for himself, his business, and anyone he encountered.

Even as his friends were berating him for agreeing to help Jim, he brushed it off as simply seeing an old friend. He knew they were reflecting Ra's concern that Milo was, as usual, taking on too much, too fast. Nevertheless, he was eager to hear what business Jim had in Cambodia. He also felt reassured that he could offer advice and not get directly involved.

When Jim dropped in a few days later, Milo looked up at his friend with a mixture of elation and uncertainty. Jim wore a look of exhaustion that settled in the shadows of his face, deeper than jet lag.

"Are you sure I should be here?" he asked when he saw Milo set up on the sofa. "Ra gave me a distinct side-eye that told me he'd prefer you were resting."

"He's just overprotective. It's fine." Milo noticed the darker-than-usual rings around his friend's eyes as Jim passed him one of the large coffee cups he was carrying.

"The number of times you've thrown yourself at death's door, I am not surprised," Jim replied.

"That's rich." Milo couldn't finish his sentence as their mutual laughter cut through the room. They knew they were both lucky to be alive.

"You mentioned your coffee maker being temperamental, so I thought I'd come prepared." Jim took a drink and then continued. "You still like it black, I presume."

"Absolutely," Milo replied. He felt grateful for the coffee and figured it would either calm his nerves or be a good excuse for his jitteriness. "So, are you ready to tell me why you are here?"

"Yes, well…" Jim hesitated.

"Come on, you've never been one to mince words. Why are you holding back on me?"

"There's a big piece of me that wants me to leave you out of this so you can heal."

"Get over yourself and get on with it. Before I run out of coffee, preferably."

"Alright, I need to get a picture of a woman who has been facilitating sex tourism. If we can pinpoint the bar she works in and have a visual of her there, we can find the hub and shut it down." Jim went on to explain how a paedophile from Ireland had been flying to Cambodia and meeting up with a child broker. The woman they were looking for would link them to the trafficking ring, where they could see how deep it went. Since Milo knew Phnom Penh well, Jim wanted help finding out potential locations for the bar. "Once we find the broker, we can connect the dots and shut it down."

For the next few hours, they poured over maps while Milo answered all of Jim's questions.

"Did you get everything you need, or do you want to go over it again?" Milo asked.

"We may have more questions. However, we have all we need for now," Jim said in an exhale.

"Alright then, how about some more coffee?" Milo asked. As he crossed the room and started the machine, it made no attempt to respond. "Or not."

Jim sat in silence while Milo fiddled with the coffee maker. He had bought it on a whim when he and Simone saw the brand name *Klitz*. It became a household joke, more so because it was temperamental and had to be coaxed into functioning. Finally, the coffee hissed out of the machine. Milo brought two cups with him, handed one to Jim, and sat down.

"Something about our previous conversation hit me on the way here." Jim paused to take a long drink from his too-hot black coffee and looked sideways at Milo. Then he continued. "You told me that my duality shifts from protecting and investigating to bingeing and going completely offline."

"Yes, that's exactly right," Milo replied. "Not so surprising. This industry has one of the highest burnout rates worldwide."

"I thought for a while you'd quit it all and spend the rest of your days behind the bar in Uganda. You were so alive and infused with energy during that time."

"That was a good fit for me. A bartender is not much different than a therapist in a lot of ways."

"All the best therapists are the ones who need therapists, aren't they?" Jim asked.

"Yes, that is one hundred percent accurate." Milo took a long breath.

"Why don't we talk about it, you and I? We only ever elude about our parallel abusive pasts," Jim said.

"Because there has been more trauma since, and we'd rather make light of it," Milo said.

Jim nodded in agreement. "I couldn't have said it better."

There was an incredible amount of adventure amidst the strife, and Milo always kept his mischievous side. Sobriety gave him a chance to see his life through the lens of abuse and addiction and like who he was anyway. He had been on his own his whole life and tried to mask it with a dependence on alcohol, toxic relationships, and substances.

When Milo was ten, his parents had divorced, and he had been pulled unwillingly into the spotlight of his mother's attention as she poured out her grief and problems to him. Being pulled between his parents widened the chasm of uncertainty around authority figures and people he was taught to trust. His mother had gone from telling him he was useless to leaning on him emotionally.

In school, his teachers had told him he was stupid, and his mother reinforced the idea, so he stopped trying. His teachers hated him because he hadn't been willing to conform. Milo, from a young age, had no problem adjusting things when he thought they weren't fair. He had also been undeterred when it was time to speak up. He had difficulties in school, and while attending his second year, he found out he had the greatest number of black marks (which had been the way they tracked every time he did something wrong). So, he hatched a plan to change the score, found a red biro, and gave himself extra double pluses.

What was absolutely ridiculous was the weight those red marks had carried when so much else was going on. The agony he had felt as a young child, living and learning in a place that had been thoroughly focused on comparisons and expectations, manifested in behaviour that was acting out. As he had continued to cover up painful experiences, he would fall into the trap of blasting them away with alcohol and then, later, drugs.

It was easier for Milo to blast away with drugs and alcohol rather than have flashbacks to what happened to him in school. He had been brutalised from the moment he got there. The emotional deficit of warmth from a nurturing caregiver, coupled with the emotional abuse by teachers, as well as the system itself that was designed to allow older boys who have been subjected to trauma and ridicule themselves access to younger children, had been horrific. Then there was the severing of emotional attachment from his parents and family, the impact of which he didn't come to realise until much later in his life.

Milo had always looked like the life of the party, but he felt like he was putting out fires. His coping mechanisms were all over the place, and he was just trying to hold it together. Being vibrant, funny, and engaging gave him somewhere to hide. While he was smiling on the outside, he was building layers of protection on the inside and numbing it all with drink. Each time he was able to sneak a drink and feel the buzz overtake him, he could feel the panic subside a little bit.

The truth about abuse is people don't always know what it is when it happens to them. For Milo, it wasn't until he was analysing his behaviour, seeing it as acting out and putting together the pieces, that he had started to come to terms with his past.

Finally, all these years later, he could safely consider from a distance the weird bubble of boarding school being an easy set-up for abusive relationships. His dad had told him to stand up for himself, "Warn them once, warn them twice, warn them three times, then punch them in the nose." That helped when the bullying was straightforward, but when he couldn't put words to what was being done to him, he was unable to stand up for himself. It took him many years to realise what happened to him was sexual abuse, rape, ongoing from the ages of seven through eleven.

When you're seven, and you're sent away for a privileged learning experience, the world becomes a large, pushy, and uninviting shuffle as you are expected to follow the schedule from place to place, duty to duty, and class to class. The whole time Milo had been forced to act right, follow all the rules and never get upset. That's impossible for most adults, not to mention a child who has just left home and has come to live in an institution (as glorious as it might be). Many children, like Milo, then face the horror of being accosted in their beds, night after night. At that age, he didn't have words for what was being done to him. It took him half a lifetime to be able to connect it to the word rape.

He had been abused by a student a couple of years older than he was. Milo hadn't understood what was happening when that individual crept into his bed. He froze. At that age, he didn't have the emotional language to understand what sex was. He hadn't known about it, and he couldn't stop it. When he had finally reported the abuse more than twenty years later, it was as part of his ongoing therapy and healing.

It had all come together at the time of the bus accident. The police had informed Milo that they hadn't been able to prosecute because the abuser was out of their jurisdiction.

Milo had also reported the housemaster for physical abuse. Mr Hewitt had treated Milo and anyone else who'd made a minor infraction to a bath full of ice. Milo could still remember the disgust and fear taking over his body as he and the other boys had been forced to line up naked. Then Mr Hewitt would take turns holding kids' heads underwater for thirty seconds. Other times he would make them hold pails of water up in the air without lowering their arms.

When he finally was able to piece together the nature of the abuse he had faced, Milo had wanted to stop them from hurting anyone else, but the police were unable to do anything about it. The inference was that they had found the perpetrator, but he was unavailable. Milo had hopefully considered the irony would be if he was in a Thai jail for committing similar offences. The lack of results was very disappointing, but Milo knew he had done as much as he could. The timing of the finality of the case had brought deeper spiritual insight, as he was finding power in personal peace of mind and trusted karma to take care of the rest.

Jim had experienced a parallel life of trauma, being raised by the system. They had often discussed the horror of what happened to children, never focusing on being united with first-hand understanding. Milo had always looked in awe at the role Jim played in international law enforcement.

Their work had crossed paths and borders through which they formed an unspoken brotherhood. Being able to feed each other information in different areas of the world was seen as happenstance and played off as a visit between old friends.

During those visits, they also shared a penchant for making light of their coping mechanisms, glossing over the rough bits with humour. Getting to know Jim had been a mirror for Milo, especially around the issue of his substance misuse being a mask for the trauma he had experienced.

Milo and Jim often talked about how all their fun experiences happened once they left school and overcame a tumultuous childhood.

Between boarding school and various nannies that were part of his proper upbringing, Milo's parents had been notably absent in his early years. His sister had been estranged from their mother, but even Milo and William, who grew up with her in their lives, felt estranged in some way. The two brothers stuck together as the adults ebbed and flowed into and out of their lives.

One day he had arrived home and found the house too quiet. It was a holiday, though thinking back on it, Milo couldn't remember which one. They were both young yet, and at the age where if you don't know what is going on, you guess. His grandfather and grandmother had just been visiting, and Milo was hoping things would settle down now that the added tension was gone.

"Where is everyone?" Milo asked William as he wandered through to the kitchen for a snack. William was in his favourite armchair with his nose in a book.

"Mum had a problem with her roses, so she had to run to the shop for something," William said without looking up.

Milo thought for a minute, "Why are you just sitting there?"

"Trying to make this feeling last forever," William put his book on his lap face-down, like he had more to say about it, or maybe that he regretted speaking at all.

"What feeling?" Milo asked as he stood between the kitchen and living room and munched an apple.

"Your chewing is annoying," William said, and he looked away. After a moment, he spoke in a softer voice. "The feeling of just being here, quiet and alone. Not on edge, wondering where the next attack will come from."

"Oh," Milo said with a light laugh. He had understood completely, although they rarely spoke of it. Uncertain of what to say next, he had made a joke. "Why aren't you reading the new book grandfather gave you?"

"Why aren't you reading yours?" William replied.

They had both laughed at the easy distraction from deeper turmoil. Their grandparents had given William a book called *Why You Lose at Bridge*. Their choice for Milo was no less hilarious. It was a book on how children should behave, highlighting the insolence of children who didn't respect their elders.

His paternal grandfather had been a strict man who expected everything to be held to a certain standard. The senior Mr Cummings was known for terrorising people, and he had been proud of it. One of his staff members had taken his own life, and after his death, his grandfather had boasted that he bullied the man into it. He was malicious and unkind to his own family as well. He had tried to push his own grandson off a cliff because he was different. Grandfather had thought a non-verbal, autistic boy had no place in his family. All he saw was an inconvenience, even though the boy was an incredibly talented pianist.

That family story had always unnerved Milo, and, as an adult, he thought there was something a bit Third Reich about it. The endless cycle of abuse had a noticeable impact on him. His grandfather had been traumatised at boarding school, and then he sent his son. The son was also traumatised at school and grew up to send his own sons into the same traumatic setting.

As he got older, Milo had recognised and tried to reconcile his own trauma. Then, when grandmother died, it was like a light had turned on. His grandfather became a totally different person. He had begun to show kindness, and they became close. In the end, Grandfather had waited to die until Milo and his father arrived when he became lucid briefly and then passed away forty-five minutes later. Milo, in his own way, had continued with some of his traditions, like shaving using a straight razor. Still, Milo's grandfather had never known his grandson's true self. He had reached the end of his life right when Milo was becoming more comfortable coming out to several people rather than everyone at once.

Grandad had been the total opposite. He was Milo's mother's father. Actually, he was her stepfather, though you'd never know it. He was a kind, brave man who loved and embraced Milo and the rest of his family. Even as a decorated marine from a conservative background, Grandad had been full of life and always supportive. Since his boarding school was near Portsmouth, where they lived, Milo had been fortunate enough to spend time in their warm home.

When he and a few boys had gone out at night to check out the nearby town, they got suspended from school.

Milo was one of the ringleaders, and he had waited with the others as they got picked up to be taken home. Milo had watched all the other parents arrive, scowling and looking ready for punishment and in the midst of them was Grandad beaming through the crowd. He had waved Milo over, then hugged him and kissed him, and he went home to have a great time with his grandparents. It was two weeks off, and Milo had relished it. There was no talk of school or punishment, and Milo had gotten the feeling that they didn't really like the institutionalised education he was getting.

He had got a sneak peek into their true feelings when it was time to go back to school. They had to be back Sunday evening before 6 pm. After church and a family meal, they had been running late. When they arrived, a teacher had scolded them for their tardiness. Granny had given him a look and sharply replied, "We'll drop him off on Monday morning then if it's such a problem."

Milo had never heard anyone talk to the teachers at his school like that before. Before he had a chance to process it, Granny and Grandad had whipped the car around, and they were headed back home. They had wanted to keep him with them as much as possible.

His grandparents knew things weren't great at school, but they had never forced him to talk about it. They simply seemed to want to take his mind off of it. When he was with them, it had always been a respite from the fight or flight mode he constantly found himself in.

Once he had begun studying child psychology, he became aware of attachment theory and social development theory. Applying those theories in orphanages that called themselves boarding schools had brought a deeper understanding of his trauma, but understanding didn't equal healing. On a physical level, he had recognised that the skin-to-skin contact and caregiver bonding he was helping implement were missing from his own life.

The only thing consistent in Milo's life was a lack of consistency. Trusting people had come later, with sobriety, though he still had his own demons to work on. He willingly talked about being an addict and a survivor of abuse, but it was difficult for him to be more public about it. Milo sometimes felt like the typical addict cliché, an abused boy who turned to alcohol and drugs to cope.

Milo understood that most people want to be seen as special and different, but we are all just the sum of our traumas. Boarding School Syndrome, a term Milo learned many years after he left school, looks at the layers of trauma unique to the situation where you are told by society you are privileged, yet you know you have experienced horrendous abuse. Being taught that you are a leader and part of high society and that children have to be severely disciplined feels wrong and affects people for the rest of their lives. Milo could attest to that. The idea that boys are so wild and unruly that they will end up like *The Lord of the Flies* has been proven wrong in real-world examples. That depressing book was written by a headmaster who held the erroneous belief that strict boarding school was required to raise boys into men.

Growing up in an orphanage or in a boarding school, Milo had learned, does damage to a child's social, emotional, and cognitive development. With the boarding school element, you are also told you are privileged, and you get to go home once in a while, so it really screws with your attachment. Being told he should feel lucky to experience boarding school created a separation of self and a narrative of destruction within Milo.

People would say, "Oh, you went to boarding school; you know the answer to everything."

And that may be true. The education level is high, so it can be perceived as arrogance. Milo was considered fortunate to have learned Latin, but that same Latin teacher used to hold his head under water full of ice cubes and pull him out by the hair when he gasped for breath as punishment for not conjugating verbs properly. So yeah, Milo would get a little sarcastic when anyone mentioned his spoilt upbringing.

Many boarding school survivors end up buying into the narrative that boarding schools create leaders, prime ministers, and successful networks. The connections you make in school are invaluable because you are attending with princes and children of powerful people. Then, the next generation doesn't want their kids to miss out. It's a mess because the cycle continues.

For Milo, it had taken twenty years to even put together the pieces of his traumatic past, and it took even longer to understand how it had shaped him. There is a Korean phrase called *nunchi*, which means the ability to read people through micro-verbal cues. It normally stems from people who were neglected as children, and they learned to be intuitive as a coping mechanism so they could respond to people. The genesis of these skills is not great because it comes from neglect. Being able to read people well comes from a need for attachment and attention that has not been received. Some Asian countries consider nunchi an art form. It is a beautiful gift born out of something horrible. Milo found the skill useful in his everyday interactions, as part of the fellowship, and as someone who worked in the mental health field.

Now, as he began to notice his dependence on pain medication, he felt the line of sobriety start to wobble. He saw the tragedy and comedy of his journey. With Jim back in town, he found himself fighting the urge to dive back in with both feet. When Jim mentioned the coke-fuelled fun he was planning to embark on at the completion of the investigation, Milo could taste the line drip down the back of his throat.

Then, he shook his head and swallowed the urge with additional meds. The pills were running out, and his doctor wasn't inclined to prescribe more.

## SEVENTEEN

# METH ENCOUNTERS ARE MESSY

He needed the meds to keep him going as he started to improve, two steps forward, one step back. Being able to dress himself and take care of his own basic needs was a cause of massive celebration for Milo. Having to obtain more fentanyl was above his current comfort level, but he was going through the pills he had squirrelled away faster than he expected.

With Jim spending more time with him, Milo felt compelled to watch who was watching him. Finding a different doctor who was willing to refill his prescription wasn't too difficult. With a sob story and the right payment, it wasn't long before Milo had a courier arrive with a new supply. Dancing around the reason for delivery, which of course, happened when Ra was home, initiated a distinct nausea in Milo that dimmed the thrill of acquisition. Ra had already questioned the dosage of his prescription as he was paying attention to Milo's healing journey. As usual, Milo had charmed his way out of any suspicion.

Jim had just walked through the door, there to catch up after a busy few weeks, as Ra and Milo had their heads together trying to figure out how to get the coffee maker going. Milo was swearing and threatening to throw the machine out the window. Ra laughed and nudged Milo over, saying it would be alright. In the end, their attempt was a success, and when the steaming stream started to fill up the pot, they both cheered. After Ra left for the day, Milo noticed Jim smiling.

"It's not too often I've seen you that relaxed. You two fit together," Jim commented.

"When have you ever remarked on who I am with?" Milo laughed so hard he grabbed his ribs in pain.

"It's either age creeping up on me, or I'm blinded from the last fuck tart you were with." Jim sank into the armchair in the corner. Across from him, Milo noticed how Jim slouched back into his chair with much more ease compared with his last visit. Something had changed, yet Milo was unable to shake the fog to think it through.

"Which one are you referring to?" Milo was struggling to trace the conversation as his head pounded and the yearning for relief pulled at his every emotion.

"Your ex, the one I called an uppity prick," Jim said with a laugh.

"Oh, right," Milo said slowly. Then he paused for a moment. "Excuse me for a moment. I need to use the facilities."

Jim's demeanour turned serious as he realised Milo was distracted and maybe agitated. "You alright?"

Milo nodded and extricated himself from the Chesterfield. It was ridiculous that going to the loo without accoutrements and assistants was a feeling of freedom. Though anyone who has needed medical treatment for a long period of time could relate. He took each step with caution as, through it all, the haze around him was a steady constant, throwing off his equilibrium and adding notes of confusion. He reflected on the damage done to his body and how he was healing physically, psychologically, and spiritually.

Swallowing two fentanyl pills, he could feel his anxiety start to fade and considered how he should be needing less pain medication as time went on, not more. Pushing himself to get moving again, he realised, not for the first time, he had not always chosen health.

Quite the contrary, he had been downright hard on himself, pushing to the limits of intoxication and putting himself in unsafe relationships and situations. Jim's words about his ex finally made it to Milo's consciousness. Alone in the bathroom, he laughed at Jim's accurate description. During his first marriage to Roger, he had gotten to such a dark place that he eventually chose a path to health, but that took years. When a relationship looks good and is mutually beneficial, it can become a trap. Add in vast quantities of drugs and alcohol, and reality can be twisted to take on a rosy hue.

Early on, the attraction between them, their interesting careers, and their parallel lives had been enticing. The anticipation of having someone to share the highs with felt good. Being part of a power couple, Milo and Roger didn't have time to worry about their relationship because they seemed to be too busy getting ready, heading off to a party, or travelling with friends.

Every year a group of them went to Ibiza, Spain, for a Mediterranean retreat. In the third year, Milo had wanted to tone down the drugging and clubbing and enjoy their time and the local culinary treats. He and Jay had ventured to the market to pick up some fresh ingredients and local wine to have a proper meal together. Roger had been quite rude about their dinner, interrupting his partying. When Jay stood up for Milo, Roger had taken off with Jay's boyfriend and a couple of friends to the club. They ended up having a split vacation. Milo, Jay, and a few others had shared a meal and enjoyed the holiday. Roger and his group had gotten completely wasted, spent the whole-time partying, and crashed the rental car.

When they got back from the wreck of a trip, things got worse. Roger had spent most of his time on the phone, looking busy. Or he'd ask Milo to join him only to make a vicious remark. Mostly Milo had tried to ignore it and internally made plans to get out.

One day he had arrived home from work to a frenzied Roger stomping around, slamming doors, and completely worked into a state. Milo set his keys down in the ceramic dish with hesitation but held on to them. One foot on the rug, the other still just inside the door, he had been of two minds. *Run and don't look back.* That thought held him in place, and it seemed so easy if he could have just kept running.

Why hadn't he gone towards Roger and seen what the matter was? Maybe he needed help. Shouldn't that have been his first thought? Milo still hadn't moved. Instead, he

217

was watching himself, realising he was already spiritually detached and was just going through the motions.

He had seen himself as if from a distance and watching live as he strode calmly into the kitchen and poured himself a glass of wine. Milo had been able to hear Roger shoving things aside in a closet down the hall, and then angry footsteps moved toward the kitchen.

"You're home finally. Have you seen my other trainer? Did you put it somewhere?" Roger had asked.

"No, I have no idea where it is," Milo replied. He had swallowed the tight feeling in his throat.

"Just perfect. Of course, you don't know where it is." Roger had turned away as Milo realised he wasn't in the mood for this domestic scene.

"I'm going to the pub," Milo had said to Roger's back.

Roger had huffed off without reply.

The pub had been conveniently located directly across the street. As Milo tucked into a corner table, the music, people chatting, and happy hour in full swing felt peaceful compared to the tension of home. Milo had just considered ordering another bottle or checking in with friends when Roger joined him, slumping into the chair across the table.

"There's no point to life anymore," Roger had said, voice dejected, shoulders slumped. Milo wondered what had happened since he left half an hour ago, so he leaned forward and waited for Roger to continue, "I've looked everywhere for it."

Milo had let out a laugh and sat up again, almost toppling his chair. "So, there's no point in life because you can't find one specific shoe. What a tragedy!"

"You belittle everything I say," Roger accused.

"If you just came here to start a fight, don't bother. You're ruining my merlot." Milo had been in disengage mode.

"You're so self-righteous, and you think you're so smart," Roger accused.

"How did we go from your lost shoe to somehow this being my fault?" Milo had asked.

"How's this for ruining your merlot?" Roger had replied. As he stood, he had swiped the newly filled wine glass and tossed the contents in Milo's face.

Emotionally, Milo had left the marriage that day though it would take a year to physically separate. Still, after the most recent outburst and a litany of endless excuses, Milo had looked down at the stain spreading down his clean, white shirt, and he had no fucks left.

The waiter came over and handed him a napkin. "Are you okay? Can I get you anything?"

"Another bottle of the same, thanks," Milo had said as he dabbed wine off his face with a napkin. Damp in wardrobe but not in spirit, he had sat there with a crooked smile, unmoved, wondering what kind of idiot he was for failing to listen to his friends about that prat. As he finished the new bottle on his own, he had ruminated about how he was fixated on things that didn't matter, like a lost shoe and how fickle it seemed when faced with the dire situations many people experienced.

Milo hadn't wanted to live in a world of self-made drama and frivolous strife. The tension around living up to societal expectations and fitting in was contrived and becoming mundane. Once he had learned there was real catastrophe in the world, he had no longer been able to stomach the contrived panic of the privileged. He had started to find peace and become more grounded through Buddhism. His travels found him more open to exploring and undertaking roles where he could be of service. It had been difficult to discern the chasm that had grown between Roger and Milo, and through a wine-soaked haze, he saw the bloody truth.

Travelling for work seemed like a good excuse to get away from it, but the reality of what was happening had come looking for him. On one flight home, he had heard from his bank, as they were concerned about a large overdraft in the tens of thousands. Milo's immediate response had been disbelief as both he and his husband were earning decent salaries. When he looked into the situation, he saw his husband was making daily withdrawals of £250. Since a gram of coke was £50, Milo had a glimpse into how bad his husband's drug problem had gotten through the financial consequences. Soaking in this new information, Milo connected to other key indicators he had chosen to ignore.

The most glaring sign was that their coke dealer had always arrived within twenty minutes of Roger's call, no matter the day or time, even if it was 3 am. He had obviously been a preferred customer. Milo had realised he could no longer ignore the scale of the problem. Coke brought out the violence and paranoia in Roger, and the longer they were together, the more often it had turned ugly.

It had taken Milo a year to get himself cleaned up as he worked to get himself out. To start with, he had opened a separate bank account and accepted more projects that took him from Africa to Asia, anywhere but the UK. While he had kept away and kept quiet, some of Roger's behaviour was catching up with him. His friends had begun to see Roger for who he was. Jay had discovered his boyfriend was cheating on him with Roger and confronted them. Jay had insisted Roger tell Milo, or he would.

Working in India, Milo had found it odd when he started receiving random, sometimes angry-sounding texts from Roger explaining that while he wasn't perfect, Milo had hurt him also. Most of the time, Milo had wanted to correct the syntax of the message or otherwise tell Roger he made no sense, but he hadn't been interested in starting intercontinental drama.

The weirdness had continued, so Milo messaged Roger before he got on a flight home that he'd be going to stay with his mum for a few days when he got back. Behind the scenes, Roger had refused Jay's demand to admit it to Milo. When Milo had messaged Jay to arrange to meet up, he added a cheeky joke, and Jay had replied with: *you don't know, do you?*

Before he had finished typing a witty comeback, his phone rang. It was Jay.

Milo had answered and jumped into chatting, but Jay cut him off mid-sentence. "...I can't believe he's not told you. You wondered why I was newly single? Well, I found out my boyfriend was having an affair with your husband."

"Yuck," Milo said, as he had started to laugh.

Tension broken, Jay had laughed too, "It's ridiculous, isn't it?"

"That explains all the strange texts coming from Roger the last little while."

"When I confronted them, I told Roger if he didn't tell you, I would. Then, when I hadn't heard anything about it from you, I warned him I'd be seeing you today. What a coward!"

"That's one word for it."

"Sorry to be the bearer of bad news."

"Bad news, fuck that, it's great news. Now I can leave for good."

"Do you still want to meet for lunch?"

"Absolutely! Can we push it back an hour? I have to move out first."

And as Milo approached many things, he had switched on a dime and got moving. He went back to what he now considered Roger's penthouse. While he was packing, Roger had asked him to sit down so they could talk out their problems. *That's rich*, Milo thought, poker face permanently in place. He considered the hilarity of hearing Roger wallow in excuses or, even better, blame him, but he was so far past done it wasn't worth it.

"Come on," Roger repeated. "You haven't heard my side of the story. Jay doesn't know what he's talking about."

Milo had shaken his head and kept packing. It was more a reaction to the entire situation, but Roger took it as a direct assault.

"You've always been so difficult anyway. You'll be back. We've been through worse." Roger had sounded so sure of himself and kept talking as Milo ignored him.

He had packed up his Le Creuset cookware, copper pots and pans, handmade Japanese knives, a few essentials, and he walked out the door without even turning back while he closed it.

After he had left Roger, there were awkward periods where Milo wasn't sure whose loyalties were where. When a relationship breaks up, you have to choose who you are going to be friends with. Everyone takes sides. There is no way around him. That epiphany was one of the reasons why Milo had begun to make a point of staying out of other people's relationships if he could help it.

He had felt gratitude towards some friends who made it easy, like Patty, who called him up once the split went public. "In case you have any concerns about how this will go, just know I'm picking you," she had said after they'd said hello.

"Thanks, sweetie," Milo said.

"Anyone who had their eyes open would know exactly why you left. It was obvious he wasn't treating you well." Then she had stopped herself. "But we're past that now, so let's do lunch."

He had made some questionable choices in the past, and he marvelled at the events that took place from that decision. Switching focus to children's aid programs and helping the most vulnerable, he took every opportunity to visit new places and participate in new programs.

As his first marriage ended, he had begun a new career and started down a path of immense beauty, sorrow, and intentional acceptance. This new path had almost ended when he was run over, but he wasn't done yet. He had seen and felt the worst and been in the most decrepit, desolate places, and there was always hope, even amid bad choices, consequences, and hard truths.

While reminiscing, Milo had somehow wandered back into the living room and sat down with a cup of coffee in his hand. Jim was shifting uncomfortably in his chair, and Milo had no idea how long he had been sitting in contemplation. Where did the conversation leave off?

"It's been a few weeks, and I am convinced you are not following doctor's orders on those meds," Jim said when he noticed Milo was mentally back in the present day.

Milo started to put together the pieces. Little remarks over the few weeks since Jim had been visiting and a change in his attitude clued Milo into the realisation that he'd been too busy to notice Jim growing suspicious of him.

"You can't bullshit a bullshitter," Jim spoke plainly. "And you know me well enough to know I'm not judging. I just know this isn't what you want. It's a slippery slope."

"Aren't we supposed to talk about the case? Do you need more information?"

"Yes, there is news on that, but I am worried about you."

"Well, I've got enough people worrying about me; thank you very much."

"Is that so? How many of them have told you to slow down on the pills?" Jim asked and then waited for an answer. When Milo didn't reply, he continued. "I am sure Ra has noticed your dependency, even if he hasn't confronted you about it. You've been down this road before."

"I am a different man than the one who considered having Christmas dinner in a Cape Town sauna, you know!" Milo said defensively. And he meant it. His meth-fuelled visit to South Africa had been a low point in his life. It was somewhat of a bar he set to compare other experiences. Working in South Africa and neighbouring countries, Zimbabwe, Malawi, Namibia and Zambia, his usual route had been to fly into Johannesburg. If he could arrange it, he'd go a week early to spend time in Cape Town. Milo's boss was South African, so he encouraged it.

After a bad break-up that had been a rebound relationship, Milo had needed to get out of the UK. He had been putting himself in risky situations and acting out. The trauma he'd experienced from a very early age was starting to come to the surface; his behaviour was morally questionable to himself, though he wasn't sure who himself was quite yet. Feeling alone in his uncomfortable memories and wrong for misunderstanding how horrible it was earlier, he had sought alcohol and drugs as an escape from his emotions.

When he was in Cape Town, he had gone to a gay sauna with a co-worker for a laugh. The co-worker left early in the evening, but Milo had stayed. Being freshly single and eager to let loose, he had been drinking heavily, doing coke or cat, and having random sex. Stumbling into a sex worker, after untold hours, he had smiled and made a joke, but the man had been obviously upset.

"Sorry mate, can I get you a drink?" Milo had asked.

"Okay, thanks," He spoke.

Working with sex workers in a professional capacity had put Milo in a unique position to speak with empathy and offer real assistance, even when he was heavily drugged or otherwise inebriated. As they got to talking, he had told Milo what was going on.

"I was just screwed out of some money by one of my clients. Now I don't know what to do." His eyes had glanced upward, flitted around, and then looked down again as he spoke, the timidity evident in his tone and posture.

It had only been a couple of hundred rands, but to this man, it was more than he could bear.

"Have you heard of SWA (sex workers association)?" Milo had asked.

"Yes, I know them. I am part of the male support group," he replied. As they chatted, he told Milo to call him Tau.

"I have the crystal, and I have to pay the dealer, but the client disappeared without paying," Tau explained.

Milo had simply handed Tau the few hundred rand he needed, equivalent to less than £15. To thank him for his help, Tau had asked Milo, "Do you want some?"

"Why not?" The words burst out before Milo could stop them. Internal Milo had his justification ready. He didn't prefer to lecture people about specific drugs unless he had tried them, so this was work-related research, right?

What had transpired instead was meth acted as a dark rabbit hole that hooked him hard and fast. A lot of people don't recommend drinking when taking meth, but Milo hadn't taken that advice. He had been in and out of the sauna for close to three months.

Staff in gay saunas are pretty non-judgemental, but even they had been thinking he was getting out of control. When they had asked if he would be joining them for Christmas dinner and Milo looked at the menu, in a moment of clarity, he had realised if he was considering eating turkey and stuffing in a bathrobe with a bunch of men he had just had random, anonymous sex with while on crystal meth, he really had to consider the depths his life had sunk to.

That had been the beginning of his thought process that this escapade would have to come to an end. Add to the fact that his boss and the secretariat of the association were telling him enough was enough; it was time to come home. He had been expected in the UK two months previous. His excuses were piling up as he was leaving work earlier and earlier to go to the sauna and indulge.

Meth is messed up in the way that it draws you in and separates you from space and time. Personal time seems to speed up, and you feel faster, harder, and stronger while the rest of the world slows down. Senses heightened, everything becomes about intense pleasure and escapism.

After three days of bingeing non-stop at the sauna, he had returned to his wind-swept apartment at Sea Point. Sitting on the porch with two bottles of wine and two strips of Valium, he had considered the meth-induced madness and knew it was time to cut off the supply. Bringing in the New Year, he had taken a full strip of Valium, though he had only needed ten milligrams to come down. As he took the last swallow from the first bottle, it had crossed his mind that if he opened the second bottle, he'd definitely finish it, and if he finished it, he might not wake up. He had decided to drink it anyway.

A feeling of calm had swallowed him as he got lost in the cerulean waves cut off by a knife edge of bright white beach. He had floated like the clouds above the waves, just a puff, and then they were gone. For a time, he had thought his life might end there, a feeling he'd relive much closer to reality in the back of a cab in the future. A sense had overpowered his awareness that this drug chasing had to end. He had received the message; this is not your path. That's when he knew he needed a change, so he booked a flight home.

He had saved the second strip of Valium for the way home and mixed benzos and drinking to get through it. As his flight took off, heading north along the coast, he had remembered looking down at the sea and realised he could do better. He got back to Brighton, got back to work, and started working on himself and confronting his trauma rather than running from it or blasting it away. Though it would take a few years yet to understand the nature of his addiction.

Reliving the experience to Jim as they laughed about Milo's extreme choices, he emphasised that if he came back from that experience unscathed, he could get through just about anything. By making light of the situation while explaining the depth of his bad choices, he hoped to dissuade Jim from poking at the number of pills he was taking.

Milo could see the rebuttal forming, so he got Jim laughing again as he rehashed the experience and the doctor's reaction when he got a health check upon returning to the UK.

He knew the sexual health doctor in Brighton in a professional capacity. An association he was working with had been in regular contact with the clinic because they were the leaders in HIV treatments in the UK. After returning from his meth holiday in South Africa, Dr Alexander had welcomed him into her office. Milo, noticing the posters advertising free at-home HIV test kits, recalled his previous visit. When the HIV tests were being rolled out, he had left a bag of them on his table in the entryway until he could bring them with him to India for work. One day a friend came to him, terrified to admit he had nicked one, tested himself, and it came back positive. Milo had helped his friend get diagnosed and see a doctor. He had also reassured him that a positive test was no big deal. He always thought the melodrama around HIV was a bit much, and as soon as people had education on the subject, they were able to make healthier choices, or at least, remain calm when they didn't. Milo knew the science, so he wasn't scared of HIV. He had told his friend what he told anyone else who had concerns, "I would have no hesitation dating someone with HIV. When you are virally undetectable, it's fine."

Milo had inwardly mocked himself for finding himself at the health clinic because of his own transgressions. For someone with his knowledge and background, to have gotten himself in this position was quite hilarious. Milo had already reconciled himself with being HIV positive, considering his recreational activities over the past few months.

"Are you here in a professional capacity?" she had asked.

"No, I am here because I might have possibly taken lots of crystal meth and done all the things you're not supposed to do, like having unprotected sex with key populations," Milo had said, using terminology from their professional relationship. Key populations included those most vulnerable to HIV because of their marginalisation from health care and broader society.

"So, how many partners? Can you give me an overview?"

"I don't know." Milo had scrunched his face, thinking of the best way to put it, knowing he'd never have an accurate count of bodies. He'd been too out of it. "What are we talking about, cumulatively? In the three-month period? Or in one night?"

"Uh." Dr Alexander had opened her mouth and then closed it again, and in her silence, Milo had continued.

"Cumulatively, I think we're talking in the hundreds," Milo had said.

"In one night?"

"Thirty plus per night is probably a reasonable estimate though I am not entirely sure," Milo had said, then added. "I was drinking while doing meth, which you're not supposed to do apparently."

"What was crystal meth like?"

"Wow, it's difficult to say. I like to underplay it in my head," Milo said. After a pause, he had continued. "Mixed with the alcohol and other uppers and downers, it was a mess. A thousand times more addictive than nicotine. One hit is too much, and a thousand is never enough."

"Sounds like a lesson learned," Jim said when Milo finished his story.

"Yes," Milo agreed, happy to have the subject of their conversation be rooted in the past. "Dr Alexander tried to send my tests express to speed up the process, and she called four hours later to let me know they all came back negative, except chlamydia."

"How is that possible?" Jim wondered.

"I have no idea. But by the grace of God go I, my

friend, because I should have had at least five or six STIs," Milo replied.

Milo stretched out, remembering the relief mixed with disbelief when all his tests had come back clean. He had survived his meth binge unscathed physically anyway, but mentally and spiritually, he knew there was work to do. Now he was sitting in reverse, marvelling that he was the same person. While he was not so great physically, he was determined to be mentally and spiritually connected for as long as his body would allow.

"You're reliving that moment a little too close to the edge."

"What's that supposed to mean?" A growing awareness even as he said the words. Milo noticed the pull to excuse himself almost as soon as the last pills had been swallowed. Since he became aware of Jim's suspicions, his internal dialogue changed. He began to feel a twinge of guilt every time he opened the medication bottle.

"We've been through a lot worse than this. Accept help for once, you stubborn prick." Jim's name-calling had a softer-than-usual edge to it. "You have to wean yourself off the fentanyl if you want to heal."

"I can admit you are right, but I don't have to like it."

"You've been avoiding your sound bowl guy as well."

The accuracy of Jim's statement caught him off guard. He still hadn't returned Nima's call. Meanwhile, he let Kanshin believe he wasn't recovered. "You really don't miss much. Isn't it time for your little holiday?"

"Yes, but you won't get rid of me that easily."

"This is starting to remind me of how much time we spent together in Uganda," Milo said thoughtfully.

Jim's eyes narrowed, and he cleared his throat.

"I meant the good parts. There were lots of those. You loved it there as much as I did," Milo said quickly.

"For a time," Jim replied. "Did you forget what happened? I think about it every time I look at you. Especially now with the news, it's getting worse."

"Indeed," Milo said.

"It didn't end well, and that's one story I don't want to rehash. I was sure I'd have to come to get you out," Jim went on.

"Okay, fair enough, no mention of the debacle that was my time in Uganda. So, let's get to why you are here. Any updates?" Milo asked.

"Yeah, we got her. Your directions allowed us to go through the back, which she didn't expect," Jim took a deep breath. "We're quite certain, based on the other information you gave us, that the bar was the hub, the main connection for tourists coming here specifically for child trafficking purposes. It was also linked to one of those foreign-owned orphanages, so that opened another investigation. The resources you provided are helping us reunite the children with their families."

"Good, that's one gate closed," Milo said.

"That's why we do what we do," Jim added.

They sat quietly for a moment contemplating the successful operation. Both of them experienced a subdued internal celebration. It was reassuring that a cup of coffee between friends could help bring down a trafficking ring. Their reflection was interrupted when Ra entered with dogs in tow, and the flurry of fur and wagging tails spurned a more positive conversation and another cup of coffee before Jim left for the day. On his way out, he reminded Milo to consider what they talked about.

## EIGHTEEN

# PENETRATING THE BWINDI IMPENETRABLE FOREST

On the treadmill, starting at a saunter, Milo appreciated all the running he did all over the world. The slowest setting set up a steady pace for his recovery. He was a long way from a marathon. During these rough first steps, he could flip through his rusty memories and imagine running through rainy London or through sand at the Marathon des Sables. One of his favourites that he could almost smell the memory of was the run he would take, surrounded by lush trees, around his home in Uganda.

The most welcoming places will kill you if you're gay. It's an odd thought, but he was trying to keep his mind off the dwindling supply of pills he had, instead accepting strangeness abounds and previous connections are carefully scrutinised. Milo could call it going stir-crazy.

Sitting still was never a top skill; he was much more of a go-out-there-and-get-things-done kind of guy. It's true; he knew his body needed patience. He also knew it needed to get moving. It might take him a while to start running again, and he might be a little creaky at it once he got going; regardless, he couldn't heal without action.

Now that he was starting to feel better, he became aware of his physical recovery as well as the state of the world around him. Neither were doing great. His work and family needed him, and he needed to support them, not get support from them. That was the bitch about getting run over; it knocked him down again as he was gaining momentum. His body didn't need a reminder to take it easy, but it got one.

He let his mind consider the clusterfuck that was his experience living and subsequently being kicked out of Uganda years before coming to Cambodia. Even now, with all the water under the bridge and a sense of gratitude for simply living, he was still in shock at the incredible life he had left behind.

Uganda had helped him get him away from his ex-husband and was, in most ways, much freer than in London. Except for his sexuality, he could be who he was. The moment he first arrived, he had felt energised, like he was in a sanctuary where time slowed. Looking back, it was so diametrically opposed to how he had been living in the UK. It allowed his heart to yearn for a life that was a better fit. Uganda became a surrogate country to become addicted to.

His first trip had been a fundraising endeavour as a board member for an organisation he became part of. Ella was already a trustee, and they had needed another, and Milo's connections in the entertainment world seemed like a perfect way to spread awareness and find donors. Of course, shortly after he joined, Ella had taken off, leaving everything in his capable hands. Though he had teased her for it for years to come, he had an affinity for the work and loved any excuse to travel.

Being asked to take photos of poor mothers dying of HIV and sending them back to headquarters to be used to make money had felt disgusting, however well-intentioned. At first, he hadn't understood the exploitation or how to better help, but he wanted to be involved in that type of work.

In the beginning, he had found it was easy to fall into a trap with a white-man saviour complex, but he had been quickly checked by Joyce, one of the powerful women he worked with in Uganda. At her suggestion, he had gone to a course that talked about choosing to be a martyr to a cause, a saviour, or a professional that acts as a facilitator in a non-colonial way. He kept that lesson close and had constantly focused on being there for others. By learning not to diminish people's capacity to help themselves, he had begun to unlearn a lot of expectations he was raised to believe.

He relished the opportunity to learn differently and had been thrilled to discuss the complicated terms people use that affect the independence, humanity, and culture of the people they are serving. He was drawn to the work that was being done and the vast unmet need of children and families in the countries he travelled to.

In an incredible eighteen-month span, he had visited Uganda, Ghana, Kenya, South Africa, Sri Lanka, Hong

Kong, India, and Tanzania. His work for aid organisations had begun to take over his life, and his entertainment company collapsed when he wasn't there to keep it going. From there, he had been hired full-time by an agency he volunteered for, and his boss agreed to let him move to Uganda.

It was difficult to put into words because it was more of a permeating feeling, but Uganda had felt like a welcoming foreign refuge. The people of Uganda seemed to Milo to have a peaceful rhythm, and it was refreshingly accepting. Paradoxically, it was deeply homophobic yet deeply inviting, and he wanted to come back as soon as he left. Once there, he had committed himself wholeheartedly to care reform. As soon as he had seen firsthand that orphanages were a money-making scam, he began to work to get kids back to their families. Most children had people they belonged with. What they needed was support and resources. Eventually, he became recognised as a UN expert on care reform. He had put a lot of himself into the work, but in so many ways, he was the one learning. Certain aspects of the bureaucracy were completely insane.

It was the street-connected kids or those in orphanages Milo had wanted to advocate for the most. His own experience in institutionalised learning propelled him to make changes in child care wherever he could. He had been one of few white social workers that could work on the street with the kids. Normally whites were seen as dumb missionaries giving handouts or someone to exploit. Milo had spoken their language both metaphysically and in actuality. He was also there consistently, which was something unheard of among some of the children who had been forced to grow up in hard situations.

In his after-work hours, he had spent his time drinking heavily. He had also gotten big into benzos, which were free, and it opened up a whole new world, one where he quickly became dependent on them.

Securing class-A drugs where they are not readily available was extremely dangerous, so Milo had avoided it. Two TV producers had purchased coke in Uganda that killed them; it ended up being rat poison. That had been alarming enough that even in the grips of addiction, Milo was wary of the supply chain and careful of what he was consuming. In the UK, it was bad for business if people died from taking your drugs so it hadn't been a concern. In Uganda, the sketchiness of the supply had made Milo very particular in the procurement of recreational substances. Then there was the risk of being found out.

He had felt alive there, yet he had to live in the closet. As a natural rule breaker, it had been a complicated decision that was clouded by the intense beauty and amazing sense of chaos in Uganda. From the highlands to the savannahs, the bustling cities and vast nature preserves, the mixture of different environments had thrilled Milo and welcomed him to explore.

Milo became addicted to work and obsessed with the lifestyle in Uganda, where he had felt alive and different. Living in East Africa was a beguiling experience. At first, he had been so career-focused his sexuality was irrelevant, and it didn't play a part in his decision-making. After a few years, he had realised he might want a relationship.

When he moved into his first house, his friend Beth had lived with him. They were both gay and avoiding being outed, so they had given each other cover. Later on, Milo became more aware of how challenging it was to hide a same-sex relationship in a place where you could be killed for it. And by then, it had felt like it was too late. He had built a house and made a commitment to live there.

Beth's arrival was another joyous happenstance where she came for a visit and never left. Her house had blown down, she lost her job and had needed a place to stay. He had been happy to have her. Together they had hiked fifty kilometres around the Bwindi Impenetrable Forest, where they saw chimpanzees, birds, and gorillas. It was intensely beautiful, and Milo had found peace amid the lush vines and thick green landscape. The interconnected ecosystem, thriving among a community of tree families, had given him hope for humanity.

It didn't feel like it at the time, but he had been settling, desperate to find somewhere to call home. In the previous years, he had moved every six months. In Uganda, he had little to no access to drugs, and he had the opportunity to settle into a life and a home. The friendships he had counterbalanced being out. He had lots of people in his life, which aided in his ability to gloss the loss of freedom to be openly gay.

He had convinced himself that having a senior job, a professional career path, and a home was what mattered. He had also held out hope that he could be part of the positive change for the country. When he found and became part of the underground gay scene, he felt optimistic and helped with the Ugandan gay pride that ran for three years. For a time, he believed he could be part of the movement in the right direction.

In Uganda, Milo found it easy to get involved in crazy things. He had accidentally become a co-owner of a bar and later bought into a luxury safari company. Neither opportunity had been something he sought out. Another time, he had been involved in a gold exporting business. He had accidentally fallen into the opportunity one night while drinking. Thinking back on it, many of his business ventures started that way.

The bar he used to go to was owned by Tigran, a wild Armenian who Milo met when he fell off the bar onto Milo's drinks. They ended up becoming good friends. One night Tigran told him the bar was running out of money, so Milo bought half the bar to help out. The next morning, he woke up with no recollection of the agreement until he had a cup of coffee and realised "there is something niggling at me."

Eventually, it came to him, "Fucking hell, I bought half the bar last night." And he hadn't been referring to the amount of alcohol he had consumed. A short while after the blurry revelation, Tigran had called him and asked, "When can you drop the money around."

"I'll be there this afternoon," Milo replied while his internal voice screamed in silence, "Oh no. I actually did it!"

After that, he had spent many of his afternoons in the bar, which had put him in the right place at the right time to get involved in all kinds of endeavours. That was how he had ended up getting into the gold dealing process. Tigran had obtained a licence to export gold from Uganda, and together they started selling small amounts from local gold diggers. The business had only lasted six months until Milo had to get out because the rules changed.

The UN had banned gold from the Congo because of warlords controlling the supply and using child soldiers. Once the blood gold could no longer flow from that country, it began to be shipped through Ugandan exporters instead. Heavy people, the kind you don't come back from, had been involved, and it got too dangerous to stay in business. The original idea was to pick up trace amounts of gold from small, local miners. Milo had liked taking a motorcycle out into the country to meet them, and often their families, but the licences had made them targets.

One South African regular in the bar, who also had a gold licence, had gone missing after getting involved in Congolese gold smuggling. Milo had warned him that buying gold from warlords was playing with fire and that he shouldn't fuck with them, but it was too late. Soon after, he was no longer a regular and had never been seen again. That was when both Milo and Tigran backed out because they didn't want to die.

The safari company had been a much more light-hearted endeavour that also got its start at the bar. One of his drinking buddies, another regular named Hassan, suggested he buy into the business, and Milo thought it sounded like fun.

He wasn't super involved, but it had been a great way to see wildlife and watch the wonder of tourists experiencing the African wilderness for the first time. They specialised in luxury tourism, which had brought with it some entitled travellers. Milo had one group of tourists that he'd never forget because of a German couple who thought they should be able to rearrange nature for their photo opp.

They had been trying to get up close and personal with a gorilla, and Milo warned them to back off. After harrumphing at him, they had stepped off the path and moved closer to the massive animal who had turned away.

"Yoo hoo," the woman, wearing a red jacket, shouted as she lifted her hat and waved it above her head.

"You'd best not rile him up," Milo had warned. "Remember, the rule guide says to keep quiet and keep a safe distance."

The couple had declined to respond and continued making a scene. The gorilla had turned sharply and was on top of them before they could scream. With a swipe of one powerful arm, the animal had knocked the couple off their feet. Then he gave a fast and angry snort and was on his way.

Picking themselves up, they huffed towards the rest of the group. "We could have been killed!" they had exclaimed.

"Yes, you were very lucky. You also illustrated why it is essential to follow the rules and listen to your guide," Milo had said, his taut mouth holding back a sarcastic remark.

"This is horrible. I want to speak to your manager," the wife had insisted.

"There is no manager out here, but there are lions, elephants, giraffes, maybe even some leopards." Milo had directed the tour onward and kept his word. The next few hours consisted of driving through the remote wilderness and stopping to take in the migration of animals.

They often stopped for lunch, at Murchison Falls, where Milo had befriended a warthog. While everyone was enjoying the shade of the nearby grove and taking in the beauty of the cascading water nearby, Milo sat on a rocky outcropping and waited for the snuffles and scratching that meant his friend was nearby. The tiny fur ball was an awkward creature. Milo had accidentally discovered it loved being scratched behind its ears. The oddball forgot he was a dangerous creature and got to know the timeframe when Milo had usually arrived. After a few tentative visits, he would rush over right away. Then, when Milo would tickle behind his ears, he'd flop over so Milo could rub his belly.

Sometimes when he was patting his dogs, he would remember that warthog and feel the peace of the union between all living things. He had appreciated the lessons of simplicity he got from his pets, the pup-like warthog and other animals. Buying into a safari hadn't been a business success, but his friendship with an oddball was priceless.

That was one of the exhilarating things about Uganda. It hadn't taken huge amounts of money to get into business. Each time he took an opportunity to try something new, it was quite a ride.

Originally, he shared an apartment with Macy and John. While there, he had returned from a trip to Northern Ghana feeling like shit. Unbeknownst to Milo, during a meeting with public health to discuss communicable diseases, he caught one. At first, he had thought it was a tropical hangover, which was like a bad hangover compounded by dehydration. His only aim was to get home, pass out, and never move again.

Macy had become concerned when he arrived home, sat down, and didn't even notice Jim was sitting in the room. When Jim had realised how sick Milo was, he helped them try to figure out what was wrong. As his fever rose, Macy had gone into mother hen mode, keeping an eye on him. Eventually, she and John had forced him to the clinic, where he promptly collapsed on the floor.

When he had come to, he was being checked over by Dr Chalmers, a British GP with a horrible bedside manner. Realising Milo was coherent, the doctor had informed him that he'd withdrawn some blood. Then, after informing Milo he was going to be leaving for the night, he had added almost as an afterthought, "You've got a rare form of malaria I haven't seen before. Good luck getting through the night. I may or may not see you tomorrow."

Not long after he left, Milo had started having slow fits. His whole body went into a complete seizure as Macy, John, and the nurse looked at him in abject horror. It had continued for a crushingly exhausting two hours. Dr Chalmers had explained that a parasite lives on the virus that causes red blood cells to explode. The following day, when the doctor had arrived to check on his patient, he had been amazed to see Milo weakly hanging on.

A little more up close and personal situation had happened when he was taking students to the north country in Uganda. Their driver had been arguing with the security guard at a roadside market they were stopped at. Milo had been able to tell they were from different tribes when all of a sudden, he had an AK-47 pointed at his head with the safety switch flipped off.

The students behind him had yelled, "Duck!" Milo looked at the guard and said calmly, "Obviously, you are under stress. If you want to talk about it, we'll sit down and have a cup of tea." That had been enough to diffuse the situation, and off they went.

He had made Uganda his home for the best part of a decade, and it became a place where he had amazing and toxic relationships. For the first four years, he had been gregarious and got out a lot. Eventually, he had started going out on safari less, stayed close to home, and became more introverted. His focus narrowed to the adoption and fostering NGO agency he oversaw that prioritised bringing children home and supporting families.

Years later, when he had settled in Cambodia, he talked to Gia about the vast spectrum of needs in social work.

"It's really just moment to moment when you see the worst of it," she had said. It was as though she could put herself there alongside him. She had seen similar, and she quietly commiserated with the level of sadness and strength of children who lived in the slums of the world.

"Yes. When you are helping a child who just escaped being beheaded, everything you think you know goes out the window." Milo had spoken from experience.

"Wow. That situation highlights the privilege most of us have; it's staggering," Gia had said.

That was the conflicting side of grinding poverty and brutality. Working with young people, street children who escaped beheadings and faced daily trauma most people couldn't comprehend had been a horrific reality. Milo had always been able to see the potential of the children left behind. The attachment issues they faced were something he had been able to relate to, and he knew they all needed love and a chance to grow.

When he spoke to Gia, it reinforced the importance of empowering people rather than the colonial nature of helping they had sadly seen so often. Most people who offered aid had an agenda or a belief that they were saviours. Milo had just been there to help, and he learned more from those kids than anyone else.

There were downsides of Uganda that had been hard to ignore, including the poisonous man who had wound himself into Milo's life and attempted to destroy it. Of course, Milo had invited him in with open arms. That was one thing he was excellent at, being distracted by good looks.

Adam had seen Milo's vulnerabilities while Milo was taken by his charisma and chiselled features. It had been a passionate and forbidden affair. When Adam had slept over and eventually moved in, they had to make his bed in the spare room look slept in and hide their intimacy from staff so that no one would suspect they were together.

In some ways, it had been a deeply toxic relationship, and in hindsight, Adam had likely never been honest. At first, everyone had loved him and welcomed the high energy to the household. Then things had started to go missing. When Jim came to stay for the weekend, he had $100 go missing. That raised their suspicions, and Beth had warned Milo that Adam was bad news. Of course, Milo hadn't wanted to hear it. Later, after the destruction was done, Milo was able to piece together more friends who had lost money and other strange circumstances that had surrounded Adam's appearance in his life. No one knew who Adam actually was and what, if anything, he told them was true.

He was as beautiful as he was toxic, and he had eventually outed Milo as gay in Uganda, where people were being murdered because of their sexuality. Milo's name and work organisation had been published in a ridiculous article in the national press at the same time an anti-homosexual act had been passed into law.

Adam and Beth had been the only people locally who knew the truth about his sexuality, and Milo had always been terrified someone would get drunk and say something. That was why he had been so hesitant to connect with someone romantically since he had arrived in Uganda. Adam had seemed irresistible, but Milo ended up paying a dear price.

He had been out of the country for work when Beth had gotten in touch with him and let him know it was too dangerous to return. The newspaper had a front-page outing, the 'Top 100 Homos in Uganda'. In a subsequent gossip column, the organisation he had worked for was entangled in a made-up love affair story, which had also singled him out in the process. It had been over-the-top and real-life satire. Milo had wanted to both laugh and cry. Admittedly, he had been a little pissed off he hadn't made the list of the top one hundred homos.

At that moment, he had lost everything he didn't have with him. His friends, pets, and the brand-new dream house on Lake Victoria. The life he had built for himself was gone.

He hadn't known where to go. The UK embassy hadn't provided any advice. So, he had decided to head back to the hotel, where he drank two bottles of wine and realised he had nowhere to go. Halfway down the first bottle, Jim had called. Having heard the news, he had offered assistance in getting Milo to safety. Milo thanked his friend and told him it wasn't necessary. The next day, he found a house in Nairobi where he had been able to stay for a while. He had Beth send him some clothes. Then, he had been able to get his contract extended in Kenya. Afterwards, he had started working as an LGBT advisor for Africa, which had felt like serendipitous timing.

What had been not so serendipitous was returning to the UK and reuniting with an ex he had been well rid of, who also got him back into drinking and drugging heavily. Initially, he had only gone to meet up with Roger to exchange some photos and other items they had that belonged to each other. Roger had wanted to catch up, but Milo figured it couldn't hurt until he had too much wine with dinner.

Then as the evening wore on, Roger had professed his love for Milo and said, "If I can't make it work with you, I can't make it work with anyone! Please take me back."

And for some reason, Milo had said yes.

The rest of the night had been a bit of a blur as Milo had tried to drown the little voice telling him it was a bad idea.

Soon enough, he would hear the same message from a louder voice that he hadn't been able to drown out. When Jay found out, he had been furious. "Are you kidding me? How much time have we spent getting away from that ass?"

As usual, Jay had been right. The reunion didn't last long. When they finally broke up, Roger had said that their mutual friend told him to be thankful because, "At least you can leave Milo. Milo cannot leave himself."

After that was his side adventure into meth, and then he got a job that took him to Cambodia, where he finally stopped running.

Leaving everything behind in Uganda had been a whirlwind.

He had experienced a sense of profound disappointment and also acceptance. That chapter of his life was closed in an abrupt and tangible way, and he had no choice but to move forward. His emotions had fluctuated from gratitude that he was able to leave somewhat safely to anger at the people who were being taken to court in the US for funding the anti-gay movement in Uganda. He had also experienced hope that he could make a difference in his new role. After all, he had lived the experience of being persecuted because he was gay.

His dream house had been nearly complete when he left the country and couldn't return. He had been building a beautiful open-concept wooden house on the shore of Lake Victoria and was making preparations to move in when the final touches were complete. The views were epic, and he had a beautiful study where he would be able to work and watch the sunrise over the lake. It felt like he was in his forever place, and he had planned on doing what he needed to stay there.

Being out of the country, with no ability to return, had made it easy for people to exploit Milo. He had been forced to sell his Land Rover for less than a tenth of what it was worth. It had been well-known that he had to get rid of everything because he couldn't come back, so he ended up selling his brand-new house for $20,000 when it was worth at least $250,000. That had hurt because it hadn't just been a house. It was his home. He had put personal touches in, and he had never even gotten to live there. He didn't even get to see it finished. Milo didn't have a leg to stand on, so he had been forced to let it go.

Returning to the UK and beginning to re-establish himself in his early thirties had been surreal because it was difficult to articulate what happened. In many ways, he was a refugee with white privilege. Many of his friends in the underground gay community in Uganda became refugees, finding new homes in Canada, where they had been celebrated for their work in human rights in their home country. For Milo, the UK hadn't been a new home. It wasn't his home at all. Uganda was home, but when he had been exiled, he fell into an empty space. While some diplomats had to be extricated because they were gay, they had a level of protection. As far as he knew, Milo had been the only white working resident who had to flee. He was conscious of his privilege, which didn't make leaving easier.

Another aspect of arriving in the UK that had been awkward was how his friends and family had treated it like a happy return home after an extended trip. It had been difficult to vocalise how he felt, which was fine because no one asked. It hadn't taken him long to realise he didn't want to live in the UK, and he wasn't there by choice. Jim had been the only person to ask Milo how he was doing when they caught up at lunch in London. The question had taken Milo by surprise. Later, Jim mentioned the haunted look he saw on Milo's face that day, not realising he had been the only friend to acknowledge what Milo went through.

Back in the UK, not by choice, he had started to seriously increase his drinking and drugging a lot more. Every hour had been cocktail hour. He could easily get drugs in Brighton, and they had helped blast out the emotion and allowed him to mask everything that was coming up.

He had also funnelled his experience into a passionate advocacy for LGBT rights and sex worker rights. The reality of what had happened to him was hard to take because he had been able to understand what was happening when it came to gay rights violations. Uganda had made him see his white privilege, and though he struggled as a gay male, the nuanced issues of sexuality for women and people of colour were something he witnessed secondhand.

He had struggled with his new role, his mental health was spinning out because of unresolved trauma, and he tried to kill himself when the pressure became too much. Surviving that was when he started taking therapy seriously.

Uganda had been a pivotal country, partly because he was there for so long. When that chapter of his life had been slammed shut, and he had conversations with many people in power who "couldn't guarantee his safety," Milo had faced ruin. He had been saved in the short term by a job back in the UK, though he was not ready to reassimilate into the lifestyle there. After six months of catching up with everyone, Milo had been desperate to get out of there.

It was exhausting to remember in detail, but he felt more powerful for having faced it and having the distance to see it from a wiser (and more beat up) vantage point. As Milo wobbled to healing mind, body, and spirit, he realised he had finally stopped running away from himself and wanted to run towards things instead. It reminded him of the powerful clarity he had when he returned home from rehab and went for his first run as a chance to relax and stretch his mind. It was a feeling of oneness that was not easy.

# NINETEEN

# TICKS, DICKS, AND BABOONS BEING PRICKS

Jim's words echoed in all of it and broke through the fentanyl-induced indifference. He hadn't escaped Uganda just to give in to a pill dependence because it was easy and felt good. Instead of holding on to chemicals that numbed him, he wanted to feel life.

The thought brought clarity, and Milo became aware of Ra banging around in the kitchen. He felt content to sit and absorb the homey sounds. Keeping people happy is an exercise in futility, especially when it comes to expectations of responding to text messages, group posts, and other social media. Milo did his best to keep in touch while maintaining boundaries for his sanity. Back in the land of the living meant back to being bombarded by hundreds of unread emails, messages and notifications non-stop, and overflowing voicemail.

Up at his usual early hour, 4 am in Cambodia was late evening in the UK, so he might be able to catch his brother for a quick conversation to put off making any progress on his long list.

"You rarely call me this late. Is everything alright?" William said as he picked up the phone.

"Yeah, I knew you'd still be up. I thought I'd check in with you rather than start the day complaining," Milo said, happy to hear his brother's voice.

"You want me to do it for you?" William asked.

"What have you got to complain about?"

"Haven't you been reading the papers!"

"Yes, I know. But if you read all the papers, you can find something funny about it."

"You only find it funny because you don't live here."

"That might be so," Milo said. The smirk on his face almost made sound waves.

"It's getting harder to navigate."

"What is?"

"How to take people. You never know what topic is off-limits or how they might respond," William said with a sigh.

"Yeah, last visit, I noticed the overall heightened tension."

"It's different for you. You can walk into a room and immediately know what people think and feel."

"It's not quite that simple, but I usually know what's up," Milo admitted. "Being able to read people is a skill that can be acquired."

"I know. You've helped me with that a lot. Still, you're a natural. When I'm having a conversation, I have no idea if it's going poorly," his brother responded.

"You've got an eagerness to know and a willingness to learn; that's all that matters."

"When you put it that way, that's probably what's missing with everyone involved in this political pandering."

"True, politics is known for its unwillingness to change. I remember years ago, I attended a speech given by Al Gore in London. Someone asked him what he thought was the greatest threat he perceived from George W. Bush. Gore's response was that Bush is incurious. He doesn't ask questions. I think that's the missing ingredient for many problems." Milo said. "Curiosity is a precursor to learning. And when we can learn from those we oppose, we can find solutions."

"Though I would have never thought that," William said. "I can see it both ways. You are incredibly curious, and look how much trouble you've got yourself in."

"Curiosity killed the cat. But I'm not through my nine lives yet." Milo and William chatted for a few more minutes before the older brother said goodnight.

Milo finished the conversation thinking about how shamelessly curious he was. He couldn't help himself. In one instance, he had been in the Heathrow airport bathroom standing at a urinal. James Bond (the actor who played the fictional character) had walked in to use the urinal beside him. After an awkward acknowledgement that is common when two men pee beside each other, Milo had tried to sneak a peek. He didn't succeed, though who wouldn't be curious in the same situation?

Sometimes curiosity could be a bad thing, especially with drugs and new risky situations. And other times, it resulted in hilarious accidents that were hard to explain.

When he had still been working in Africa, he was away from the office and needed to get on a conference call, so he stopped in a well-shaded lounge for a beer and a cigarette. After getting a drink, he looked for somewhere he could sit and listen to the meeting without disruption. To the left of the bar was a staircase that led to a dark room he thought was a smoking room.

Relieved to be out of the heat of the day, he had stretched out his legs and let the a/c chill his skin. He lit a cigarette and dialled into the call. As people started joining the call, Milo had realised he wasn't alone. Across the dimly lit room, there was movement. Eyes adjusting to the darkness, Milo made out the silhouettes of two men. He had cringed and let out a squeak as the larger man bent over the smaller one and put his hand up his bum. Then, before Milo could extricate himself from the situation, the two had begun having sex right as the conference call got underway. So, on one end of the phone, they had been talking about program implementation, and the sounds coming from Milo's end would be considered unprofessional in any setting. He had to apologise profusely and sidle out of there while doing their best to prevent themselves from bursting out laughing.

That was the way life worked out, especially for Milo. He'd be doing something mundane like trying to have a quiet phone call and come across something he couldn't unsee. Another time he had been working as an aid worker alongside Jim in Batticaloa in northeast Sri Lanka during the civil war. For most people, that doesn't sound mundane, but that was par for the course in Milo's career. The child soldiers knew they were there to help and left them alone. They went into the pointiest situations to try to make a difference for the people.

The children were taken from remote regions and recruited as soldiers. After they were released and brought by the government to a boarding school to be cared for, those in charge wondered why they were acting out. Milo had been sent, on behalf of the organisation he worked for, to help the survivors. Jim went along gathering information. The officials running the school were looking for answers as to why the boys were misbehaving.

Milo said little to anyone except the children. In talking to the boys, he could see the agony in their eyes. Living a life under conditions of civil war had a negative effect on children. That much was evident. Milo felt that the kids had a somewhat justified hatred of their very existence, and they needed support.

He and Jim had been spending the night in a guest house and having some beers. They got along well, though they disagreed about why they were there.

"We need to get angry that these children's rights are being violated," Jim said.

"I totally get that, but I don't think it gets you anywhere," Milo had replied. "The way we made change in care reform successfully was with gentle advocacy."

"What drives anyone to pick up a gun and commit mass murder? We need to remind ourselves of our humanity. These tremendous acts of violence are happening with greater frequency. And all I do is investigate it," Jim had said.

"You do more than that. But people are not born racist, sexist, or homophobic. They're taught it. If you can acknowledge they learned those things from a hurtful place, you can move past it," Milo said.

"That's one way of perpetuating a more harmonious way. Does that lead to forgiveness?" Jim had passed him another beer as they continued the discussion.

"Forgiveness is not always necessary. You can't rewrite the past. Memories and dreams merge, so can't we just pick and choose what we remember?" Milo said.

"Interesting concept. Is that how you get through the darkest stuff, by going deeper," Jim had asked.

"The inevitability of human suffering. It makes you understand what practising peace means in a broader context," Milo had said. Then he had added, "And the inevitability of the call of nature, I'll be right back."

He had stepped outside to take a piss when he heard a grenade go off mid-stream. Stopping the flow while trying to zip up and get back under cover could have been an act of grace and wonder, if he had got the timing right. As it was, he was stuck in the opposite realm; pain and terror as he zipped his penis into his pants and had to make the split-second decision on which was the more immediate threat: The stinging sensation radiating from the tip of his trapped foreskin won out, and he pried the zipper off his penis without much delicacy as his nerves shuddered in anticipation of the next threat. When he got back inside, Jim was on the way out to look for him.

Thinking back, that might have been karmic payback for a time he was working as a medic, field training in Kenya. One guy came in with a tick on the tip of his dick. In a misguided attempt at humour, Milo pulled out a lighter and said, "No problem, we'll burn it off." He barely had time to see the look of shock on the guy's face before he turned around and attempted to run out with his pants still around his ankles, not realising Milo was joking.

By this stage in his life, he figured weirdness followed him, like a honey badger, wherever he went. Seeing a honey badger in action proved to him that anything is possible. He had been in some insane situations, but he could find a way to see the funny side, usually because he was the one who got himself in trouble, usually unintentionally. He had a vision of himself as a honey badger refusing to let go of a tyre twice his size, aggressively going after it without thought of backing down. Everyone on a safari wanted to see the big animals: elephants, lions, giraffes—but it was the honey badger, the asshole of the savannah, that had entertained Milo the most. Those badass creatures will happily take on any beast, no matter the size difference, and Milo had seen one bite a lion on its face.

Milo had come across that way too many times. Maybe that's why he could relate. His family thought he would either be prime minister or head of a crime syndicate. After what he'd seen in his life, he realised there was little difference, and he didn't have the appetite for corruption or bullshit, two top qualifications for both jobs.

After Uganda, his BS metre was on high alert, and he was no longer blunt when people danced around the issue of human rights. He had attended a parliamentary discussion to testify about the validity of same-sex unions. After the first day, he had spent time decompressing and trying to mentally prepare for the next round of ageing white men/politicians discussing the human rights of others.

His friend Melinda had messaged him for moral support, and he asked if she had time to talk.

"It's great to hear your voice," Milo said when she answered. "How are you and Evan?"

"We're doing great. When are you coming to New York to see us?" Melinda asked. She had then followed up the question with three more about his health and wellbeing.

"These proceedings are taking a larger toll on me than I anticipated. Listening to one prominent man confidently spout multiple fallacies, I felt like biting my way out of the corner," Milo had said. "The lack of awareness on human rights is terrifying considering these are supposed to be the decision-makers."

"Sounds like an easy way to make yourself crazy," Melinda said.

"Isn't it just? God, he was up his own ass," Milo had said.

"Politicians should not be in charge of human systems," Melinda had commented.

"That's a good line; I might have to borrow it," Milo had said.

"It's yours, dear," Melinda had replied.

"Thank you for listening. I didn't realise how riled up I'd let it get me," Milo had said.

"You know I am always here. Get some rest, and we'll talk to you soon," Melinda had said.

"Say hi to Evan and take care, you two." Milo had felt more composed after he got off the phone. It regularly annoyed him when he let some ignorant buffoon rile him up, and he was glad to have had Melinda to chat with about it.

There were some similarities between parliament and nature. Once, he had come back from a wilderness hike, hungry and eager to soak in the surroundings and his bag was being ransacked by a baboon. Caught by surprise and eager to retrieve some piece of his lunch, he had picked up a can of soup and lobbed it at the baboon in an attempt to chase it away. With a quick swipe at the air, the baboon had caught the soup can and threw it back, hitting Milo in the head. He used to think he could still feel a dent where it hit him, but now he'd been dented in the head so many times, he lost count.

Limping into work, as the sun shone on the already bustling Gia Wellness Centre, he considered that was why he saw so much of himself in the honey badger because it takes whatever comes at it head on. And while Milo would rather talk it out over a cup of tea, he would still stand up where needed and face uncertainty with authenticity.

Stepping into the office he heard the resident rescue macaws squawking out expletives.

## TWENTY

# THE CIRCUS OF LIFE

The Gia Wellness Centre was also part of his continued recovery, his failsafe of sorts for years down the road. He figured if he owned a mental health and rehab centre, he couldn't possibly relapse. It would be bad for business. Tying the success of the business to his health made for some funny pressure, and Milo liked that level of irony in his life.

Trying to manage his aftercare was a bit of a circus considering most usual avenues were closed for the time being. Breaking your body during a global pandemic is inadvisable. However, Milo was so used to working with people and in situations that were hilariously mismatched he had learned it was best to roll with it.

One of the more memorable times in his life that the ludicrous became real was when he had been forced to give closing statements at a child rights conference from his hotel bed when he was sick with dengue fever. Before everyone joined him in his hotel room, he had dropped to the floor of the bathroom, face pressing against the tile floor, miserable. His burning body, aching with the new knowledge of why dengue Fever was called break-bone fever, had begged to remain immobile.

Shaking with fever, it felt as if all his bones were being snapped. Through his pain, he had started to hear a bell, ding-dong, ding-dong like a hammer. Assuming it was housekeeping, he had pulled himself up to open the door. He had it in mind to tell them he wasn't well and would be staying a few extra days, and could they please tell reception. He had been due to leave the next day and travel south to check on programs that had recently been implemented. When he opened the door, he was lost for words.

Twenty people from the conference he'd been at were at his door.

"What are you doing here?" he had mustered the energy to ask.

"Well, we decided if you couldn't make the closing remarks at the conference, we'd come to you," someone said, and they all started filing in, past him. Milo couldn't tell who had spoken, and he had wished he was dreaming.

He had crawled into his bed, and everyone gathered around him. Every inch of his body ached. Dengue fever had felt like his body had been turned into kindling, bones splintered and then set on fire. The intensity made it impossible to focus on anyone or anything else. As he huddled there, he had wondered why they weren't leaving.

"Would you like to give the closing remarks?" The same voice spoke again. Milo couldn't focus hard enough to see who spoke.

"No," he had said as forcefully as he could. "I'm dying. I have dengue fever. I can't make any remarks right now."

There had been an awkward silence and no one in the room moved. Everyone stared at him expecting him to go on. Finally, he had managed to say, "This has been a very special experience for me and I think everyone has learned a great deal from what was presented." In his mind he was screaming, please for the love of God, leave me be.

Eventually, he had said some semblance of what they wanted to hear while emphasising, "I am really ill, you need to go." And they had left him to his misery. When the door shut and he was blissfully alone again, it came to him that in this instance he would have preferred a polar bear. At least an Arctic adventure would have been more chill.

That was probably the sickest he had been up until his recent accident. He had had lots of scrapes and bruises in his younger years when he struggled to find where he fit. Back then, he stood for himself, even while finding his footing.

That determination came in handy now as he pushed to tap into it to direct his healing without relying on substances to numb the pain. As he became more aware of adapting to his condition while returning to work and life, Milo found he had slight amnesia, couldn't remember every incident, and forgot conversations. Sometimes he was worried about his declining cognitive abilities, and then he would remember a moment with crystal precision to the point he could viscerally experience it. Those moments were little miracles.

When he had worked in India, it seemed to go that way as well, from one extreme to another. He worked with incredibly talented individuals, building relationships that had become lifelong friendships and others who were the most corrupt people Milo ever had the misfortune of working with.

When he had arrived, he got the feeling that the country director of the organisation he worked for at the time was dodgy, so Milo had gone to visit the programs without her there. As part of the program, they had built a home for disabled children in one of the villages. This project had won an award for best project for tsunami recovery and was heralded as a success in the international aid world. Manjit, the country director, had sent Milo an email saying that the project was delayed due to flooding. The attached picture was a laughingly bad image of the house, photoshopped with a water line around the building.

In an attempt to find out what was actually happening, Milo had gone on his own, unannounced, to go see the property. What he found was that the chief of the village was living in the house. When Manjit caught up with him, she had begun making all sorts of excuses saying there must be a misunderstanding.

"There hasn't been a misunderstanding. This place has been nicked by the chief. This is supposed to be a flagship program, and it is a total disaster," Milo had said.

"Well, there are no disabled children living in the village," Manjit insisted.

Shaking his head, Milo replied, "Give me fifteen minutes." Then, he had walked into the village looking for someone who spoke English. When he did, he had asked if there were any disabled children living nearby. An hour later, forty or fifty children had gathered in the village centre, so Milo dragged Manjit and the chief down to where they had gathered and said, "Here you go. There are loads of children who need help."

Both Manjit and the chief had been quick to reply, "Oh, we promise we will change it to what it was supposed to be."

As Milo walked away, he had known that nothing would change and they would have to lie to the donor that everything was going really well. There were some things you couldn't change, no matter how absurd it seemed.

Soon after that disaster of a project, he had gone to Tamil Nadu, where he came across a desalination project taking place right where children lived. Though he was by no means an expert in chemistry, he was exceedingly concerned that there were kids playing in industrial levels of potash. Everyone had insisted that it was perfectly fine. He found out it was more than objectionable; they were poisoning the land and water, as well as the children at the nearby school. It had been appalling to Milo to witness the *laissez-faire* attitude of the general population towards health and safety.

Thankfully, he had managed to stop that.

On the opposite end of the spectrum was another program in India where they had helped over 30,000 street children access education. It wasn't the number or the success of the program. It was the inspiration that every individual brought. As unscientific as it sounded, there had been magic in seeing children light up as they learned to take control of their education and their lives.

It had been the first time Milo had seen children participate in all aspects of operations, including the budget. They were a true community, and the pure joy they experienced in every step of the process had shifted Milo permanently. Through their eyes, he had finally understood how the simple things in life were the richest.

The innate curiosity and relentless trust in the universe were such special qualities he saw in children everywhere.

He had become close friends with the program manager, Rohan, who had taught Milo a lot, including how to focus on putting everyone on an equal footing. It was the main reason their program was so successful because the children they served were considered equal. The only argument he had ever had with Rohan was to get air conditioning in the office.

Rohan had insisted if their colleagues and the children on the streets had to live without a/c, so could they. It was only when Milo suggested they needed it to maintain computers and office equipment that Rohan relented. Milo admired his determination and relished his time in India working with Rohan.

He had been in awe at the results they were seeing as the team tried to help kids learn and improve their lives. He had learned so much from them, and yet the thing that stuck in his mind from that period of his life all these years was that trust was earned. The street children they worked with had no reason to trust anyone. It was only time and assisting them in getting an education on their terms that had allowed Rohan, Milo, and the rest of the organisation to become part of their lives. After his first month there, Milo relished his morning walks to join the children in their day. While the day got off to a bustling start, Milo could make his way down the well-worn path.

As an early riser, he had often arrived before everyone else, and he would find a table in the shade, sip his coffee, and watch the morning unfold. The children arrived bright and cheery, and sometimes they would leave early and catch up with him on his way to work. One morning he remembered the sun shining orange along the horizon, and this small, wiry, adorable kid ran towards him, jumped, and scrambled onto Milo's shoulders for a ride to school. At that moment, he had felt the joy of life emanating in and out with every breath, as well as a unity. He saw the simple innocence of children.

Every step he had taken since was seeking to see that spark of joy in people everywhere he went. In the practice he created, and in the fundamental values of the Gia Wellness Centre, mental health care was available for all children. And that meant a focus on each individual finding jubilation in the world. While he had left India years ago and had long since forgotten the boy's name, the moment stayed fresh in his heart.

Advocating for children came naturally. When it came to advocating for himself, it was a complicated wave of ups and downs. His journey of living clean was adrift on a sea of cataclysms. Milo realised that sobriety was going to be a lifelong process of living clean moment by moment. The clarity was profound and often overwhelming.

The second half of life seemed to Milo to involve

mostly saying goodbye before he was ready. Death's fingers were forever reaching out to take someone important from Milo and his loved ones. It took him too long to accept uncertainty is reality; it is with you 24/7. Uncertainty can be ignored until it becomes unavoidable. Milo had a few things he was certain of, but you can't know for sure. Just because you say something doesn't make it true. Just because you spoke to someone yesterday doesn't mean you'll be able to tomorrow.

Then there are people so close, regardless of distance, that it seems impossible they would not be available to reach out and connect with. Milo had already lost key people in his life. Losing David was distant from Milo's realm of possibility. He had one of their regular two-hour calls, and nothing in it gave any hint that it would be the last time they would speak. They had a light-hearted argument about whose turn it was to visit next.

"You come here. I came when you were in the hospital in Thailand," David said.

"I told you not to," Milo replied.

"Only because you're stubborn and don't like people caring for you. You were glad I was there," David said.

"Yeah, you made what was a miserable recovery fun."

"That's what we do for each other."

"You even got me up and helped me around. Remember how I was limping around when we went shopping?" Milo asked.

"And you made me get that impractical fancy shirt," David said.

"It looked great on you. Even with your comfy shoes," Milo teased.

David wondered if he would ever have occasion to wear it, and Milo encouraged him to let loose and wear it out one day. Then, David changed the subject and asked Milo how he was recovering in all ways. They went on to more serious conversations about health and wellness, their families, and life.

A few months later, the phone rang at 3 am. A phone call at that time can mean one of three things; it's either an emergency, an accident, or a booty call. When Milo saw Jay's number, dread washed over him.

"It's David," Jay said with a shaky voice.

"No," Milo squeaked.

Jay explained David's sudden passing to the best of his knowledge. They briefly discussed their mutual friends and how they had all remained in touch over the many years and adventures. Like Milo, David had travelled the world and led a rich and amazing life.

"Did you know he became a travel agent?" Milo asked.

"What?" Jay responded.

"Yeah, last time he visited, I was talking about taking a trip, and he started giving all this information about flights and the best times to book. I asked him when he became an expert, and he told me he got really into the algorithms of the travel industry, so he took a course to become a travel agent so he could understand it better," Milo explained.

"That's incredible and also so like David. A few years ago, he took an olive oil sommelier course," Jay said.

"He does have a penchant for fine cuisine, and now I know where he gleaned that knowledge from. When we ate together, he was very particular about his oil and balsamic combination," Milo said, and a calm feeling spread through him in his memories of their friend. "It's hard to conceive we won't share a meal with him again."

"We'll think of him whenever we dress our salad," Jay said after a quiet moment. Then added. "I never thought he'd go before you."

"Why?" Milo responded.

Jay laughed for the first time since he called. "You have to ask? He was Mr Safety. You were—well one of the most risk-loving bitches I've ever met."

"True." Milo let out a laugh.

"How many times have I almost lost you? You got sober after decades of being the one who would carry on drinking or drugging until the very end, only to be run over and left for dead."

"That's a rather bleak summary, but not invalid. I can't believe he is gone."

"Yep, it's just you and me now."

Milo didn't have any concrete ways to come to terms with David's death. Day by day, he continued to consider what David would think about different things he was going through. Fitting his nickname Grandma, David was who Milo went to when he needed anything. Not even death could break Milo's natural inclination to ask David his opinion, and every time he went to dial his friend's number, he had to remember David wasn't there.

In his grief, he distanced himself from Ra, his friends, and his family. He could sense Ra walking on eggshells and didn't have it in him to reassure his husband. Milo knew everyone was waiting for him to drop off the edge, and he didn't care. He liked a good edge, and he was happy to stay there, staring over it into the abyss of life without David. For a time, no one could reach him. He buried himself in work and being busy. His employees didn't know what was happening in his personal life, so he hid behind the mask of operations manager.

Jim reached out by text and phone, and Milo ignored both. He wrongly assumed Ra had contacted Jim out of worry. It was less of an attempt to shut people out and more of a tool of self-preservation.

His commitment to sound bowl therapy training was part of his regular schedule and one thing he couldn't avoid or put off any longer. In an attempt to prolong his despondency, he took the scenic route. Nima was outside waiting when Milo arrived.

"You've been oddly quiet on all fronts, haven't you?" Nima noted as they made their way inside.

The softness of the familiar space eased Milo out of his emotion and into the healing frequencies. It was like muscle memory, the amount of time and training that he had put into learning sound bowl healing over the years. The calm lightness of his surroundings steadied Milo. He described how David's loss had affected him and how he closed himself off, trying to compartmentalise the sadness.

Nima and Kanshin listened while Milo acknowledged it had been too painful to even consider not being able to hear his friend's voice or that there would be no more holidays together.

"Mourning does not have to only consist of grief. Use your grief to spark joy. Let it out through the vibrations of our practice today." Kanshin's voice was gentle as he led the way through the doorway between the collection of sound bowls along the back wall.

Nima nodded in agreement as they entered the classroom at the back of the shop. The three of them were in silent synchronicity, moving into their regular routine, each setting out eight to twelve bowls. The traditional cymatics taught by Kanshin included complex combinations of frequencies, and the three of them had practised together for hundreds of hours, perfecting the patterns.

The physical and acoustic experience of familiarity washed Milo with acceptance and peace. The anxiety and terror of having David wrenched from his life were replaced with the soothing presence of his dear friend's memory. When the session ended, Milo was visibly more at ease.

Upon arriving home, Milo met Ra with a hug and a reassuring nod when Ra asked him.

"Are you alright?"

Milo was on an ongoing journey to accept uncertainty and appreciate people in all stages of life. Through meditation, other spiritual practices, and working around the world with friends from many cultures, he became deeply moved by the reality of the complex or layered identities many people have. With families who live abroad, travel frequently, or are biracial, it could be hard to have a sense of belonging. For Milo, growing up in military communities and being a forces brat kept him from being immersed in the popular culture of any country. As a Brit living in Uganda, Cambodia, and elsewhere, he was aware of the colonial history of the world. He was fascinated by the fact that people wanted a definitive answer to the question, "Where are you really from?"

He didn't have an answer to that question. For many, like Milo, there was no place. He was born in England, moved to Scotland, Germany, back to the UK, and Norway. His life had taken him around the world, but the idea that 'home is where you hang your hat' didn't apply. Instead, he had people in his life that anchored him. Home was the people he loved. As the years went on, he was losing some of those anchors.

David was an anchor for almost twenty-five years, and Milo felt his loss in a staggering weight that took months to fully comprehend. Maybe he was deluded, and he would never fully grasp the importance of his friend. David was Milo's ever-present compass. In any weather, no matter where they were, he knew David's thoughts, and they could finish each other's sentences. Calling his mum and brother to tell them of David's passing had been excruciating.

His granny and grandad were his first anchors, and they had embraced him. They had been a united force of nature and the first place he felt the sheltered safety of a nurturing home. His most vivid recollection of their love and support was when he had been ready to come out to his family. Sharing his sexuality had happened in a trickle and then all at once. Although he loved them dearly, he had been uncertain how the older generation would respond.

Granny's immediate response had melted away any uncertainty. "I'll always love who you are, my dear boy."

Grandad had echoed her sentiment, and they surrounded him in a hug that he could still feel. When he had lost them, a few short years from one another, Milo felt detached, like that anchor let go, and he floated off kilter for a time. Yet he carried with him their lessons and laughter.

As his spirituality transformed through Buddhism, the toxic people in his life could no longer have the same effect on him. Most had been entirely removed by that time. Even as an expert in psychology, it was difficult for Milo to grasp the strangeness of how people become immobile in their beliefs. Once people find a comfort zone, they will defend it in preference to a false sense of security.

Sometimes a false sense of security can help people feel comfortable, though different people have different layers of comfort. Milo, Jay, and David were perfect examples, as when it came to security, they couldn't have been more different. Jay was the most famous of them, and David was the most careful. No one would question that Milo was the risk taker. They disagreed often, yet it was the similarities they noticed most, and Milo wondered why more people couldn't respect other views. He also found it strange how people would become so unmoved from their position.

People have more going on than they let you see. Milo knew first-hand that the stalwart CEO who seemed to solve everyone's problems had once been a junkie passed out in a McDonald's bathroom with a needle sticking out of his arm.

Now that he had started to rebuild his life, he reflected on Jim's conversation about why they were so drawn to social work and child protection, even though it was a cruel and heartbreaking position to be in. A part of it, for both Milo and Jim, was that no one had protected them as children. And now, with renewed optimism, Milo could pick apart his intense desire to protect children and enact care reform as a way to preserve that joy for life.

As a professional, it was easy to understand how his loss of innocence as the victim of abuse took away that pure joy. He had to work to get it back, which was why he worked so hard to protect the most vulnerable.

The abuse he had faced made him question himself. He came to also see how it started the ball rolling of finding himself in the thick of it. Milo understood how finding himself in sexually compromising situations could be connected to his formative experiences, where he had learned that if he sexually pleased someone, they would go away and leave him alone. Essentially, that had led to him putting himself in the position to be abused by older men when he had first moved to London.

There was no one in his life he could talk it through with, and he wasn't emotionally equipped to deal with it. When he had been raped at the age of nineteen, he received the response he had somewhat anticipated. Instead of protection, Milo had been shamed and told: "He was probably asking for it." That comment from someone who was supposed to be a friend had confirmed to Milo what he already knew, that he must somehow deserve what happened to him, he must be asking for the unwanted attention, and if he just kept quiet and kept everyone at a safe distance, he could protect himself.

For years, Milo had searched for words to describe what it is called when you're too drunk to say no or unconscious while someone takes advantage of you. Taking advantage is such a nice word for rape. Milo felt taken while he was being blamed and shamed. His friend Xavier had taken him in and given him a place to stay during a vulnerable time. When he woke up in Xavier's roommates' bed, he had glimpses of the previous night. He remembered not-consenting, and he remembered the roommate started anyway. Mainly unconscious during the incident, it hadn't been until much later that he started piecing parts of it together. At the time, with the help of alcohol, he had switched off during the assault, much like he had done as a child.

The next morning Xavier had acted like Milo hooked up with his roommate and was angry and accusatory. Without the proper words to defend himself, Milo had gone over and over it in his mind, concerning himself with the nuances of consent. The one thing he was sure of was he hadn't been asked, and he hadn't been willing.

He had no one to take down the stigma of victim blaming for him. It was a process that unfolded in an ugly way. For a time, he withdrew sexually, and he had actively avoided any intimate relationship. When he had eventually opened himself up to Roger, he had been laughed at and shut down, so he never brought it up again. Even internally, he blocked the trauma for years. It had been a betrayal that went beyond rape. Xavier's blame had added rejection to the trauma and added to his chasm of distrust.

His drinking and drug use got worse and worse, in part because he hadn't been able to understand those behavioural connections. Milo was inherently distrustful of people. Having been targeted for sexual abuse, his first reaction was to assume ulterior motives. Milo became hyper-sensitive to the motivations of people in his life because they often wanted something out of him.

He learned to protect himself by pushing people away. Even with his close circle of family and friends, he had a small part of himself that worried he would end up alone again, and he wanted to protect himself and prevent anyone from getting close.

Meanwhile, he was intent on keeping those he loved close. Getting his health back was a second chance and a constant reminder of the gift of time with those friends and family. Above all, Milo didn't want to be the empty seat in his son's life.

# TWENTY-ONE

# GROWING PAINS

Sitting with Jim for their last morning coffee and bitching about the highs and lows of life, Milo had a sense of normality return for the first time in a long time. It was odd as it brought with it a wave of melancholy about the relentlessness of normal, especially amid grief and devastation. Yet he leaned away from it, wanting to enjoy his remaining time with Jim. He could cry later.

"Lost in thought?" Jim asked.

"Yeah, something like that," Milo paused before choosing to continue with humour. "Are you still heading out for your hedonistic holiday?"

"Absolutely, it's my way of coping. I'd go mad if I didn't let off steam every now and then," Jim replied.

"What is it about coke that has made it your go-to drug of choice for so many years?"

"It's tasty and makes me feel invincible," Jim

commented. "Plus, it is the perfect accompaniment to any alcohol."

"Ha! Too true," Milo spoke from experience. "Did I ever tell you about the time I combined wine and cocaine for a fundraiser?"

Jim laughed so hard it took him a moment to regain his composure. "No, pretty sure I would have remembered that."

"Yes, well, it was a rather unorthodox fundraiser," Milo said sheepishly. "In the early years, when social work was a pro bono extension of my entertainment industry connections, I quickly got tired of the traditional money-raising events. In an attempt at creative fundraising, I came up with a brilliant new theme for a party: Wine and a Line. For a premium, guests received a bottle of wine and a gram of cocaine."

Living in a penthouse in London gave him the perfect venue, and he had always loved the role of host. The event was a hit, and before long, Milo had to contact his dealer to be sure he'd be able to acquire the appropriate amount of powder. The alcohol wasn't a problem. He'd find any excuse to choose some exquisite wine, though he wasn't sure there was a proper pairing in place.

He had gotten in touch with the dealer well in advance to pre-order a much larger-than-usual order.

With such a drastic change to their regular, frequent order, the dealer had to ask, "What's up?"

Milo had kept it simple. "We're doing a fundraiser. Wine and a Line. We're trying to raise money for children dying of AIDS. We'll need forty grams."

"That's incredible," Buddy had replied. Then silence.

Milo wondered if he'd lost connection. "Tell you what. I'll sponsor the fundraiser. I've got a soft spot for anything that helps kids. If anyone likes the product, send them my way."

"They're probably already your customers, but okay. That's very generous of you." After he hung up, Milo had wondered if he'd been gracious enough. He had been caught off guard a bit and chuckled at the idea of a drug dealer sponsored event.

It wasn't a fundraising endeavour he planned on repeating, but it did give him the opportunity to see compassion coming from a drug dealer, which seemed like a relatively rare event. It reminded Milo that he had witnessed great compassion in strange places before, even amid the horrors of genocide and the aftermath of war.

Jim had belly laughed throughout the retelling of the event, and they said goodbye feeling light-hearted and fulfilled. Milo was relieved to have kept his melancholy to himself. Instead of feeling down, he would be optimistic about what was to come.

The ground was ever-shifting, so Milo was used to being flexible to achieve what he liked to call aspirational ideas rather than goals. Goals seemed too concrete and easily dashed. Instead, he took things day by day. With Jim gone, life was finding its way back to a more low-key routine.

Whatever your intentions, the best-laid plans often go to shit. Milo didn't have to look far in his life to find the ramifications of errors in judgement, even with the best intentions. Remembering those situations was one of his favourite ways to laugh at himself. It also served as a reminder when others caused him harm; before he got offended, he wanted to know why it happened. Sometimes we unintentionally fuck up, and Milo knew that. Thinking back on it, Jim had been around during a lot of Milo's missteps. Having him in Cambodia was reminiscent of their earlier friendship during his time in Uganda.

He'd never forget the feeling of ineptitude he had when he had an encounter with a green mamba, a gorgeously vibrant snake whose venom is lethal. In the back garden in Uganda, he had met all sorts of creatures wandering between the neighbouring yards.

It was a quiet afternoon, and Milo had been heading back to the house when a sleek chartreuse body slithered across his path. Without thinking, he had used his walking stick to pick up the snake and hurl it as far from him as he could.

In that horrifying instant, Jim popped around the side of the house. Just as Milo had hurtled the snake through the air, Jim called out hello, and an angry venomous mamba came raining down right in front of him.

"NO!" Milo had shrieked the instant realisation set in. Jim did a quick side shuffle before the snake spotted him, and they had both bolted back into safety and closed the door behind them.

Jim had loved retelling the story about the time Milo unleashed a green mamba on him. Milo was certain each time he heard it, Jim had made it more crude.

The whole thing could have been avoided if Milo had brought his guard dog with him. Munch the Rottweiler was miserable and had hated every creature except Milo. She had also liked to bite people's bottoms. It sounded funny, but it was not. It had become a problem to the point where she had to be kept in another room when people were visiting, and Milo had been the only one who could handle her. He knew her lashing out had come from a place of pain. She had been a bit of a bitch and a big pain in the ass, but he could relate, and she had nowhere else to go.

Blade, the optimistic German Shepherd, who was the friendliest guard dog ever, had been his loyal companion in Uganda. Strange as it might sound, the happy-go-lucky attitude of Blade had encouraged Milo to pay attention to his own mental health. Having a joyful dog whose face seemed to be permanently smiling had pressed Milo to find his natural perma-grin, which he usually sought through feel-good substances. Blade had taken whatever happened with a wag of the tail.

None of his dogs since had the same totally positive outlook on life, though Pierre came close. He seemed to put up with whatever came his way in life. He was like Ra's furry shadow and just as mellow, only missing Blade's lopsided grin and forever-wagging tail.

Milo had always appreciated the presence of the animals and noticed how people tended to mirror their behaviour after the animals they most resonated with. Different pets Milo had brought about interesting reactions. While most people were either dog people or cat people, Milo had an affinity for all animals and welcomed birds and reptiles, as well as mammals. They kept him grounded and helped distract him when he was down. The Gia Centre's animal partners were two rescue macaws, and they definitely ran the place.

Offering mental health services during a time when people were forced to stay isolated was both more necessary and more challenging. As Milo's bones were knitting back together, a lot of people reached out to him as they were falling apart. Lockdown around the world drew many to reach the end of their ability to cope. At the same time, the pandemic changed how the Wellness Centre could provide services, and it was unknown how long they could financially continue to put things on hold, adapting to changing policies.

On Gia's birthday, he was intent on taking a few days to himself to reflect and still, he was putting out proverbial fires. He was eager to hear from Celeste and Ava, to see how they were holding up and reconnect with them. Their plan for a reunion in New Zealand had been put on hold, so they were resigned to a video chat for the time being.

Even so, seeing their beaming faces helped lighten his mood immeasurably, and he reminisced with them about Gia. Celeste shared how she and her wife had a birthday tradition of starting the day somewhere new, whether it was a new café for breakfast, a new place to hike, or, when possible, travelling to somewhere they'd never been.

"She always had a different type of cake every year," she finished.

"Yes!" Ava agreed. "She's been that way as long as I can remember. That's how my boys celebrate Auntie Gia's birthday, by trying a new type of cake every year."

"I love that! She never did like picking favourites," Milo recalled. "And she'd always pick the underdog."

"Even with cakes. She'd pick the ones that weren't as popular, like coconut and cherry because she wanted to give them a fair chance," Ava said. The three of them erupted into laughter at the memory.

When the giggles subsided, Milo noticed their eyes were glistening with happiness. As the conversation picked up to carrying on with life without someone important in it, he felt gratitude for these women who anchored him to his dear friend. Talk turned toward the Gia Wellness Centre, and both women inquired how things were going.

Milo knew the question was coming and felt torn. He had a lot riding on the company, and the memory of Gia was wrapped up in it for him, to a degree. It was a sticky topic, but he loved them, so he gave an analogy. "It feels like running uphill in sand."

"Well, you've done that before, and you'll do it again," Ava said.

"True," Milo mused, feeling reassured by a rush of kindness blowing over him.

"Yeah, aren't you planning on doing that marathon again?" Celeste asked.

"Yes, I am. It's something to work towards while healing," Milo said.

"So, you'll be choosing to run uphill in sand?" Ava remarked.

"And paying for the privilege," Celeste added.

"Fair point. Now don't you two start ganging up on me," Milo said.

"Oh, Celeste is just having a go at you. We think you're fabulous, and you'll come through all of it fine," Ava said. Celeste nodded.

"Face it, I am fuzzier now since I was driven over and left for dead. There are so many different aspects of the business, and I want to remain focused on the initial mission."

"Your fuzziness is only noticeable to you. You'll be able to manage," Celeste said.

"No, I will have to adapt," Milo replied.

"That's not a bad thing. You've been doing that all along."

"You're right. I have."

"Gia would tell you that you're overcomplicating things again," Ava said.

"I was just thinking the same thing. I hear her voice in all of it," Celeste added.

"Me too," Milo replied.

"Yes, totally. The Gia Wellness Centre is incredible, and it will thrive, you'll see," Ava said. "Thank you for keeping my memories fresh. Now I have to go. The youngest and the oldest are picking on my middle boy."

They said their goodbyes and encouraged Milo to stay safe. He laughed. "Not to worry, Ra has banned me from riding motorcycles. Apparently, he wants me around for a few more years."

"Smart man," Celeste said.

After the call, Milo sipped his second cup of coffee and avoided checking emails. He was soaking in the positivity of the conversation and was reflecting on Ava's comment about memories.

Some memories were still so clear, even as life went by in a blur. Whereas others seemed to be locked away. Events that should have been important enough to remember, like his graduation, were vague, like a half-remembered dream.

For a breath or two, he sat in silence, settling within himself. As he quieted his mind, he got a random image of the white rhino, once wild and free, now on the brink of extinction. In the Lake Nakuru National Park, as he was trekking through the Kenyan wilderness, he had seen the prehistoric-looking creatures graze on the savannah, a seemingly rock-solid addition to the landscape. Now, the only white rhino he saw was the vodka that flowed from people's glasses. For Milo, he was no longer looking for stability at the bottom of a bottle, yet he still stood awestruck at the impermanent nature of what seemed solid as a rhino.

For one strange moment, he felt a well of sorrow hit him, and tears pushed to the brink of his eyelids. He held them off, stunned at his urge to weep for the rhinos of all things. Grief for the loss of many people he cared about manifesting itself as ecological concern was part of it, but the wilderness mattered just as much. It was perhaps that paradox of nothing lasting and the tenacious determination to make it last a little longer. That was part of grief, the wondering what might have been.

Milo realised he had been growing around his grief for Gia and Daniel and trying to use it to propel himself forward. He wondered if he could do the same with David. Milo reflected on how he and others could experience terribly tragic losses and miserable circumstances and still be able to cope and live joy-filled lives. He noticed that when he experienced significant trauma, his expectations started shifting and changing.

Grief and recovery, like coming out, was an ongoing process. Milo saw and experienced how it could consume him. There came a point when Milo made the conscious choice to move past the what-ifs, wondering why those left behind hurt so much, and focus instead on the ongoing journey of the soul.

Some people are wired for post-traumatic optimism. They take what's happened to them and end up with a more positive outlook in life. It gets underplayed, but Milo had seen the amazing things people achieved after suffering great loss. He counted himself among the optimistic, and though it hurt and he wept for the people he loved, he preferred to remember them with a smile. The grief bit doesn't have an ending; it evolves and changes. It can be soul-destroying, but people grow around their grief and try to use it. People experience terribly tragic experiences, and instead of suffering from PTSD, they live life with greater vision and, like Milo, take on new and exciting roles as each day becomes a blessing.

With the Gia Wellness Centre expanding into new cities and new partnerships, Milo was exhilarated by the acceptance of his ethical therapy model. It was also daunting to continue without funding, yet offering fully subsidised access to services for survivors of abuse was an essential aspect of the company. Growth and clearly increasing demand meant making choices as an entrepreneur that were best for everyone involved.

Combining a scientific approach to the holistic Eastern methodologies he had been introduced to was balanced with the operational considerations and logistics of running a business. When he first went into business for himself, his father had given him some words of advice: "You're the captain of the ship, and no one is your friend."

It wasn't the way he saw himself. Still, he knew there was a grain of truth to it. In reality, at work, everyone immediately saw him as the CEO, not as Milo. He'd always be the boss, which made it hard to be a person. People didn't notice he had shit going on in his life. He knew he was seen as successful, but most days, he struggled simply trying to be okay.

This stark contrast helped him help others because he saw how easy it was to overlook layers of hurt, trauma, and anguish people experience because they are so used to hiding it. Now more than ever, we need to know that people are going through shit in their lives. Milo understood how people felt when they were not okay, and they wanted to know what it felt like to be okay.

## TWENTY-TWO

# REAR VIEW

After a prolonged absence from each other, Milo could finally travel again to see and be with his family. He and Ra went to the UK, where they reunited with his family, starting with Ella and their boy. As he wrapped his arms around his too-grown son and held back tears of pure joy, the simple bliss of a hug was a gift. The four of them set off on an adventure of their own. Once the world woke up from dreary days and being locked away, travelling for a while was a way for them to reconnect and learn together. Milo now, in some way, would be retracing life's most incredible locations, but this time insulated with a family and the contentment one feels when in their bubble of peace.

Even though everything is shit sometimes and nothing is certain, he felt the peace of their energy, and the turmoil seemed easier to handle.

Before they left, they visited his mum and gathered in

the garden as she flitted from plant to flower with names that he instantly forgot. They sat catching up and talking about the shock of David's loss.

On the grey-lit, slate patio Milo swallowed his gloom.

"It's true what they say; only the good die young," his mum said, dabbing her eyes.

"I'm sure David would be the first to tell you. He wasn't that young," Milo said with half a smile.

"He was such a delightful boy," she said, ignoring him. "Oh, how he will be missed."

"I couldn't agree more, Mum," Milo said.

"Well, wonders never cease. There's a first time for everything," his mum said, with a hint of a smile.

After a whirlwind visit and a family adventure that spanned the continents, Milo and Ra headed back to Cambodia. As the sun went down during their last flight, Milo looked down and saw the sea undulating through like a steady constant healing, finding a measure of peace amidst universal tension.

"Well, I'm not moving for at least a week," Ra said when they arrived home. He sat down in his favourite chair after he had adequately spoiled their pets, apologising for being away.

"Yeah, then you will be planning the next one," Nathan teased.

"What was the coolest thing you saw?" Simone asked.

"There was so much, I don't know where to start," Ra said, looking at Milo to help out. Milo shrugged and went to get more coffee as Ra continued. "The one thing that surprised me the most was how much I learned about Milo that I didn't know."

Now everyone looked at Milo. He laughed. "I've been around."

"You should write a memoir," Kali said.

"No one would believe it. Plus, I can't see myself sitting behind an oak desk going back historically." He stood up, balancing cups and saucers in one hand, imaginary quill pen in the other, taking on an over-the-top posh Victorian tone. "Milo Cummings was born in Richmond, Yorkshire, to a family with a proud military heritage."

"It would be more like an action movie," Simone added.

"No, it's more like a wild guide for the sober curious. How about Drink, Pray, Love?" Piper suggested.

"Adventures of a Serial Entrepreneur," Nathan said, waving his hand with finality.

Laughter all-round as he brought his arm full of dishes to the kitchen. When he returned, they were still debating the genre of his life. Milo leaned back as his friends bantered. His big dog, Fendi, lazily licked his hand while Louis, their little Pomeranian, hopped on his lap for a pat. Good to be home didn't even begin to cover it. He turned to his husband sitting behind him. As they caught each other's eyes, the corners of their lips turned up.

Ra, who had been shaking his head from his spot in the corner of the room, spoke up in his earnest and endearing way. "No, it's more like Milo doesn't need any more projects."

"That's true; you're the one person in the world that opened a cafe to ensure a steady supply of coffee," Nathan said.

"The Klitz was on the fritz, so he started a coffee shop," Simone added.

The room was full with the sound of their laughter. His friends each saw a different aspect of him, though it was always his husband who would get to the heart of it. Milo looked at his husband, and his smile showed he agreed with him; his look intended to convey, with no words, that he adored Ra and also despised how well he knew him.

Whether he was across the room or across the country, it was Ra that was his anchor and partner in all aspects of life. Together, they showed Milo that love and trust existed. Through Ra, he saw the basic goodness of the world.

Surrounded by their animals and human companions, Milo felt content. He had the big dogs, Fendi and Miu, on either side of him. Louis was lying at Ra's feet, and Pierre was running back and forth between them. Chanel wandered in circles, tail wagging for a while before Milo sent her to go settle in her bed rather than knocking into everything with her tail.

Without even noticing it, he had his dogs to get through all stages of his life and be there for him in steady support. The creatures in his life who had been there for him all along reflected loyalty. Silent and steady through all of it, he had animals by his side.

The universal love and joy that he had seen from animals was something he strived for. The animals in his life had loved him without expectation or judgement. They were also a constant reminder that there are factors in life that are totally beyond your control. Even as he was once again pulling the pieces together, he appreciated their chaos and warmth.

Even before he found sobriety, he saw the same traumatic response in children all over the world. There were so many children who were victimised and abused and didn't have the support to get out of their situation. He could see that young people with addiction issues always had trauma they were trying to bury.

Working in social work internationally and with families supporting children, Milo saw how deep the need was. There were so many incredible, invisible people working to help make things better. From Milo's personal experience, the work was endless.

Oftentimes, to Milo's endless frustration, the actual programs set up to protect children made the situation worse. In one area he was working in, the children had nowhere safe to play. A prominent aid organisation had a playground built in the area with a large fence and a chained gate closing it off.

After spending an inordinate amount of time trying to get in touch with someone who would give them permission to use it, Milo took matters into his own hands. He simplified the problem by removing the gate and allowing free access to the playground. Seeing the children laugh and slide, swing and glide, was worth whatever consequences would befall him, though nothing came of it.

In a much more serious outcome, one program that was an attempt at reducing child trafficking actually increased it significantly. Other times, he worked for organisations that ended up supporting orphanages without knowing it. In child welfare, there are a million ways to get it wrong, and only a few get it right.

Working in India, home to more than one billion people, gave him a clear image of the vast scale of the issues. It could be a bit overwhelming, especially in big cities, finding child trafficking and child labour victims and then trying to discover where they came from. Depending on the age and what happened on their journey, the child could provide little to no information. At most, they could approximate how far they travelled to get to their city. Any details helped, though getting them home was hard.

Having clarity now made unravelling the blurry early years an interesting effort. It was futile to expect it would all come flooding back to him in a neat and tidy way. Nothing about his life had been neat and tidy. He was either throwing himself into something new and exciting or running away from something that had gone awry.

Just like most sailing accidents happen in moderate weather, a simple set of errors can become serious straightaway. If the boat capsizes and you get stuck under the sail, it's like glue. No matter how prepared you are, something can still go wrong. When you're experienced, you can see the events as they will happen. That's why Milo was constantly watching other boats whenever he was at sea.

It was also a lesson he wanted to teach his son. While it could be a challenge for Milo to be present in his son's life while living half a world away, they worked it out. His son knew Milo would answer his phone at any time, day or night, if he called his dad.

As it happened, his son's ringtone sounded while Milo was back in the office.

"Hi, Dad. Can I ask you something?" The small voice put a big smile on Milo's voice.

"You know you can ask me anything," Milo replied.

"Well, that's good because this one is tricky. I'm not sure what the question is."

"What's going on?" Milo asked gently.

"The other kids at school say that the world is too big to do anything about the environment. But I think we should try to save the earth. Is it pointless to try?" he asked with resignation.

"If you don't think one person can make a difference, try sleeping with a mosquito in your room," Milo said.

"So, how do you do it?" his son asked.

"If I see somewhere I can make a difference, I try to help," Milo responded.

When their conversation ended and they said goodbye, Milo sat in contemplation for a long while.

Walking home from the office after working into the evening, the familiar street and the walk he'd done a million times seemed to be at a peaceful equilibrium. Living and running a business in a vibrant neighbourhood that was so knit into his life provided a fascinating backdrop to experience life's foibles. It never ceased to amaze Milo how quickly people got on with life after a major catastrophe or trauma. Once the immediate threat has been diffused, the up close and terrifying adrenaline response seems to wane into acceptance or is cordoned off to be forgotten. The basics of life require unceasing attention, and people that were once close become players in past lives.

Milo was contemplating that one day he would just be a memory, and with all the water under the bridge, he wanted to spend his remaining time on earth in a meaningful way with the people that mattered to him.

His reverie was interrupted when a pedestrian in front of him started to weave off and back onto the sidewalk. The break in pattern of the everyday bustle caught his eye, and Milo followed for a while to make sure the stranger was okay. When he realised the man was definitely inebriated, he picked up the pace. The man rounded a corner into the street, and Milo reached out and pulled him out of the way just in time. A car whizzed by right where he had been standing and missed them both by inches.

"Don't fucking touch me!" the man yelled, spinning towards Milo. "Are you trying to steal my coat?"

Before Milo could muster a stunned response, he was attacked. In a flurry of movement that seemed impossible from a man who had been stumbling into his death moments ago, he came at Milo, arms and legs swinging. Milo's agility had been mostly recovered, so he was able to block or avoid the onslaught, but he misjudged one movement and got a swift kick in the nuts.

"I was just trying to stop you from being run over," Milo gasped.

Screaming obscenities and slurred accusations at Milo, the man went on his way. Groaning, limping, and muttering under his breath, Milo finished his trek home.

Counting everything that he'd done to his body, Milo figured comparatively his testicles had been through the most. Though the most recent incident left him no worse for wear, he decided to get checked over. After multiple surgeries on his testicles to remove tumours and replace the originals, his doctor was thorough in ensuring everything remained healthy.

Though everything ended up being fine, the doctor called the Royal Phnom Penh Hospital for some further tests. Milo stood nearby, listening to one side of the conversation as the doctor tried to delicately explain the need to "scan the scrotum for any abnormalities."

It was amusing to watch the exchange as the doctor tried to tactfully explain what was wrong with his patient. He became increasingly frustrated with the communication breakdown and finally shouted into the phone, "Let's keep it simple. It's his balls. He needs to have a scan of his balls."

That got the message across.

# AFTERWORD

"Our moral compass is the product of the work we do to understand and apply spiritual principles. When we move away from what we know is right, we feel frustrated and trapped. When we forget what is true for us, we lose our way and drift dangerously. On the other hand, when our understanding of the truth is changing, we may feel much more lost than we actually are. That compass is very much at work and is leading us in a new direction. Through these periods of grave doubt and uncertainty, we find a new surrender, a deeper faith, and often a very different sense of who we are."

Narcotics Anonymous Fellowship. Living Clean: The Journey Continues. Narcotics Anonymous World Services, Inc.

*The days are long and yet they echo lightly.*
*Your time here is indelible.*
*I seek peace in your absence,*
*yet struggle with your understanding and compassion,*
*that bleeds into my thoughts on an understanding that*
*    you're by my side.*

*I'm tormented by your loss, yet inspired by your presence.*
*Our shared history will end one day,*
*but for now it's here, present, and it aches my body*
*and grows my lust for wanting each moment to matter.*
*You're not gone, but rather by my side.*

*I crave that to be more, I wish your brilliance shone on now*
*as much as it shines in my perspectives and small thoughts*
*    and actions.*
*I can only ever imagine a world where you're still here with*
*    me, seeing me grow.*
*And yet, paradoxically, that growth is because you're not*
*    here, but next to me.*
*It's our anniversary. I wish sometimes I'd stopped in time*
*    with you.*